I0541381

Haven
By
N.S. Howard

Published by
Melange Books, LLC
White Bear Lake, MN 55110
www.melange-books.com

ISBN 978-1-61235-061-5
Haven, N.S. Howard, Copyright © 2009 - 2011

Names, characters, and incidents depicted in this book are products of the author's imagination or are used fictitiously. Any resemblance to actual events, locales, organizations, or persons, living or dead, is entirely coincidental and beyond the intent of the author or the publisher. No part of this book may be reproduced or transmitted in any form or by any means, electronic or mechanical, including photocopying, recording, or by any information storage and retrieval system, without permission in writing from the publisher.

Credits

Editor: Nancy Schumacher
Copy Editor: Mae Powers
Format Editor: Taylor Evans
Cover Artist: A. Bratt

Haven
By
N.S. Howard

When the world of Haven was rediscovered 240 years after the colony ship Regal crashed landed, reporters Scott Pearson and Cindy Lorncroft were quickly sent to find interesting new stories. What they uncovered instead was a behaviour considered uncivilized and immoral by the Alliance Worlds' Charter of Conduct Office, igniting charges against the Haven government.

www.nshoward.com

* * * *

The Praxton Series

To the reader: While Haven can be read as a stand alone novel and is complete by itself, I continued to use part of the storyline for another series. The Charter of Conduct Office and the Alliance Worlds are used in the upcoming Praxton series.

I hope you enjoy Haven, and I would be happy if you decided to read the Praxton series as well. However, pleased be warned the Praxton novels are more erotic nature and involve bondage. Having said that, you will find reading Haven gives a good background leading to events that occur on Praxton.

Haven
By
N.S. Howard

PART ONE—THE WAVE

We tend to think of our culture as the sensible and judicious one; that others are not only peculiar in their habits and foods, but even their very way of life is wrong and perhaps sinful. Throughout the ages, civilizations would try to influence others by sending out messages of what is appropriate. Sometimes the methods used have been in the appearance of entertainment, news and diplomats. Other methods used to spread indoctrination have been in the form of missionaries, and if that failed, armed force. Language, religion, diet, even socializing have been changed and bent towards the new and improved way of living.

Haven, early years

Jason Elliot. The Steermaster of the starship Regal. The Steermaster is second in command to the captain.

Ensign Elaine Trestle: Elliot's girlfriend and later wife.

Corporal Duggan: Power engineer on the Regal. Distant relative of Aaron Duggan.

The Hood: One of three starships sent by the Starlight Collective.

The Mobridge: One of the three starships sent by the Starlight Collective.

The Regal: One of the three starships sent by the Starlight Collective.

Starlight Collective: A religious order on Earth that sent out colony ships.

Captain Marvin Anderson: A minister of the Church of the Starlight Collective and the captain of the starship Regal.

Haven: A planet just past the edge of human occupied space. It remained hidden for about two hundred years before being rediscovered.

Ross Gibson: Religious leader who led a small splinter group. Father of John Gibson.

John Gibson: Led the remainder of his father's group back to the main group on Haven.

* * * *

Earth

Robert Dural: power engineering student in York City University.

Glora Bitmon: Diplomat assistant, works at the Conciliate General (part of the Charter of Conduct Office). Robert Dural's girlfriend.

Dr. Margaret Reshew: Bitmon's boss.

Scotty Pearson: Reporter for NightHawk News, a scandal based newsmagazine.

Cindy Lorncroft: Reporter for NightHawk newsmagazine. Forced to go an assignment with Scotty to Haven.

The Wave: A disruptive particle force from the galactic centre that destroyed all electrical and electronic equipment in human space. Natural phenomena.

Mars: Capital of the Sol Alliance.

Charter of Conduct: An all encompassing document that spells out laws for the Sol Alliance (and all Alliance Worlds). It supersedes any planetary laws and is designed to reduce conflict in human space by having all people follow the same laws and customs. The Charter of Conduct Office can order planetary constitutions changed, charge political leaders with crimes and has the full support of the Alliance Forces. Only the President of the Alliance Worlds can overrule Charter of Conduct Office decisions.

President Liz Cartier: President of Earth during the Wave crisis. Mother of Marcus Cartier.

President Marcus Cartier: Drafted the first version of the Charter of Conduct and established the **Sol Alliance Emergency Forces**, later becoming the **Sol Alliance Forces**. First president of the Sol Alliance. The Sol Alliance was union of Earth and humans living in the solar system. Later when the Sol Alliance took over other human planets in the galaxy the name Sol was dropped to become the **Alliance Worlds**. The president is elected by the House of Representatives, and those members are elected by Alliance world members. Earth, with the largest population, elects most of the House of Representative members.

Perplex: The first planet that Sol Alliance used force to take over for failure to follow the Charter of Conduct. The ease with which the Sol Alliance Forces captured Perplex set an example to other planets that were resisting joining the Alliance Worlds.

Regis: One of the last worlds to oppose the Alliance Forces.

* * * *

Haven, Eight generations later.

Aaron Duggan: Premier of Haven.
Irene Thompson: Duggan's assistant and girlfriend.

Steermaster Troy Ravener: Lorncroft's contact who took advantage of her.

General Louis Burgess: Senior officer of the Alliance Forces.

Diplomat Dr. Roger Beaumont: Sent to negotiate terms with Haven to join the Alliance Worlds.

Haven
By
N.S. Howard

Chapter One

On the starship Regal, traveling towards the galactic centre, approximately 400 light years from Sol.

By the year 2353 various divergent groups of humans had colonized several planets. The Regal was a group of three colony ships sent out by the religious group the Starlight Collective, to locate a habitable world.

"Sir. There seems to be a visual abnormality in sector four." Ensign Elaine Trestle swivelled in her chair to face Steermaster Jason Elliot, giving him a slight smile.

Jason Elliot had already noticed this time the gravity wave fluctuations were more than just interesting. He walked over to where Ensign Trestle sat and studied the viewer. Under magnification, he saw some distortion of the star fields – like looking through a sheet of contorted glass.

"Lieutenant Mason, send a message to the Hood. Inquire if they are seeing any abnormalities in sector four and if so what they make of them." Elliot had a second thought. "Ensign Trestle, is that interference only in sector four? How big an area does it cover?"

"I'll check right away, sir." She turned back to her screen.

"Lieutenant Mason, would you also inform the captain we may be having a situation and his presence is requested? And then contact Power Engineering and let me speak to Corporal Duggan, I believe he is in charge this shift." He turned back to his station and turned on his intercom in response to the blinking incoming message light.

"Steermaster Elliot, this is Corporal Duggan in Power Engineering."

"Corporal, are you getting any peculiar readings on your gravity wave generator?"

"Yes sir, we are. They're still within spec, but I have had to make some minor adjustments the past few minutes. Like something was opposing the wave front. There is also a change in the electromagnetic field generation. The harmonics in the higher dimensions are unstable."

"I see. Please inform me at once if there are any changes; monitor as closely as possible until I contact you again."

"Yes sir."

Mason approached his station, looking surprised. "I have the Hood sending a communication, sir. But it's too soon for a reply to our inquiry."

"Send it through. Did you get a hold of the captain?"

"Yes sir. He said he would be here as soon as possible."

Elliot switched on his intercom.

"...we are experiencing absolute havoc in our field generation, both gravitational and electromagnetic." The visual flickered off and on, revealing the communication officer looking worried and harassed. Electrical sparks, like miniature lightning bolts, could be seen randomly striking objects behind her. A shower of noise filled in over her voice. When it cleared again for a few moments, Elliot could hear shouting in the background. A new voice, filled with panic, came over the speaker. "Shut down your fields! Shut down your fields! Something is..." More noise covered the voices, then silence.

"Steermaster Elliot, this is Power Engineering. We are experiencing some difficulties in maintaining field controls. Situation seems to be getting more difficult, though nothing we can't handle."

Elliot thought the voice was speaking a little too rapidly for a situation that could be handled easily. "Stand by please."

Trestle came over. "Sir, that cloud, or distortion, is all over in front of us. It's covering everything in front of us and it's moving in our direction." She managed to keep her voice down, but he could hear the tension as she spoke.

Mason came running up. "The Hood has just exploded! It's gone! I'm trying to contact the Mobridge, but they're too far away. They're probably just reaching the distortion now."

Elliot thought hard. *Damn! Where is the captain?* "Power Engineering."

"Yes sir."

"Commence emergency shutdown of all fields immediately. Shutdown the fusion generator. I want everything off line ASAP."

"Sir?"

"Now. Move it!"

"Yes, sir!"

"Mason, sound the emergency alert. Inform all that we going to shut down all power immediately, including lights and gravity."

"Steermaster Elliot, what the blazes is going on here? Mason, stay that order on power shut down until I say so." Captain Anderson entered the bridge, his face looking flushed as he focused his attention on Elliot.

Elliot spoke rapidly, determined to change the captain's mind before Mason communicated to Power Engineering. "The ship is in immediate danger! We must shut down all power! The Hood has exploded and the Mobridge is in trouble."

Trestle interjected, "Mayday from the Mobridge life support computer. Direct communication is gone."

"Do as Elliot says, shut down all power. Now!" The captain now stood beside him on the bridge, lowering his voice. "Jason, you better be right about this."

"I'm not sure I want to be if what happened to the Hood is about to happen to us …"

"The Mobridge has exploded! It's gone. Oh my God! Oh my God! It just exploded!" Trestle jumped up and away from her station.

Elliot watched as she tried to control her emotions and then heard the captain shout behind him.

"Inform Power Engineering to get the fusion generator off line immediately! Ensign Sherwood and Gredal, shutdown auxiliary power except for life support."

The order came just as the lights dimmed and gravity began to fade. "Everyone buckle in at your stations. Gravity will be gone completely in less than ten seconds."

Elliot knew one of the problems with a ship the size of the Regal was that it was difficult to change direction or stop in a hurry, and now both the ship and the distortion raced towards each other. He was worried about the passengers and hoped the emergency distress calls went out before the power disappeared completely. As soon as it was possible they would have to find a way to communicate to the rest of the ship. The bridge was isolated from main ship, sitting just above the main hull.

The distortion wave hit. First was the anticipated strange sensation of weightlessness, expected as the gravity fields collapsed. Then a curious feeling of gravity returned, not in just one direction, but instead from several areas at the same time. A peculiar sense of a tug of war washed over the crew, followed by a second impression of being in a high voltage electrical field.

Elliot could feel his hair standing on end and he noticed one of the crew members jerk her hand from the console from an electrical shock. "Bridge personnel, keep away from all conducting surfaces. We are entering a highly charged storm of unknown magnitude."

The ship seemed to be spinning, but Elliot wasn't sure if it was due to the ship turning or it was due to strange gravity field pulling at his body. The dizziness was hard to avoid, but he fixed his eyes on the blank screen in front of him. He heard an electrical discharge and then the smell of ozone. He glanced about and saw electrical sparks jump from the walls to equipment, occasionally in the air itself.

"Sir, my console is smoking." Trestle looked right at him and not the captain.

"Stay calm. Avoid breathing in the vapours. There's no power to the console, so there should not be any immediate fire danger." The electrical discharge continued, increasing in strength. Smoke would appear where circuit boards were present. Occasionally lights would flicker on, or the sound of a small motor could be heard. Otherwise, he could only watch the strange electrical storm lighting up the room. The only other light came from the softly glowing walls and ceiling that were treated with a chemical that gave off light in the event of a power failure.

Elliot was glad of the foresight that some unknown engineer thought they might be needed. Then he remembered another 'just in case' design built into the ship. "Bridge personnel, in the event you are feeling a bit queasy in the stomach, underneath each seat cushion there is a drawer that contains a first aid kit, including pills to settle your stomach and a sickness bag." He immediately heard the sound of two drawers being opened. He wondered how long the storm would last.

* * * *

The ship remained at the mercy of the wave of distortion for several days. The crew occasionally left the safety of their seats when needed. Thirst could not be stayed too long due to the bouts of smoke, and emergency water bags were passed among the crew.

The captain sent Mason to investigate parts of the ship under strict guidelines. Each section then sent out messengers to another section in the same fashion. Eventually reports came back. Hundreds of cases of sickness, some minor injuries, and unfortunately, several deaths reported, so far. Most of these were from people with artificial hearts, the electric pumps running too fast or not at all due to the intense electric field. The ship seemed to fare better, circuit boards were ruined, but there was no obvious damage in power engineering and the hull did not appear damaged.

Elliot woke to see Trestle floating above, looking at him. He smiled at her and then noticed there was a change in the air; the storm had passed.

"Sir, the captain has gone to power engineering. He wants you to handle any concerns here." She hesitated a moment and then gave a nervous smile. "Are we going to be all right now?"

"I hope so. If power engineering is functional, then we should be okay." He didn't express his thought that if power engineering wasn't functioning, they would all die a rather slow death. Elliot was glad Trestle couldn't read his thoughts. She looked like she was on the edge of an emotional outburst and he wanted to make her feel safer. He sat up straight and cleared his throat. "Corporal Lingerst and Ensign Ravel."

"Yes sir." The two men approached him by slowly drifting towards him.

"I need you two to find a way of getting air purification running again. Report to me within the hour on your progress."

"Ensign Sivel, I want you to go to guidance and control and see if it is possible to put a spin on this ship to create some gravity. Don't proceed until you have checked with me or the captain first."

"Ensign Trestle, why don't we go to the ship's lounge?"

She followed him the best she could, slowly pushing off chairs and walls to the door. "Why the lounge, sir?" She sounded a little suspicious of his intentions.

"There is a view window there. I want to see if we can recognize any of the stars, and thus locate where we are." Elliot was attracted to her, but he wasn't sure of her feelings.

"Oh." She looked at him, biting her lower lip.

In the lounge, they looked out at the sea of stars that slowly moved across their view as the ship did a slow tumble.

"Can you pick out any identifying stars or groups?"

"No sir. Unless that bright one is … no, that can't be. This one is a binary. It's easier to see possible formations by view screens."

"Yes, but that may not be in use for a while."

They went to another window to look at a different group of stars, but it seemed impossible to recognize any of them.

He drifted towards her slowly and she tensed as he stopped right next to her. He then slowly rested his hand on hers. She continued to look out at the stars for a moment longer before turning towards him. After the week they had had, touching her rejuvenated his batteries. He felt her fingers grip him tightly on his shoulders and then her head buried into his neck.

"Please, don't let go of me," she whispered.

He wanted to kiss her but knew he had already breached the boundaries of an officer with her. Instead, he held her for long minutes.

* * * *

A few hours later, a damage assessment conference was called among the higher officers. Some gravity had been established by causing the ship to slowly rotate about its axis. This caused the wrong areas to be the floor sometimes, as all areas that were the hull of the ship became the bottom. Still, it was significantly better than everything floating.

Captain Anderson spoke slowly, addressing them with respect. "First I want to thank you all for the job you have done in these past days. As I have no idea what will transpire from here on, I'd like for us to keep our posts but you are all permitted to speak casually and address each other, including me if you wish, by name. The grace of God has spared our lives. I think it only right to let our faith and belief guide us from here. You are all officially at ease. Does anyone have anything to report?"

"We have no electrical power yet," Jason said. "Our main generator has been damaged. However, a backup is being put in place so we should have power within a few hours. It seems to have escaped damage because it was stored within a metal cabinet. This appears to have provided the necessary shielding. We are fortunate that many backup and replacement circuit boards were inside metal cabinets as well. I would suspect many of these boards survived as well."

"That is good news, Jason." The captain turned to Mason. "Aaron, what have you established about our ability to communicate?"

"Not good, Captain. The replacement boards are not reliable. They have trouble holding on to a set frequency, and allow an appreciable amount of distortion. In addition, we do not have an antenna; all were destroyed during the storm. I could jury rig up something, but coupled with our circuit board problem I am not optimistic about their range."

"And now, Rosario, how does power engineering look?"

"Well, the good news is that the main cores survived. They are triple protected and needed only minor repairs. We will be able to generate electromagnetic and gravity fields again. In addition, fusion power can likely be re-established, once additional repairs are done."

"But there is some bad news as well?"

"Yes, there are significant problems in using our fields for travel. First, many of the circuit boards have been damaged. The replacement boards seem to be functional because they were stored in metal cabinets like those for electrical power. However, it appears that we are unable to calibrate them to the exacting specifications needed in field wave generation. Most of our test equipment has been damaged and unfortunately, backups were not protected from the storm wave.

"Furthermore, the ship as a whole is short of view screens. Nearly all of them have been damaged during the storm wave and we are short of backups. The result is we cannot monitor all of the functions of the field generators. If we were to try to bring the field generators on line, we wouldn't be able to control it or monitor it correctly. And without proper calibration the fields will be unstable, perhaps not sufficient to even generate a collapsed phase for more than a few seconds."

"That is not good news. To summarize, we can generate a field that may not support travel?"

"Correct. And I should point out that even if we can sustain a field for travel there wouldn't be any way to know where the null space point would be located. In other words, we couldn't know where we would be heading to or how far we have traveled."

The silence stretched for several seconds, and then Jason spoke. "But you do feel we can initiate an integrated field?"

"Likely, though not of good performance."

"Captain, we cannot remain here indefinitely. Environments aboard Regal is jury rigged and will not likely be able to sustain life beyond a few weeks."

"That is true. You have a suggestion to make?"

"Yes, since we are also unaware of our location what would the harm be in trying to initiate an integrated field? If the ship can withstand the travel then anywhere might be better than here."

The discussion continued for another hour on Jason's suggestion. The captain finally came to a conclusion. "The consensus is we have to do something. Remaining here will accomplish nothing. Therefore, we will follow Jason's suggestion and try to establish an integrated field. Rosario, prepare for initiation at fourteen hundred hours tomorrow. Mason, please inform the crew and passengers of our intentions so that they are kept current on our progress. The passengers should be told only that we are testing our drives so that they will not get false hopes about our predicament. It wouldn't hurt to ask for a bit of prayer on the Regal's behalf. It seems we are going to need more that just luck to find a safe haven."

* * * *

Two weeks of blind travel was taxing on all the crew. The passengers, however, were largely unaware of all the difficulties. Gravity had been re-established, though it seemed to vary a bit over time and as one walked around the length of the Regal. But the ship was traveling, supposedly to their new home.

"Captain?" Mason approached him slowly and then glanced around to see if anyone else was in hearing distance.

"Yes Corporal."

"I did the summary you asked for. As you asked, I didn't include any food supplies that were of questionable quality. Unfortunately, the lack of refrigeration caused quite a bit of spoilage, and apparently some of the electrical discharges ruined some others. In all we have about two or three week's left."

"I see. And the water and air recovery systems?"

"They are running at about sixty-five per cent efficiency. But they are dropping, sir. The air filters are not too bad, but the water units aren't holding up. Listrom, in engineering, has been the one working on them and he estimates about two weeks before they give up completely."

"Then the bottom line is we have perhaps three weeks left of life support."

"Yes sir. Sorry to have to bring you such difficult news, sir."

He smiled. "Quite all right. You did well. The good news is we have the Lord on our side so far. I think we will do just fine."

The ship's crew was a religious group chosen by the Starlight Collective. This was a requirement to serve on one of the ships leased by the Starlight Collective. The captain was a minister of the church but there were other church members who looked after the chapel on the ship.

The captain approached the chapel's minister and asked if he could use the chapel so he could lead the crew in a special service. The minister readily agreed and the captain arranged for a weekday evening service. Over the intercom, he requested for any crewmember that was available to join him in the chapel. While he was surrounded by over half the crew, the others were on duty and for the most part were able to listen to the service over the ship's intercom, he asked the Lord for a safe haven for the ship's passengers and crew. He believed such a place would be found, why else would He have protected them from the storm? He bowed his head and led the prayer.

The next day the Captain sat alone in his study drinking his tea when Jason knocked and then entered.

"Sir, you asked me to inform you when we are going to make the next jump."

"Thank you, Jason." He then reached out and picked up the book on the table.

Elliot looked at the Bible. "Captain, may I stay and pray with you?"

They waited together, finishing the pot of tea in near silence when Trestle knocked on the door and then entered. She looked excited.

"Captain, the jump was successful! We, we're near a star system! With planets!"

The Captain and Jason looked at each other and then shook hands, grinning at the fantastic news.

"Hallelujah, Jason. Hallelujah!"

Trestle's grin turned into a laugh of happiness as she watched Elliot yell hallelujah in return.

Elliot grinned for a moment longer before he turned towards the door. "Excuse me, I better return to my station and check out our exact proximity to the star system." He paused beside Trestle. "This is great news, Elaine, just great." He held her hand a moment before disappearing down the hall.

The jump left them a short distance outside the star system, and the captain immediately ordered the ship to use its fusion drive to move towards the inner planets. The ship was positioned high above the plane of system, which made travel a bit easier since they didn't have to worry as much about the small planetary bodies that drifted in orbit around the sun. A few hours later Regal reached the edge of the system with eight planets circling a dwarf star. The journey seemed to take forever as they passed first gas giants, a medium size planet and finally they found a possible candidate. One of the planets gave tell tale signs of oxygen, carbon dioxide and water vapour in the atmosphere. Telescopes were trained on the planet that revealed colors of white clouds over brown, blue, green, yellow and other shades on the planet surface. While that by itself didn't prove the planet could sustain life, let alone human life, a cheer rose when the image was shown to the rest of the ship's occupants.

Soon the captain called another meeting among his officers. The crew was getting excited about the new planet, and he thought he needed to make them aware of the needed preparations.

"Ladies and gentlemen, we have reason to be optimistic about our new planet." He looked around at their smiling faces. "However, we have some serious work ahead of us. I need the shuttles to be inspected now. It is possible, or rather, likely, some of them have suffered some sort of critical damage, and it is probable all of them will need some sort of repair. We have to also check on what resources we can transport down to the planet's surface, if in fact it proves to be habitable. I want everyone to realize that this planet may not be the home we are looking for; it may not support human life. If that is the case, I expect each and every one of you to act in a responsible manner and help passengers and other members of the crew deal with the disappointment of looking for another solution." This brought a sombre look from his officers. They knew that if this wasn't a suitable planet, it would be the same as a death sentence. The Regal's life support system had perhaps only a week left.

The Regal itself had several shuttles attached to it, wrapped around on the outside that were to be used to transport people to the planetary surface. Unfortunately, when the crew went through the hatches to examine the shuttles, they found the damage to them was far worse than they expected. The hulls were still air tight, but all the electronics as well as the main propulsion were damaged to the point where it was hard to find a single usable part in any of them. The fact all the shuttles suffered similar damage meant they couldn't use parts from one to make another serviceable.

16

Elliot talked to the captain in the study. "I did some checks myself, sir. Unfortunately, it appears the first status reports were accurate. The shuttles are unable to make the journey to the planet surface."

"I see." The captain looked up from the report he was reviewing. "I have decided to establish orbit around the planet in any event. I doubt if we have enough time left in our support systems to make another jump."

Elliot was silent for as he reviewed what the captain said. To go into orbit meant there would be no other choice but to go to the planet. If they couldn't find a way to the surface the Regal would become an orbiting coffin for them all. "There is some good news. The planet can sustain human life if we can get down there. Our stock of genetic material, both plant and animal, survived very well. I suppose that was due to being stored in deep freeze area of the refrigeration equipment. Our food generation equipment has been damaged, likely beyond repair; however, some of our manufacturing equipment is in good condition. So, once again, if we can find a way to get down to the planet, we may be able to manufacture the parts we need to survive."

"Good to hear that. So the problem is to find a way to get to the planet surface. By the way, I have decided to follow the crew's unofficial name of the planet. From now on we can call it Haven."

"Haven it is, sir." He smiled. "God brought us this far. He will help us find a way to complete the journey."

"Thank you for saying that. It is something to keep in mind at this stage."

Elliot stood to leave. "There is one other matter, sir. As required by regulations, I must report any relationships I have with junior members of the crew. I am currently spending my leisure time in the company with Ensign Elaine Trestle. With your permission, sir, I would like to continue to see her."

"Of course, you two have my blessing." The captain smiled. It wasn't much of a secret. In fact, with death so nearby since the Wave struck, many affairs had blossomed throughout the ship, even among the crew and passengers that normally was frowned upon. Elliot was one of the very few who had actually followed the regulation and reported a relationship with a junior member of the crew.

* * * *

The Regal continued its orbit around Haven. Company was kept by the two small moons as the captain pondered on what to do next. It would be next to impossible to try to land a mother ship on a planet, including the fact that a ship of Regal's size would virtually crash land and never could leave the planet's surface. The Regal was a rigid structure, designed for space travel. The gravity field generated by the ship itself was carefully monitored to ensure it was balanced for the length of the ship. The planet's gravity would be much greater and could easily cause the hull to shatter; the rigid hull might not have enough flexibility to bend with the forces. However, the captain knew he didn't have a choice in the matter. Besides, he believed God would be watching out for them. All the same, he decided he had better ask for computer simulations on trying to land the Regal.

Several of the simulations had the Regal breaking up during the landing. However, Elliot found a solution was possible if they first removed the shuttles from the outside of the ship, and then they brought the Regal in tail first, using the fusion drive to slow its descent. Not textbook by any means, but it looked like it might work.

"And then, sir, when we are approximately ten thousand metres above the surface we allow the Regal to tilt on her side. At this point, if we were to fire maximum retardation on the lower thrusters, the ship would hit the planet surface with minimum damage."

The captain stood behind him where the animation played out on the computer screen. "And how many times have you run this simulation?"

"Two dozen times."

"The success rate?"

Elliot looked up. "Almost sixty percent, sir. That was with me using the controls. I'm sure you could do much better."

"Thank you for your sentiment. I think it would be prudent if I was to try it myself a few times, though."

The captain announced that they were going to drop out of orbit and land. He said it as if it just another announcement but everyone in the ship suddenly held their breath and then started talking.

The captain was certain now he made the right decision to land the Regal. There was no other option. The computer simulation was something he kept trying to work on. Try as he might, his average success was not much above Elliot's, hitting about sixty-five percent. He sat back and sighed. There had to be some trick to this he had over looked. A knock on the study door brought Lieutenant Mason into the room.

Mason gave the captain the latest reports on the planet and then looked at the simulation with interest. "Why does it topple over like that?"

"The Regal is almost thirty-five hundred metres long. The top of her and the bottom are experiencing two different wind conditions. If we try to correct too strongly, we put extreme stress on the hull and it may rupture. That has happened several times in this simulation. On the other hand, once a wobble starts, it gets progressively worse as we get deeper into the gravity well. I'm trying for the fine line of control of the wobble without stressing the hull too much. The Regal wasn't designed for flight inside gravity. Normally that isn't a consideration, but this is not a normal situation. The hull of the ship was designed to be rigid. That helps for our space drive and maintaining our own gravity field but it seems to be a fatal flaw here."

She looked at animated ship drop towards the planet. As it lowered, the top started to wobble in one direction and the bottom in the other. Soon the ship was out of balance and then it broke apart.

"Any thoughts?"

She was silent for almost half a minute and he was ready to repeat the question when she spoke.

"Sir, you are just dropping straight down here. How about trying to put a spin on it? Like a gyroscope? It may not have to be fast but it should stabilize it."

The captain typed in a new set of commands. Once again, the computer showed the Regal dropping down to the planet though this time it spun on its long axis. The ship still wobbled but not nearly as much. Near the surface, the spin slowed and stopped as the ship tilted on its side and then landed on the surface. Excited the captain ran the simulation several more times. The success rate climbed to over eighty percent.

"Well done, Lieutenant Mason! You may have given us the key to make it to our new home!"

The captain felt they had a good chance for the first time that they could make it down to the surface. "Haven, here we come!" He just wished he knew where in the cosmos they were.

Chapter Two

Elliot and Trestle approached him together. He looked up and smiled. In the past day, there had been a record number of marriages on board the Regal. The passengers had largely used the minister of the chapel to perform the ceremony while the crew had usually gone to the captain.

"Elaine, Jason. Now what might bring you here in my study?"

Elliot looked nervous. "Sir, we, Elaine and I that is, would like to ask you if you would marry us. That is if you approve of us marrying. It would be an honour, sir, if you would be able to do this."

The captain laughed. "Relax Jason. Of course, I would be glad to marry you two. I think you will make a fine couple. "When would you like to this? As you know we will attempt to land on Haven within forty eight hours."

Elaine spoke up. "Yes, we know. Actually, we were hoping that you would marry us on Haven itself."

The captain raised his eyebrows. "I see. There is some danger we won't make it alive down to the planet you realize."

Elliot now looked a bit more relaxed. "Sir, I can't believe we have come this far not to make it now. We have every confidence that you will get us to our new home."

He looked at the smiling couple standing across from him. For them to put off their marriage until they reached Haven meant a lot to him. He felt good inside, confident they would make it to Haven alive. "Thank you for those words and those sentiments. I think this calls for a special toast" He turned towards a cabinet and brought out three glasses and a bottle of brandy.

* * * *

Touchdown on the planet surface was to occur mid morning. They choose a continent that straddled the equator, picking an area near the ocean. The land there was also relatively flat, and might help prevent the Regal from breaking up when it landed.

The huge ship fired some of its control rockets to begin its descent. Slowly at first the orbit began to decay, and then with increasing speed it fell towards the planet. The captain guided the Regal down, relying on computer projections and his own intuition to follow the ideal path to the surface. The hull moaned as he slowly turned the massive ship tail first and began to rotate it. How fast to spin it was partly guesswork as the computer was not able to calculate it precisely due to variations of weight along the hull. The captain slowly increased the spin until he "felt" the Regal was stable. There was still a slight wobble but it did not feel too threatening.

"Fifteen kilometres, sir." Elliot called out distance from the ship's bottom to the planet surface.

"Thank you, Steermaster. I will commence turning Regal on her side at ten kilometres. Mark please."

"Fourteen thousand, thirteen thousand…" When the altitude reached eleven thousand, Elliot changed his count to hundreds of kilometres. "Ten-eight hundreds … ten-seven hundreds …"

When Elliot reached "ten-ten hundreds", the captain directed the Regal to topple on its side. The hull began to groan from the outside gravity pressure. Creaks could be heard along the great hull as Elliot resumed his counting.

"Sir, Ninety-five hundred …ninety-four …" Towards the end Eliot could barely keep up with the downward count as the planet's gravity pulled the ship faster to its final resting place.

He continued the countdown until he reached nine hundred, when he looked at the captain, his hands and face covered with sweat, holding his finger above the control panel for a moment, and then pushed down on a blinking yellow symbol.

The thunder could be felt through the hull; the ship seemed to be buckling under the strain as emergency alarms rang out.

"Sir! Sixty seconds to planet surface!"

The captain stared at his screen, there was nothing more he could do. The thrusters were going full board, past their safety levels. Red lights flashed everywhere on his console. He closed his eyes and prayed.

Elliot and the captain expected the ship to hit with a thud, to break apart during impact. That was okay as long as the people inside survived the crash-landing or rather most of the people survived. Instead, the ship landed with a 'whomp', almost an anticlimax. The hull did not breach; it held intact in the end, surprising the captain and Elliot who had watched the computer simulations often enough to calculate this landing was one in forty-seven. For the Regal not to break on impact meant the entire ship, three and a half kilometres long, had to land flat, stem to stern almost at the same time.

Before leaving the ship, they tested the atmosphere again, although it really didn't make any difference. They had to leave the ship regardless.

The planet was not well advanced, at least in the area they had the Regal land in. Plant life was abundant but not much in the way of nourishment. Trees were more like large bushes than what they would have liked and were not good for building material, providing only small, bitter fruit. There was plenty of fish and sea life and although the small fish were easy to catch, there were also large predators they had to guard against. Another problem was that almost half of the fish had a soft shell around them and those proved to have a toxin in them. On land, most of the creatures avoided the area around the Regal. They varied in size from the very small to almost elephant proportions. There was insect life that acted the same way as the variety on Earth though there was a definite absence of birds. The odd flying creatures were more like flying squirrels and bats. Carnivorous animals were not uncommon but they seemed content to leave the new arrivals alone. All the same, a security fence was placed around the Regal.

One blessing was the climate. Being near the ocean and located in a temperate zone the weather was a bit on the damp side with the temperature warm to hot.

A meeting was called after the initial exploration was conducted among the various leaders. The captain and Elliot represented the ship's crew, with the church appointed leaders for various positions representing the passengers.

The expedition leader and now the Premier, as he was to be designated on the new planet, struck a small gavel to start the proceedings. Nagel Thompson smiled as he sat down. "First, let me formally thank the captain and his crew for bringing us safely to Haven. Let the record show that we acknowledge their courage, wisdom and faith to give us our new home." The applause from the dozen people around the table filled the small meeting room.

The discussion became less cheerful after that. Plans were drawn where to put the first cemetery for those who had passed away on the voyage.

Elliot reported there was damage to much of the ship's equipment and resources. The cargo hold looked intact but much of the equipment suffered damage the same as the Regal. The food generation machinery was unable to convert various plant materials into edible provisions. Besides basic food groups, there would also be a shortage of vitamins and medicine.

"To put it simply, all we have to eat are these rather simple plants that grow here and some types of the fish in the ocean. We can convert the food by using some types of chemical reaction, but I'm rather dubious to its success." The fish itself was not an unexpected suggestion; still many of the people aboard the Regal were against eating any form of life outside of plants. Elliot finished his report and sat down.

Thomson glanced at his notes again before speaking. "There will be some hard decisions to make and we will have to be prepared to do things we wouldn't expect to have to do. Let me start by saying the key to survival according to ship's emergency survival guide is food, water and shelter. We do have shelter, in the form of the Regal, though that may prove to be inadequate in the future. Water, I'm told, is available from the streams that feed into the ocean. We have to find a better way of accessing it than by carrying in various containers though. As far as food is concerned, we have a problem. Dr. Ann McKinley, can you enlighten us here?"

A young blonde woman, perhaps thirty, cleared her throat and quietly spoke. "As it was pointed out, our food conversion machinery is not usable. We may be able to repair it in the future but not before we would starve to death. The plant life here will provide some nourishment, various roots, berries, fruit and so forth will at least fill our stomachs. Unfortunately, the plants here are lacking in so many vitamins, minerals and proteins that we will die of malnutrition. The fish are rather abundant here and are easy to catch. Eating the whole fish, the ones without a shell, will give us many of our required nutrients. A diet from the plants and the fish will allow us to live for some time, though to be frank, all of us will suffer to some degree and others will die, due to lack of all of the essential minerals. The fish here are different than those of Earth, and miss some of the required nutrition that our fish would have provided."

She looked around the room; the eyes were hard looking at the sombre news. Already the thought of eating fish was causing some concern, as many of the religious order were strict vegetarians and vegans. What she had to say next was going to cause an uproar.

"If we want to survive on this planet, at least in a healthy way ... let me put it this way instead. If we were to eat only the fish and the plants here, I doubt there would be anyone alive here in one hundred years. The birth rate would drop, child mortality would soar and soon the population would be too small to sustain itself." She let that sink in before she continued. "The only way, the *only* way, for us to survive as a population is to eat food as our ancestors did. We have in storage seeds for grain, wheat, corn and a host of other crops. We also have in storage the embryos of cattle, goats, chickens, dogs, insects and a host of other Earth's life forms. If we were to activate these, they would help us greatly towards our nutrition problem."

Ross Gibson leaned forward on his arms across the table. "Are you suggesting we raise cattle and other livestock to eat? My God, we took those embryos along to make our new world more Earth like, not to slaughter them like savages. I am surprised that you, Ann, as a Christian would even suggest such a thing. Furthermore …"

Thompson spoke up. "Please, do not speak without permission from the chair. We will also refrain from making personal attacks as well. Dr. McKinley has been merely giving us information to work with. If you have a better suggestion or more information for us to consider please bring it up."

The meeting dragged on and Thompson had difficulty keeping the discussion under order. In the end, they decided to vote for a poll among all the inhabitants of the Regal.

The results of the poll surprised Gibson. Over eighty-five percent favoured using McKinley's suggestion, many of them saying they must do whatever was required to save their children. The results were read at yet another meeting.

"I see you have the support of the vast majority, Ann. It seems I was a bit hasty in my earlier criticism and I apologize for my earlier comments. Perhaps you are right, that God is leading us along this path. However, I, and others, have decided to place our faith in God a different way. We will assist the rest of you when we can, as we care about your welfare, but we will be striking out on our own. We will live, as we believe God intended us to, no disrespect intended, and have faith the Lord will provide. Effective immediately, I resign from the council." With that, Gibson stood up and after a brief pause walked out of the room.

The next day over four hundred men, women and children left the safety of the Regal and headed inland. They took a small portion of rations and some extra clothing and blankets with them. With Gibson in the lead, they marched away.

* * * *

Two weeks after Gibson and his followers left, Captain Anderson stood on the makeshift podium, surveying the grim looking faces. "I know spirits are a bit low right now, but I have an announcement to make that is cause for celebration. Next weekend we are going to have a wedding. Elaine Trestle and Jason Elliot will be the first couple to get married on Haven!"

There was silence at first, then murmuring in the crowd that broke into cheers and applause.

"I will promise you it will be a reception that will be remembered for a long time. So make sure you bring your dancing shoes."

* * * *

One Year Later on Oasis City, Haven

"How is that baby of yours doing, Elaine?" asked Elaine's friend, Katherine, who came up behind Elaine as she sat near the exit ramp of the Regal.

Elaine smiled and folded back the blue blanket from the makeshift stroller. "He's just a delight. I hear you're expecting, are you hoping for a girl now?"

"I am. Jonathon has his son and now I would like to have a daughter next, the Lord being willing."

"It's great they're able to find a way to use the wood from the trees to make buildings. It seems half the women here are pregnant and we're going to need homes outside the Regal pretty soon."

"Jonathon is busy clearing the south valley and said the soil will be great for farming."

"I heard. Jason checked the seed supplies last week and said they might be planting within a month." Elaine reached over to touch the cheek of her baby when Katherine pointed where a dirt path led towards the river.

"Isn't that Gibson's son, John?"

"Oh my Lord, it is." She stood up and looked at the scrawny nineteen-year-old man leading a small group of downcast humans.

* * * *

Nagel Thompson sat across from Gibson, trying to encourage the younger man to speak about details that he didn't want to remember.

"All I ask is that you allow us back into the fold. We made a mistake and cannot survive on what this world will provide."

"Of course you are all welcome back. We missed having you during the past year."

"Thank you for your kindness."

"And the others? How are they?"

Tears glistened in Gibson's eyes. "They have all died, sir. We are all that are left. Forty-three of us."

"What happened, son?"

"My mother died a week ago. We prayed for her and my father fed her anything she could take down. But it wasn't enough. She kept getting weaker and weaker." He paused to wipe his eyes. She just slept away and then didn't wake up."

"And your father and the others?"

"Most of the others died of starvation. After we buried my mother, my father asked me to lead the rest of us back to the Regal. I thought he just didn't want to be in the lead because he felt he had failed." Gibson's jaw quivered. "I found him that afternoon. He had eaten poisonous mushrooms."

"Dear God." He watched Gibson cover his face and sob.

* * * *

Jason Elliott swung the axe and watched the tree fall.

"Looks like we have enough timber for the town centre now."

John Gibson leaned on his axe, breathing deep. "I hope so. I'm about done in."

Jason waited a minute before responding. He admired how hard Ross worked his small frame. The doctor had examined all the surviving members of John Gibson's group and figured most would never fully recover their health. Jason understood the reasons for the health problems but Ross had suffered mentally as well, looking haunted and grim. He lived alone in a small cabin in the Regal, rarely joining any social activities.

"That's okay. You did a lot of work."

"Thanks. I want to do my share."

"You do that and more."

John pointed to area of the chopped down trees. "This will be the site of the Williams General Store. Next to it will be a clothing store."

Jason remained quiet. Gibson spoke of his dreams as if they were real, often giving predictions of events both soon and far into the future. So far every one of his prophesies had come true. He rarely gave a date for upcoming events.

"Well, I guess that means Haven will be growing."

"Oh yes. Lots of children." He closed his eyes as if remembering a picture and then smiled.

Within a few years, families of five, six and seven were not uncommon. Construction of buildings was rapid as techniques of using native trees as materials increased. In a few more years, trees from Earth would be mature enough for harvest and they would become the new building material.

Haven was growing. It was ironic for Elliot when he saw the Regal, a symbol of high technology, lying like a snake among a frontier town built of wood. He wondered about the future, and if they ever hear from Earth again. He turned his horse down the path to see what the captain wanted.

Captain Marvin Anderson was waiting just outside the small farmhouse. The two former mates from the Regal had adjourning farms and saw each other often.

"Captain, how are you today?"

"Just fine, son. Come on in and have a drink."

The Spartan house did not have many creature comforts, though the captain was noted for his liquor he made from a still.

"So, Captain, what did you want to see me about?"

"You know, Jason, you are one of the few people to call me captain. Most have dropped the title. But I believe that you kept calling me by my old title has led me to my true calling."

"And that would be ..."

Anderson went to corner of the room and brought to the table a wooden model of a boat, of ships long ago with masts and sails.

"Ah, the model you kept in your room."

"Yes, and I want to build one just like it to sail in. We need to explore the ocean and the captain is the man to do it." He grinned. "When it's time to harvest those trees, I want some of that wood."

It took another three years before the ship was built. It was not as large as Anderson would have liked, but it was launched and he proved to be a smart captain whether at space or the ocean.

Jason and his family went to see him before he left.

"Jason, this is a fine world God provided for us. I wonder what His plans are for us?" He smiled. "Your boy is gonna be a tall one."

Jason looked at his ten year old son, only half a foot shorter than he was. "Yeah, like most of the kids here they're going to be taller than their parents. Ann said the boys will be nearly six footers and the girls will be tall too. She said the environment and healthy food is causing them to grow as tall as our great grandparents."

"Yeah. Some of the prophesies by John Gibson seem to be holding out." Feeble John Gibson would occasionally tell of his dreams of his father coming to visit him that told him the future of Haven. Some dismissed his tales of that of a disarranged man who couldn't let go of his strong willed parent. Others pointed out his predictions were coming true, including the appearance of the supernova in the night sky exactly three years after they touched down on Haven.

"Makes one wonder, doesn't it? He also said we would be found by Sol again and lead them to the future. Whatever that means."

Anderson laughed. "Just vague enough to mean anything and everything." He paused as he looked towards the sea. "Amazing to think when we arrived here we almost all starved to death. What a change. What a change. And for the better, to boot."

The Wave

Exploration and travel between the stars was made possible by the discovery that space could be condensed. The vacuum could be manipulated by generating fields of electromagnetic and gravity waves, and then unifying them as one force to bring space to its primal state, the eleven dimensions suddenly accessible to the spaceships. At this point, a ship could blaze through space that suddenly didn't exist at all. The distance between stars literally shrunk to nothing, the only barrier was the enormous power that was required to realign space-time.

The human race spread out from home, looking for new planets that sustain life. Many were found, some rejected as being the home of advanced life already. Still, several were settled by Earth's burgeoning population. On some worlds, the human race found it easy to adapt to, others required help from both Earth and technology to survive. Each planet was different, and it was impossible to understand everything about it until people tried to live there.

One thing all these new worlds had in common was the desire to be free of all of Earth's laws and restriction. The pioneers wanted their own constitution. Earth didn't challenge such a notion directly. It did demand that its laws were valid wherever people were even though it couldn't enforce these on the disobedient worlds. It fumed even more as trade routes bypassed it. Earth only had people and knowledge to barter with and could only watch as its best left for other places. Even the rest of the solar system preferred the outside worlds. Mars, the Asteroid Allies, Titan and the Free Traders all got better returns for their money and resources when they dealt directly with the outside worlds.

Then the Wave came. An explosion of unknown magnitude deep within the galaxy center sent a spreading sphere of mysterious particles that raced outward, and when it reached the region of human space, destroyed any spaceship it touched. Outposts were ruined as anything electrical was instantly destroyed. Planets were safer, but not immune as satellites were ruined and electronic devices failed. All high technology devices failed, computers, and anything that contained electronic circuits were likely reduced to garbage. Space suddenly became a hostile place.

Scientists didn't agree on the exact nature of the Wave; it seemed to have properties that a single particle couldn't duplicate, yet acted as a single substance. Eventually the Wave passed by, only to be repeated by another weaker wave a few months later. A final, and the weakest, wave came and went. Theories were bounced about to explain the phenomena, but it was difficult to prove any of them without instruments to do tests.

Civilization almost ended then. Whole cities were without power. Food and fresh water became scarce. Riots and gang warfare became common as people struggled to obtain the necessities of life. Many died of thirst, hunger, and disease, some elderly and disabled people were never able to leave their apartments, the higher floor suites imprisoning them. It took years before there was return of law and order. Power plants had to be rebuilt and slowly civilization was restored. Not without costs, of course. In the meantime, billions of people perished and many more became sick and disabled.

All the stars became isolated once more. It appeared at first Earth was going to suffer the most because of the dense population, but the other worlds of the solar system became desperate for any help as their high technology resources failed to survive and made their worlds inhospitable. Using only rocket powered space ships, Earth reached out to its neighbours in the solar system, offering any assistance it could. Some of Earth's population openly objected to helping the rest of the Solar System when they had problems of survival of their own.

Meanwhile cynics claimed the President, Liz Cartier, was clever enough to realize the opportunity this presented to Earth to dominate Sol. But in a famous speech she ignored the opportunity to force the rest of solar system to bow to Earth.

"… I want to extend help to any and all of our neighbours in the solar system. Earth will not ask for any favours or allegiance in return. We will give as much as we are able. Why are we doing this? The answer is simple. Despite our differences, we are all human, we all have the same ancestors, and we are one people. Therefore we must act as one people."

Most people were impressed in her openness to help, the speech was held up as example of people helping each other. It was reprinted thousands of times. The saying 'We are one people' was held up as example of Earth's desire to be generous to others. But it was the last line, a short sentence that was almost forgotten that was to change everything; 'Therefore we must act as one people' became a goal for her son. It was never proved that the last line was her ultimate goal all along, but no one doubted her ability to see a problem and solution at all angles. It was also interesting to note she wrote the entire speech herself.

But she made the offer appear genuine and never asked for any favours in return, but the rest of the solar system never forgot the help they received in their time of need. This later led to the creation of the Sol Alliance. Earth supported the move to establish Mars as the capital. Lost in the excitement of Earth giving up its seat as the official head of Sol was the creation of the House of Representatives. The House was the real strength of the government, often forcing the President of Sol to do what it wanted. And Earth's huge population controlled the House.

Under the leadership of Marcus Cartier (son of Liz Cartier), Sol prospered. The President of the Sol Alliance carefully set policies that allowed technology to return as a way of life for the people of Sol, and the mystery of the Wave began to unfold. Sol, after half a century of isolation, was ready to reach out to space again. Sol sent out an envoy to its nearest neighbour, Perplex. The offer of contact was spurned. Some were shocked by this slap in the face. Not Cartier. He had, over the years, pushed for stronger social laws, rights of people, environmental regulation. The credo, 'We must act as one people' kept reappearing in official documents. All of this supposedly to help prevent chaos in times of trouble. As part of a plan to attend to emergencies in case of another Wave, he created the Sol Emergency Forces. This organization grew quietly, eventually becoming a large, well-trained armed force. He was very much prepared for Perplex.

* * * *

After the envoy was rejected, Cartier still planned to establish some sort of formal embassy on Perplex, if they were willing. Eventually after much negotiation, Perplex agreed to an exchange of embassies for the purpose of trade. Perplex was the closest inhabited world to Sol and it seemed reasonable to increase trade there, but an underlying distrust of Earth still existed.

Other worlds were also being contacted to see if they were open to new, closer relations with the Sol Alliance. Some worlds had not survived well after the Wave, their population barely enough to prevent genetic problems. These worlds were more receptive to Sol. More successful worlds didn't desire a close relationship with Earth.

In fact, they often ignored their closer neighbours as well. The Wave had destroyed much in its wake, reducing the human population outside of Earth by over half. The worlds that survived decided they didn't need anyone else any more and isolated themselves, not wanting to risk being dependent on outside help anymore.

Perplex was a world slightly larger than Earth, but with only two continents and a smattering of islands. The Peoples True Government, a military supported dictatorship, was suspicious of Sol, but couldn't justify not allowing some formal recognition. Thus, it agreed to an exchange of embassies. Initially this was to be a trade delegation staff of approximately a dozen people. Within a few months, Earth had upped this to over a hundred, some to help with people wanting to immigrate to Perplex. Many of these extra staff were spies and while Perplex's government was aware of them they weren't concerned what Earth knew about their world. After all, what could the Sol Alliance do?

A year after Sol had made contact with Perplex, President Cartier made a special broadcast to the Solar System. He announced, with considerable regret, that human rights were being abused on Perplex and Sol had the heavy responsibility to protect its children. Citing that we must "act as one people" with great reluctance he sent off the Sol Forces to Perplex, the name Emergency was dropped from its title.

Perplex had never thought of having an armed force beyond controlling its own population, and the arrival of the heavily armed fleet overwhelmed the resistance. Fighting was brief, key targets were known thanks to the work of the spies earlier. Government leaders were arrested and sent to Earth for trial. A provisional government was set up in Perplex, and the people of Sol rejoiced that it had saved a people from a cruel government. It was not the first planet that was to be saved. There was some resistance on other planets that did not want to be part of the union, but most planets quickly accepted the agreement Sol offered in friendship. They could be free to do what they wished of course. All they had to agree to was the Charter of Conduct. The Charter spelled out what was acceptable in society in terms of law and social behaviour.

Besides the Charter of Conduct, each "Associated World" was allowed to send in a number of members to the House of Representatives, determined by their population and gross trade with Sol. There was also a cost to join the Alliance; some worlds felt the cost was unreasonably high. However, to agree to the Charter of

Conduct and not join the Alliance was risky. Everyone wanted a say in the Charter. And not to sign the Charter was akin to saying the world was hiding a dark secret. The alternative was to be taken over by force.

Regis was a prosperous world that was well armed and refused to agree to the Charter. It also rebuffed Sol's request to do an inspection to see if proper conduct was being observed.

Fighting was intense when 120 Sol ships met with 175 Regis ships. The Sol ships were better armed and manned by better trained personnel, and gave the larger Regis forces all they could handle. Those 120 Sol ships were soon supported by an additional 100 ships. Regis Armed Forces found itself losing heavily to the better trained and armed enemy, and reluctantly surrendered when another 100 ships arrived from Sol. The government of Regis was charged with war crimes and was taken to Earth for trial. Regis was the last world to oppose Sol with some planets sending an ambassador first to Mars to avoid any possible conflict.

Chapter Three

Year 2595,Toronto, Earth, 245 years after Haven was first discovered.

Robert Dural, a fourth year student at York City University, frowned at the screen. *Damn, I'm going to school to study magnetic/plasma corona power generation, instead I'm immersed in the social ramifications of technology on society. Why in the world do I have to take these time consuming courses when I should be studying five dimensional harmonics? What a joke.* But his report was due in four days and he was only half way through his rough draft. He took another drink from his tea and with an annoyed sigh started back in his work.

"…while there were some tensions between various Imperial worlds, commerce dictated that there had to be a large degree of harmony. In particular, the strength of Sol, both economically and military, enforced the cooperation of the member worlds. There was some speculation that the Imperial Alliance was already under stress due to some worlds wanting to establish their own identity, and not to be tied to Sol other than as equal partners. (More details of this can be found Thomas' Political Transcript Papers, Volume 6; Carne's Mines Give Financial Clout.

Library number R103A472/HJK7834/V6492229). However, speculation such as this often fails to take in account on the strength of Sol itself and usually focuses only on Earth, often interchanging Sol and Earth as if they were the same. Earth, with its huge population and restrictive ecology laws was struggling to maintain its role as the leader of the Imperial Alliance. Mars, the Asteroid World Allies, Titan and the Free Traders had slowly increased their trade with the worlds outside the solar system and wanted to move to even greater independence from Earth. Earth's efforts at forming an economic membership was spurned and it seemed that Earth was to continue drop in status among the 23 worlds …"

The knock on the door startled him. He glanced at his watch, surprised it was four pm. "It's open. Come on in."

Glora Bitmon bounced into the room. Her brown eyes, as usual, had a mischievous glint to them. "Whatcha up to Robert D? That report you were whining about the other day?" She peered over his shoulder. "This still your rough draft?"

He nodded, breathing in her perfume as he did so.

She pressed a key on the computer. "Show previous page." The computer obeyed her voice command and the screen flicked to show his earlier work. "Not bad. This your own work or are you copying text?"

"Mostly my own. I am going to indicate how when Sol became isolated from the rest of the worlds, then the other members of the Solar System had to forge an alliance with Earth. They couldn't manufacture enough goods themselves and also Earth still had most of the brains for new technology. Like, all the big universities were still on Earth."

"So the Wave comes out of nowhere and isolates all the worlds. Earth and the rest of the Solar System form the Sol Alliance. Mars become the capital, and everyone prospers under the arrangement. But how does that tie in with your report on how a balance must be measured between technology and society?"

"I haven't got that far yet."

She punched him on the shoulder. "God, typical guy. No planning ahead. I'll just figure it out when I get there attitude." She sighed. "Come on. You promised to take me to the game. If they play well, I might even help you with your report."

"All right. Getting tired of sitting here anyway." He stood up. Taller than most men, he stood only two inches above her five and a half feet. Her height attracted a few stares when combined with her figure.

As he shut off the computer, a fleeting thought crossed his mind. *What would have happened if Sol hadn't become isolated?* That question had been puzzled by many scholars over and over again. The conclusions were never agreed upon except that when the Wave was over after forty-five years Sol had become the dominant force. And though Mars was the official capital, it was Earth that would influence nearly all decisions in Sol to its liking.

* * * *

The game was a good one, Glora's brother scored two field goals and the home team won twelve to eight. Robert walked with her after the game to her flat. The evening air clean and fresh, smelling like the night air should even though they were walking inside. Technology in air systems took into account the time of the day, occasionally making the air smell like it did after a thunder storm.

"Did you hear they found another world?"

"No, when?"

"A few days ago they made contact with some planet that wasn't even on the list of worlds before the Wave. A pioneer ship that got hit by the wave on its journey. I guess they got lucky and found a star system that they could reach."

"Wow, they were lucky. Only about two percent of any ships survived when hit by the Wave and all of them were close to a home world. Where is this planet?"

"I can't recall where they said. I guess it's got a real small population. They're sending a welcoming ship there right away."

"Welcoming ship. Strange name for something that arrives with enough firepower to destroy a planet. 'You will be our friends or we will kill you.' A think I heard of an expression that the ancients used to describe our welcoming ships. Gun boat diplomacy."

"Well, that's true. Still it is exciting. I wonder what the people are like. Stranded from civilization for over two centuries."

"You mean stranded from our form of civilization."

"What do mean by that?"

"Well, Earth, or Sol, insists that all worlds follow a certain way of life. You know, the Charter of Conduct. But if you study the past history of Earth there was a different way of living that wouldn't be tolerated now. So maybe this world is civilized, but not to our standards."

"Hmm. You have a point. Sometimes you surprise me with your insight."

"Is that a compliment?"

"For you, yes." Then she laughed and ran ahead of him to her apartment.

You know, Robert, this piece below almost sounds like it should be a prologue at the very beginning of the novel.

Chapter Four
Oasis City, Haven, year 2596

The Premier of Haven was not showing the same excitement as the rest of the population. True, he did find it interesting that a ship had contacted their world by radio broadcast a few months ago. He understood it was some sort of science exploration interstellar vessel that happened to hear their beacon. They exchanged pleasantries by voice and then were promised the Sol Alliance would be in contact with them in the future. When that would be was up to speculation. Premier Aaron Duggan was not one prone to jumping to conclusions and for the sake of those he was representing thought he better lead by example. He had looked up the historical notes about Earth; what good they were was hard to say. A lot can change in two hundred plus years.

"Aaron, I hate to break your concentration, but you have a meeting in ten minutes with Roger Healy." Standing by the doorway of his office, Irene Thompson held up a schedule book. She was of medium height, fair hair, and had a figure that drew second glances from even the church elders. Besides being the Premier's secretary, she was also his girlfriend.

He sat up straight behind the desk. He had only just started going out with her and still was trying to impress her. At six foot four, well muscled from years of ranch work, he was considered by many of Haven's women as the number one bachelor.

Duggan had been ranching with his brother, but decided to take a few years off when his older sibling married. The house suddenly became too small and the walls too thin. His heart wasn't entirely into the business anyway and on impulse ran as a councillor in the elections. He won. Four years later, he ran for the Premier's job and claimed victory again. Irene was already the secretary and helped him ease into his new position. She was attracted to him but didn't give him too much encouragement. Their first date was at a church social, a bit awkward for both of them as they could feel the whole congregation watching them. Still, they felt comfortable with each other, both on a personal and professional level.

"Healy. He still wants the inside track on that road construction project by Crostairs. He does good work but I don't want to get the Melchuk boys' noses out of joint." He looked at her again, quickly glancing at her legs. Her skirt was not on the conservative side, just slightly above her knees. And her shoes had a heel almost an inch and a half high. To some it was scandalous that she would wear a skirt so revealing at work. No wonder the poor Premier was attracted to her. But Irene was comfortable with the new style of clothes, and was not going to let the more conservative members of the community dictate what she could wear. Oasis City was the largest city on the planet with almost six hundred thousand people. It was more cosmopolitan than the rest of the towns that surrounded it. There were several other cities on the planet; New Rome was the closest that had a population of about four hundred thousand. Each area sent two councillors as representatives, while the cities each sent four representatives, and the region as whole elected the Premier.

"Well, you are the Premier. That is until they change the title to President." There was talk that 'Premier' didn't properly identify his role. As the region grew, Premier was thought to convey a title of only one community instead of the planet. And since the office was now a full time job a new status was in order.

"Yes, well, technically I should put it out to tender. But time is important too. We can't leave the bridge in such disrepair much longer."

"So what are you going to tell Roger Healy?"

"The job is his, providing he hires the Melchuks to do the damn work."

"That would work." She gave him a smile, spun on her heel and left the office.

* * * *

Roger Healy, a mountain of a man at six foot four and two hundred and seventy pounds, wasn't happy giving any work to a competitor. "Damn it, Duggan, I can't afford to give work away. It's either all of it or nothing!" He slapped his palm on his lap.

"Mr. Healy, the title is Premier Duggan or Mr. Duggan. Or just plain Mr. Premier. Just because we went to the same school, doesn't give you give you the right to ignore the formalities of the office."

"Shit, Aaron, I don't mean no disrespect. But I'm just trying to tell you how it is in the construction business." He rubbed the back of his hand on his beard.

"Sure, that's okay. But I can't give you the whole contract without having bids on it. You either share the contract, and you are getting the lion's share, or we'll decide by lowest bid. That's how it is. Take it or leave it."

"I'll have to think about it some. Give me a couple of days to work it out."

"Fine. No later than Thursday."

After Healy left, Irene came back in. "How did it go?"

"Good. He wants to think it over, but he'll come around. He doesn't have much choice. To get the whole thing, he'll have to make a low bid just to be sure it's his. So in the long run it will be to his benefit to give up part of the work." He looked at her blue eyes. "How about lunch?"

"If you're buying."

* * * *

Toronto, Earth, year 2596

"Robert, I can't help it if they call me to Denver on short notice. We can go to Banff another time." Glora bit her lower lip as she looked at him.

He bit off his first reply. It was bad enough there were a couple of other guys he knew of as competition. But she was constantly changing their plans due to some business emergency. It wasn't often he had a free week from class assignments and not to mention how hard it was to get a place to stay in the mountains. He looked at her expression and it seemed to him there was more she wanted to tell him.

"Well, I know you don't have much choice. I'll go and relax at home." He sat down on the over stuffed couch. Her apartment was beautifully decorated and showed some expensive offerings. She had a well paying job with the Office of the Conciliate General, specifically the department called the Overseeing Committee for Earth of the Charter of Conduct. The office was responsible for social practices among other things, including the interpretation of the Charter of Conduct. He noticed her standing by the false window, a large screen that gave images and sounds of what a real window might show. She turned away from him, appearing to be trying to make her mind up on what to say next.

Robert knew he should have seen this coming. First, she cancelled the Banff trip, and now the hesitation before she let him down easy. He prepared for her to tell him that it was great knowing him and it would be nice if they could remain friends. Damn. He should have tried harder, not so tied up in his studies. She looked better than ever it seemed. She was wearing the latest fashion in Sol; a skirt with an uneven hemline that went from her knees to her hip. An open net sweater stretched tight over her top. He felt he was dressed too casually next to her most of the time. This time he was wearing old plastic pants and an open T shirt. He knew he should have worn better clothes today; maybe that would have made it harder for her to dump him.

"Robby … I was wondering if you would like to fly up with me to Denver? I know it wouldn't be as much fun as Banff and I would be busy during the daytime, but we would be able to do stuff during the evening. What do you think?"

He was flabbergasted. That implied perhaps sharing a hotel room together, definitely an advance in their relationship. The Banff hotel was able to offer only single beds in two closet sized rooms. Before, even when they had sex, she didn't want to spend the whole night with him.

"What's the matter? Offer not good enough? I can throw in a dinner or two."

He realized that he was staring at her with his mouth open. "That sounds great. I mean the trip, not the dinner thrown in."

She laughed. "Great. Go home and pack." She looked at what he was wearing. "Maybe we can do some shopping there too."

* * * *

Glora Bitmon looked about the hotel room, then at Robert Dural. He was acting like he was ready for a great vacation, grinning away as he tossed the luggage on the bed, then proceeded to open the nightstand table doors, sit on the bed to test its comfort, only to bounce up again and look in the bathroom.

His excitement was contagious and she found herself grinning at him. "Haven't you ever gone on a holiday before?"

He looked back at her, still with a smile on his lips. "Of course. But it feels different this time. Maybe it's the altitude, lack of oxygen and all that."

"Lack of oxygen?"

"High building in a high city. But it just might be you putting me in such a good mood." He walked over to where she stood, put his hands on her waist, and kissed her. "Enjoy your meeting," he said with a smile.

She just rolled her eyes. "You have no idea how dull these meetings are."

* * * *

The meeting seemed to drag on and on. Glora found herself checking the time, her attention wavering from the speaker at the table. She wondered what Robert was doing, wandering about Denver without her.

"… justifies the possible exclusion of article 14.1 B. I think we will all find it pertinent to review Dr. Bishop's synopsis of the Wellington Law on Citrefer 2. It is interesting to note that, with the possible exception of the Citrefer Free Traders, this law has wide spread support by the population. This despite Dr. Bishop's study which showed the law is not completely in synchronization with the Charter of Conduct, that there are parts of it that may not prevail in the high courts." Dr. Armand Niven signalled an end to his lengthy talk by taking a drink of water.

After a few moments, there was stirring in seats, a few scribbles on writing tablets, or the silent motion of fingers on the keyboard, depending on user preference.

"Dr. Niven, are we to conclude that you feel we should not take any action at present, that we should just allow this open flouting of the Charter?"

Loretta Widmark was known as a staunch defender of the Charter of Conduct, wanting every possible infraction rectified immediately. If she had her way governments that refused to take corrective action would be brought to court as soon as possible and the maximum penalties sought. There would be no negotiation or flexibility in the interpretation of the rules. She sat with her heavy arms crossed in front of her ample body.

Glora thought of her nickname of Lotta the Clown and hid a smile by looking at her tablet.

Pierce Gabon sighed. "Ms. Widmark, are you saying that the Charter of Conduct does not support freedom of choice?" He held up his hand to forestall her from speaking. "Please, let me continue. The Charter does not have hard edges to it, it was meant to be current two hundred years ago and must be current two hundred years from now. There may be a small deviation from parts of it, and if the local population supports it, and if it does not cause exclusion of other worlds, does it not still fall within the intent of the Charter? The Wellington Law does not, in any way prevent …"

Glora listened as well as she could to the discussion. Her superior, Dr. Margaret Rishew, was also at the meeting and would be the one who would make a statement that might support one argument or the other. Or, as it happened in the past, try to run between the two sides and come up with a compromise. Glora's assignment was to take notes and to give Rishew additional information on request. Several times during the day, her tablet would receive a message from Rishew requesting information that was not at her finger tips. She would quickly access various libraries from her tablet to obtain the data and relay the information back to Rishew. It was a test of her resolve to stay awake sometimes during these overly long meetings, paying attention to the discussion so that she would understand exactly the nature of the requests from Rishew.

Lunch was finally called by the chairman, and Glora, along with the other two dozen other participants, stepped out of the room. She was thankful she had a full hour to herself and didn't have to run errands for Rishew. Rishew often called on Bitmon to do extra errands as well during breaks of the conferences. Despite being one of the junior members of the Office of the Earth Overseeing Committee for the Charter of Conduct, Bitmon had been favoured with several important assignments. But for now she was content to phone Robert and find out how he was spending the day.

"How's the meeting going?"

"Boring. Dull. I'm having trouble keeping my eyes open. Where are you? Some bar?"

"More like a lounge. I'm grabbing a bite here and then I'm off to do some sightseeing." He picked up a glass of beer and took a drink.

She watched him hold up the dark liquid and wished she could be there with him. She was trying to take it slow with her relationship with him; she had even tried dating others to put a check on her feelings. But it was getting to be a losing battle.

Her best friend, Carmen, was no help. "He's good-looking, tall, nice, smart, going to make lots of money … is there something you're not telling me about him? Like, is he a convicted murderer? Grab him while you can," she said. But there was more to it than that. He was six months younger than she was, not a big deal just something she noticed when he behaved younger than she. Or was it just because all guys acted like boys now and then? Then he was also going into power engineering, which meant he could end up on a star ship. And her job was on Earth. So was there hope in the long run? She decided two days ago to find out, to give it a chance.

"Enjoy your drink. And I'll see you back at the hotel." She closed her phone, turned off her tablet and went to a food court for something to eat. She wasn't hungry yet, but she decided she better eat something before the afternoon session started. After scouting the various menus, she settled on a combination of various fried seaweed with an imitation cheese sauce. It was at least a healthy choice though she found the kelp a bit overdone. She still had some time and phoned another girlfriend, getting some advice on what to do about Robert.

The advice was to try to seduce him, or get him to seduce her. After she hung up she did some people watching, looking at what some of the women were wearing. She decided that maybe it was time to buy some more casual clothes, get some stuff that was fun. That usually helped when she found herself thinking too much about the serious side of life.

The afternoon meeting didn't move along any better than the morning one. But it was shorter than expected and at three-thirty she found herself walking down the plaza to her hotel. She had an hour at least to kill before she had to meet Robert and resolved to find something new to wear.

The first few stores she checked were duplicates of the ones back home; about 500 square feet of the same clothing presided over by the same type of sales clerks. The next one was a bit smaller, and she was greeted by a lady in her fifties. Normally that was a sign that the goods sold were for older consumers. But her smile seemed genuine and Bitmon noticed there were two younger customers inside as well as another, younger saleswoman.

"Is there something in particular you are looking for?"

"No. Just something different than what most of the chain stores are carrying."

"Well, you came to the right place. This store is a one and only. My name is Emily and I am the owner. I personally buy these clothes for the shop. What do you want the clothes for, business or casual?"

"Casual. I'm here on business, but my closet is getting a little flat for casual clothes."

They went through a few styles of clothes before Emily began to understand what she liked. "These pants are a bit different, and would go well with this top here. Both are shift yellow in color." She held them up, twisting them a bit so Glora could see the yellow change shades as it moved.

"I don't know. The pants are cut a little severe."

"Try them on, you'll love them."

She took the pants to the small dressing room, more of a closet than a room. She manoeuvred her body so she could change and pulled the pants on as far as they would go. They weren't overly tight, but fell short of riding on her hips. She felt her back, noticing that her bottom was barely covered. She checked her stomach, and was glad she had only seaweed to eat at lunch. The yellow top was short, and had oversized armholes without sleeves.

She stepped out of the dressing room and went to the view screen. The full-length viewscreen acted like a mirror, giving a mirror image of her front, and then with a push on a button, images of her side and then her back. Small cameras hidden behind her and at her sides captured various images.

"Isn't that a great look? A short top with low riding pants really makes your body look long and slim. And that's a great color for you too."

"I feel a bit exposed in the middle here." She ran her hand over her stomach, glancing in the view screen to check again how much of the top of her cheeks was exposed. Only a fraction, well within current fashion styles.

"Don't. You're young and pretty, so show yourself off. If your girlfriends don't beg you to tell them where you bought them, I'll give you double your money back."

"All right, I'll take them."

"I thought you would, and I have something else you might like." She held up a white blouse that had long sleeves in one hand, and a blue pair of pants in the other.

Glora liked the blouse immediately, having the right amount of frills to it. The body was long with an elastic waist. The pants looked too small, by a bunch.

"These are called skin pants, dear, the latest fashion on Mars. What's trendy there will be hot here next week. Try them on, you'll like them."

Somewhat reluctantly, she took them to the dressing room. The blouse was as she expected. The pants certainly stretched as she found the material easily changing their shape to mould to her body. They had a high waist and disappeared under the blouse.

The view screen showed what she suspected, the thin material had moulded to her perfectly, and if they were of skin color, she would appear to be naked below the waist.

"Aren't they comfortable? Here, lift the blouse so that the waist sits at the top of the pants, then let the rest of the blouse fall over. See? Isn't that a great look? You'll need different shoes, with a little higher heel."

"Yeah, these are for work. I'll have to admit this looks good. And this is the latest fashion on Mars?"

"Absolutely, that's where I imported it from. They're manufacturing them on Earth, but supply is still limited."

"I can't believe I'm going to buy these. I feel great in them."

"That's wonderful, dear. But before you go, I want you to take a look at this dress." She held up an orange dress with a streak of blue in it. It looked form fitting with a scoop of a neckline, the hemline at a bit of an angle.

"Hmm. It looks nice."

Emily turned the dress around, revealing a large oval hole in the back.

"Oh, that is interesting."

"Try it on. I promise you that you'll be the hit of any party wearing this."

When she tried the dress on, she certainly found it interesting. The neckline dropped a bit off center, exposing her bosom more than she normally did. The hemline was at an angle, going from two to six inches above the knee. The back was more intriguing, the hole was oval shaped, starting at the right shoulder blade and ending over her left side.

In the viewscreen, the dress looked even better, clinging to her just the right amount.

"This is really nice too. It's a bit too open in the back though. Maybe I should wear something underneath it."

"Oh, no. Nothing underneath. That is the point of the dress. Do you want to be a wallflower, or attract attention? So your backside is exposed a bit. I think it has the right amount of tease. Live a little."

"You're right. There are times I want to show off. I'll take it."

"See, I knew I would find you some nice clothes."

She paid for her purchases, more than she had planned but it was still within reason. She followed Emily's advice and went to a shoe store she described and bought two pairs of shoes that would go with her new outfits. That was way more than she had planned to spend.

She looked in a window of an exotic shop that offered means to change the color of one's skin on a temporary basis, such as brown, white or even green. There were also some pills that promised to enlarge breasts, shape buttocks or to add muscle. Then there were 'natural' chemicals that offered to reduce breasts, buttocks or to reduce your size without dieting. Hair re-growth was another item featured, and other remedies for removing unwanted hair. She would like bigger breasts but the pills were expensive, along with the possibility of some minor side effects. The results varied to some degree and were hard to reverse. Besides, Robert seemed to like her natural size anyway. The other problem with all the pills and gadgets that could do wonders for a body was that the government slapped a heavy tax on such luxury items, making them hard for most people to afford. Still there was a good market for these wonders, and as the ads said, 'no excuses for not looking sexy.' What happened was that people as they got older were more willing to spend the money to make their bodies to look younger. As a result, clothes that used to be marketed only for those in their twenties could now be sold to those in their forties. And if a person spent a lot of money to look younger and have a better body they were quite willing to spend even more money on the clothes to show it off.

She headed back to the hotel, toying in her mind, which outfit to wear when she met Robert in the lounge. Which would shock him more?

He was watching a game on the bar's view screen when she walked in, gathering a few stares. She chose the low cut pants with short top, reasoning that he could see it better in the low light than the skin pants.

Of course he was so intent on the game he didn't notice her until she stood in front of him.

"Hey, you made it. Wow, where did you get that?"

"You like it? I bought it after work today." She blushed a little as he stared at her exposed stomach. The pants were short enough that they only required a single button to close them up.

He motioned with his finger to turn around.

"It shows a bit of your bum there. Looks really sexy."

"Not too much, does it?"

"No, just right."

The waitress came up. "What can I get for you?"

"Fountain of Youth, strawberry flavoured."

"Sure, coming right up. Where did you get those pants? They look great."

Chapter Five
Chicago, Earth year 2596

Scotty Pearson tapped his fingers on the wood coloured glass tabletop next to his chair. He held a writing tablet in his other hand and looked at what he had written. Not bad so far.

Scotty had sandy coloured hair that curled any which way it wanted. At five foot four he was average height but had a small weight problem he tried to hide by wearing loose clothes. He rubbed at his two-day-old beard, feeling grubby in his sweatshirt and jeans. He wasn't too concerned, and had seen worse days.

The Scandal Lounge was a hangout for many reporters of various magazines and news media. This was one of the few places where writers of the less respected outlets rubbed shoulders with their colleagues, including those in more established media.

Pearson looked about, spotted the waitress, and waved at her. She hurried over looking tired but still gave him a smile.

"Patricia, you're looking as beautiful as ever. When will you marry me?" He looked her up and down, from her designer tank top to her see through pants. The tank top had a soft glow to it, giving a shimmering effect around her curves, and was just long enough to cover the top of her pants for a degree of modesty.

"When you wake up, Scotty. Are you drinking rum or beer today?" The sandy-haired guy's pick up lines usually amused her, but not today. She was not in the mood.

"Rum. How about sharing a drink with me?" Pearson was in his thirties, divorced twice and was always trying gambits with pretty women. He succeeded far more often than he had a right to expect.

"Maybe another time. I'm ready to go home right now." She glanced at her watch. "But I still got another two hours." She sighed. "My feet are killing me." She turned and walked back to the bar.

Pearson watched her walk away, noticed her high heeled shoes and figured that was a good enough reason for her tired feet by themselves. He flicked his tablet off, deciding he had done enough work for one day. There were a lot of reporters in the lounge who would normally love to steal his work but there was an unwritten rule that that type of behaviour was not allowed here. Still, it didn't hurt to be careful. And he certainly would only type his work on the tablet and not use verbal dialogue here. He had two more drinks, chatted away at a couple of rivals and tried to pick up another young lady before deciding to call it a day. Well, most of a day. It was still only two in the afternoon. He jumped into an elevator, went down forty floors to the third main level, and then used the pedway to transport him a mile across town. Another set of elevators lifted him to his office.

"Hi, babe. Anything new?"

"Name is Shelly. And if there was anything new aren't you supposed to be the one to find it, Scotty?" The receptionist turned her chair away from him and went through the motions of looking for something in a desk drawer.

"Hey, don't be upset. I'm just trying to be friendly. Is the Dean in?"

She stared at him for a couple of seconds, found it impossible to take him too seriously or stay mad at him for long. She softened her voice. "*Mr. Rolluck* is in the screening room. And don't call him the Dean, he hates that."

"I know. That's why I do it. He won't forget me that way. Thanks, Shelly, for putting up with me."

"That's why they pay me the big bucks."

"Hey, want to go for some drinks after work?"

"No, I don't think so. Lots of house work to do."

"Too bad, I was even buying."

Pearson went down the hall to the screening room, so called because a large screen gave a preview of what the newspaper planned to show the next day on its web site. Dean Rolluck, executive editor of NightHawk, sat critiquing the layout and stories one last time before it was sent out. Tall and slim he spent a large portion of his day pacing around his office as he yelled out commands to his computer.

This was the best part of the day, seeing all the hard work his people had put in the past days that accumulated to produce this day's edition. He felt a moment of pride.

"Mr. Rolluck, you wanted to see me?"

The moment of pride vanished. He looked at Pearson with a steely gaze. "This morning I did."

"Oh, well, I had a hot story to check out, and couldn't make it in the office this morning."

"That so? Well, it will be interesting in seeing your notes on that one."

Pearson felt he was being painted into a corner. This morning he was too tired to get out of bed, the card game lasting most of the night. "What did you want to see me about?"

"You do pretty good work when you set your mind to it. Some of your stories have even captured a large audience. But, and this is a big but, you waste too much time recovering from various extracurricular activities. You should be concentrating more on your work."

"Yes sir. I know, Mr. Rolluck."

"I'm going to give you a big assignment, despite my better judgment. If you screw this one up, or if I hear that you're wasting time, you'll be out on your ear. Do well, and there might be a nice little reward."

"Thank you, Mr. Rolluck, you can count on me."

Rolluck looked at Pearson after the last comment. "Right. Did you hear that they found another world?"

"Yeah, some planet away from the mainstream. Small population."

"Right. But this planet was on its own for over two hundred years. They obviously haven't been following the great Charter of Conduct. I suspect there may be a story there, maybe several. Maybe several great stories. These people will have habits that'll have grown quite apart from ours."

"So you want me to dig up material on this planet?"

"More than that. Much better than that." He smiled as he laid out the plan. "There's a ship that's going to Drapper. I have arranged for the ship to take a minor detour, and that wasn't cheap, to drop you off at Haven; that's the name of the planet. With a bit of luck you can beat the government's welcoming committee. And get a big jump on the competition – we got the last cabin."

"Are we allowed to go to the planet before the government officially arrives?"

Rolluck grinned. "It turns out that unless the planet is being sanctioned by the Alliance Worlds anyone is free to go there. The government hasn't come across the situation of an unknown planet with humans on it before and don't have any policies concerning it. It's a loophole we can take advantage of."

Scotty was stunned into silence for a moment. *Good Lord! He's getting rid of me by sending me out to who knows where in the cosmos. That S.O.B.* He put on his best face, determined Rolluck was not going to see him squirm. "This sounds like more than just a simple story."

"Like I told you, it could be a big one. I would love to send a bunch of reporters there, but that would spook them. So it's you." Rolluck then held out his trump card. "And Cindy Lorncroft."

"Cindy Lorncroft?" *If it was one thing worse being sent away by myself to the uncivilized galaxy, it was being sent there with Lorncroft.* He recalled she had refused his early advances and had made it plain she thought he was lower than a snake, telling him, "Don't talk to me. Don't look at me. Don't even think of talking to me or looking at me." All he had done was rest a hand on her waist and ask her out for a drink.

"Right. Cindy Lorncroft. You two will be going there undercover, as a married couple on their second honeymoon or something like that. It'll give you two a chance to poke around without arousing suspicions."

Pearson digested the information. A couple of weeks cooped up with a pretty woman like Cindy was not bad, not bad at all. Unfortunately, Cindy, the witch, could be most unpleasant to be around with her sharp tongue. As far as Haven was concerned, the stories should be there, and not likely a problem. But he didn't like the gleam in the Dean's eye.

"Oh, one more thing, Scotty. Ms Lorncroft is a niece of a friend of mine. If you are going to try any hip and grind with her, consider yourself fired. Even if she initiates the proceedings, which I seriously doubt. Her father is a bit conservative in his views and I don't want to have to make up excuses when I go golfing. Do you understand?"

"Oh. Of course. Never crossed my mind."

"Right. Scotty, it's time for you to grow up. These extracurricular activities of yours have to stop. Try to be a professional on this assignment."

* * * *

Scott Pearson waited in the outgoing lounge of the spaceport. The hard plastic bench didn't appear to be designed for sitting a long time, and he squirmed on the seat to stay comfortable. He flipped through the news media he had downloaded on his tablet, this one attempting to be less flamboyant than the one where he worked. At least the main articles did not deal with a sea monster attacking people on the beach accompanied by photos made up on some computer. Not that he would put down the "paper" he toiled for; the pay was excellent and what he wrote wasn't only interesting, it was often as close to the truth as some of the more serious news media. Still he considered it would be nice to have a little more respect by his peers.

Scotty had the feeling he was near the end of his current job and he couldn't afford any more screw-ups. He resolved he was going to leave Lorncroft alone and try to be a proper reporter. Maybe it was time to grow up a little. It shouldn't be hard to leave her alone; she may be good looking but her personality was less than attractive.

He shut off the tablet and scanned the area, spotting Cindy coming through the security check and as always, she exhibited a lot of energy.

"Cindy, I was getting worried that you weren't going to make it. Wedding jitters?"

She gave him an icy stare. "Hardly. I had to update my medical file for the passport."

"Well, we might as well board the shuttle. Don't want to miss the big boat."

Without saying anything, she turned and walked to the gate.

* * * *

The shuttle normally took three hours to intersect with the Starship Constance. Cindy sighed when Scotty sat next to her and she pointedly looked away from him out the window.

"Look, Cindy, we have to try to get along if we are going to have any success in drumming up stories."

"Fine. We can get along providing you remember a few things. One, we aren't really married. Two, my opinion of you hasn't changed since I first met you. That means, if you can't figure it out, no touching, no leering looks and no sly comments. Got it?"

He stared at her for several seconds. "Fine, be that way. No skin off my nose." Privately he had rather stronger thoughts about what she just told him. But if she wanted to play the bitch, he could play a game as well.

The space ship could hold over five and a half thousand passengers and crew. The passenger compartment was less than one-half of the ship's volume, the rest devoted to trade goods and the power generation. Each passenger berth was small, but was well appointed and decorated in rich plastics. The ship also had restaurants, gift shops, bars and recreation facilities.

Pearson sat in the small suite trying to finish off a list of possible stories to work on while on the ship. The journey would take twenty-two days subjective time, plenty of time to do some work. He didn't know where Cindy had disappeared to; she mumbled something about being too excited to stay in the suite and headed out to do some exploring. He was an old hand in traveling and wanted to get some work done before he headed out. He looked at his list, and added another item.

* * * *

Cindy was slim and of medium height with part of her Eastern India heritage showing in her face. She thought of herself as a writer, and though that was true in a technical sense, she had trouble finding stories that caught the readers' attention. Rolluck had hired her as a favour to a friend, and now the rumour around the office was that she probably was going to be let go as she couldn't seem to learn what to write for a tabloid. She knew she was in trouble and decided to inquire about Haven. She asked if she could go there to find a story and had even checked out a possible ship travel route. It did require a diversion from it's normal path but for a price they were willing to do it. That apparently impressed him. She flinched when he told her that he would consider it and then told her later that it was a go if Scotty Pearson went as well.

She drifted into the lounge. She hadn't enjoyed much success in striking up a conversation by the food courts. True, she could get people to talk there, but not much of a story was hiding there. And she did want a story; she wanted a story so bad she could taste it. She was sure Scotty was going to come up with a bunch of stories, he always did. But she didn't want to be just a tag-a-long to him. Cindy wanted to get respect by getting a good story on the ship, before he did.

She walked half way into the lounge, and then stopped and spun about, looking around. Her short skirt was loose fitting and flared slightly as she turned. Her top's material draped from her shoulders, which simultaneously concealed and revealed. The effect was eye-catching, and she noticed several heads turned in her direction. She pretended to look for someone in particular, sighed, then took a seat at the bar.

"A Breeze, please."

"Sure, coming right up. Looking for someone?"

"Yeah. A friend. But I don't see him. I guess he got tied up in other things."

"Well, why don't you just relax here? Booze is on special 'till seven."

Cindy sipped her drink for a few minutes, looking around the room. The bartender was wandering up and down his bar, occasionally wiping a surface.

"What are those guys doing? Some sort of a game?"

"That? Oh, just a game called seven run. Those guys are all off duty crew members and they like to shoot some pool to pass the time."

"Looks interesting. Do you suppose they'd mind if I joined them?"

"Hey, I'm sure they would love your company. But before I introduce you, remember they are not supposed to fraternize with the passengers."

"They won't get in trouble will they?"

"Naw. They just have to be discrete."

The bartender walked over to the group and came back with a dark skinned, heavyset fellow. Rather on the short side, he scratched at his greying beard as he was introduced.

"Corporal Willit Bushmar," she mimicked. "That sounds important."

"Un, no ma'am. I'm just in charge of the day crew in the generator room."

"Ma'am? Call me Cindy, please. Can you teach me how to play that game?" She pointed over to where the others were standing.

"It would be my pleasure."

The game consisted of using pointed sticks to knock balls into pockets. The game was similar to the game of pool played hundreds of years earlier on Earth, but the table was smaller, three by six feet, and with slightly different rules.

"Now, you have to have at least one ball bank off the cushion before you can sink one. Try bouncing off this side first, then hit this ball." He pointed the path to take.

She leaned over the table, quickly checking the back of her skirt with her hand to check how much was showing. Not enough that was too outrageous, she decided. It was certainly getting attention from the rest of the crew and they were all set to give her advice, as long they deferred first to the Corporal. "Willby" was easy going, but he wanted his men to know who was in charge. "Darn, I missed the ball completely. Are you sure this is how you play this game?"

The men all took turns shooting, leaving her with rest of crew for a several minutes at a time. The conversation flowing easier as the drinks made their way.

"So you guys must know some real interesting stories, stuff that never gets reported back home."

"Well, there are some strange things out there."

"Tell me. I'm real interested in that kind of weird stuff."

* * * *

Pleased with his initial list, Pearson walked down to the gambling casino. He didn't make much in the way of bets, but looked out for others who seemed to run out of luck or credits. He noticed a few that had finally called it quits but they didn't have the right look to them; not enough 'I'll win next time' and too much of 'I never should have made that last bet'.

An hour of waiting produced his best candidate. The gentleman in question was well enough dressed and didn't seem to be too upset about losing at the table. He casually walked out of the casino and into the promenade, glancing to the left and the right. Then he made his decision and crossed over to a small bar.

Pearson followed him at a discrete distance and then went inside the same bar. The man sat at a small table and had ordered a drink from the underdressed waitress; Pearson chose the table next to his and ordered a beer from the same waitress. A couple of minutes passed then Pearson stood up and went over to his neighbour.

"Excuse me. I noticed that you were in the casino a few minutes ago. Was your luck as bad as mine?"

The fellow appraised Pearson a moment before replying. "It's not all luck, of course. There are methods to counter the house's advantage. But to reply to your inquire I suppose lady luck was not on my side today." He held Pearson's eyes as he spoke, looking for a clue to his motive.

"Mind if I join you? I have a few hours to kill before I have to meet my wife and I'm new to ship travel. I was wondering if you could give me a few tips."

"Sure, why not. My name is Gerry."

"Gerry, you can call me Scotty." He offered his hand. "You seemed an old hand at space travel, what's it like when you reach outside the solar system? I mean, is there any danger?"

"Well, I suppose there are some inherent dangers whatever one does. But it really is quite safe. Are you thinking of those old tales that are sometimes reported in the media?"

"Is there any truth in those rumours?"

"Where there's smoke, there's fire? Not in this case. All those stories that were reported were just that, stories. But there are plenty of other things out there that go unreported."

"Really? Such as?"

Gerry laughed. "You are curious. Well, there's a region between Tobertii and Madison that acts like a time quicksand. Ships that have gone through that locale have experienced an accelerated time phase, nothing serious. Perhaps about fifteen percent faster than relative time. That doesn't get reported because it doesn't cause any real problems, but the space fleet is plenty aware of it." He shrugged his shoulders. "There are lots of space abnormalities but they aren't of interest to most people. Some science magazines report them, but most people don't bother to read that stuff. Or even understand it."

"So it's really quite dull out here? Nothing really strange or dangerous?"

"Well, there's lots of interesting things out there, but as I indicated on the space abnormality, it's usually something only scientists would be fascinated in, or could understand."

Pearson had done this type of interview before. He had his tablet on record mode since he came in the bar. Gerry had a good story and just needed a bit of push to reveal it.

"Sweetheart, could we have another round please?" The waitress smiled as Pearson held up his cash card. "Both drinks on me. Come on Gerry. There must be an interesting story that a non-scientist can appreciate."

"Oh, there is. If you insist, I know of a few that I have come across; some told to me by acquaintances. But it's hard to say to their accuracy."

"Go on. I won't hold you responsible."

Chapter Six
Oasis City, Haven, year 2596

The Premier nodded to various people as he carried drinks from the bar back to the table. To a couple of men, he said, "Hello, how're doing," and to some ladies he gave compliments on their dresses. The biggest of problem was keeping a smile as strangers came up to him to say hello or to offer advice on a whole range of subjects.

He finally reached his table where Irene Thompson waited.

"I'll bet the ice has already melted in those drinks. Did you stop and talk to everyone here?"

"At least once, some twice." He sat down heavily. "The drinks are extra sized with another shot. I figured this way I won't have to go up to the bar as often."

"Why didn't you just bring back a bottle for yourself?"

"What, and let everyone see what a drunkard I really am?"

"Well, before you pass out, are you going to ask me to dance?"

Aaron walked Irene to the dance floor. The music was slow enough he could hold her close enough to talk.

"You seemed to be on edge a bit the past few days. Is this contact with the Alliance bothering you?" Irene lowered her voice as they swung by another couple on the crowded floor.

"Yeah, a bit. I don't have a good reason for it but I feel nervous about this upcoming meeting with them. I mean lots of things must have changed in the past two hundred and forty years since we crossed paths. Too many what ifs are running through my mind."

"Well, they'll be here in less than three weeks. Maybe we can plan some sort of response to different situations. Say, did you hear that we are getting Haven's first tourists? A couple that are on their honeymoon are going to stop here. Isn't that exciting?"

"On their honeymoon? Here? Why would they choose us? Must have been a last minute decision."

"Hey, we aren't that bad a place to visit."

"That's not what I meant. It just seems peculiar to come here even before an official party arrives."

"I suppose you have a point there. Anyway, speaking of official parties we have only a few weeks left to work out what we are going to do."

"Yeah, there are some problems to work out. Some of the councillors want to discuss every detail and then vote on it. I'm going to push for a small welcoming committee that will have the authority to set up everything. Council then can give approval of the plan, or change it."

"Who would be on the committee? Councillors or community leaders?"

"Both. One councillor and two appointed, by me, community leaders."

"I wonder what sights we should show our visitors? Tourism is not a big industry here."

"It'll have to be somewhat open. They may have their own agenda."

She looked at him carefully. "So that's it. That's what gnawing at you."

"What? There's something always bothering me."

"But this is really disturbing you. I know, I can tell."

"Maybe you can. So what's bothering me so much this time?"

"You know what it is. It's their own agenda. You don't trust their motives, do you?"

"No, I don't know what they really want. They claimed they just want to reunite humanity. That sounds like an agenda to me that we won't like."

* * * *

"It's hardly fair that you get to stay in bed when I have to go to work," Glora complained.

"It may not be fair, but consider what my conscience is going through. It's hard to sleep feeling guilty like this," Robert replied, stretching grandly on the bed.

Glora scowled. "You sure don't look like you're feeling guilty."

"I could take your place at work but I'm lousy at staying awake during meetings."

"So am I. You know, you should go shopping here. They have some interesting shops on the sixty-seventh level and you could stand to spruce up your clothes a little."

"I know. But I don't have much credit right now and I hate shopping."

"Low credit? Come on, you had credit for that cancelled trip to Banff. Do what you want but if you don't get some new duds soon, I'll be embarrassed to be seen with you. Tell you what – we'll go shopping tonight after dinner. I like shopping and my enthusiasm will carry you along."

Glora left before he could come up with another excuse. She realized to herself the relationship had taken another level. Last week she wasn't sure if she should go out with him, now she was going to buy clothes with him.

The elevator stopped and she stepped in, one of eight people. All but one was dressed for business – a middle-aged man who looked like he was ready to go to sleep. By the time he got off on the recreation floor ten more people had boarded.

She watched the news on the monitor as the car plunged down, slowed to a stop and shifted sideways for several minutes before resuming the journey downward. She stepped out onto the foyer and made way to the pedway, glancing in windows of the shops along the way. She paused at a coffee shop to obtain a tea and sipped at it as she stepped on the moving platform. She had lots of time, and stayed near the outside to window shop, while others closer to the center whisked by her. The shops were all of a business nature, advertising various services that catered to commercial enterprises. Not much of interest to her, but her thoughts were elsewhere.

Her stop took her past the closed stores where she did her shopping yesterday and she peeked at the place where she picked up her outfits. She was even more pleased than before with her purchases, knowing what she wore last night was perfect for the lounge as evident from the side glances from both men and women. A few of the men were caught looking too long and smiled at her, while a couple of women came over and asked her where she got her pants. It was great being the center of attention and Robert staying close, being protective with her. She found her hand resting on her lower stomach, remembering that she was bare from her rib cage down to almost everything. She was nervous that her pants were going to slip down when she was dancing. She suddenly noticed where her hand was and quickly moved it away, hoping no one was watching her.

She reached her destination and quickly stepped off. She was determined to stop replaying last night in her head; there was work to do, and it was time to start focusing.

The elevator took her up to the meeting room; Dr. Margaret Reshew was waiting outside the entrance. She caught Bitmon's eye as she approached.

"Glora, I'm glad you're here early. I need you to do some background work."

"Of course, Dr. Reshew."

"The Klogend item on the agenda has been dropped due to changes in their government. So that brings up the Haven issue much earlier than anticipated, I didn't expect this to come up until next week at the earliest. Now it will appear as an agenda item after lunch."

"Haven, the newly discovered planet?"

"Yes, can you come up with as much data as you can on this world? The people, population, government type? Anything at all that will allow us to make an informed decision. Our welcoming committee is already in transit, but we must send them some direction before they arrive."

"I'll get right on it, Dr. Rishew."

"Excellent. Take the morning off from the meeting to do research and meet me here at noon. We'll go over the information to see what we have."

Glora walked over to where the elevators were located and touched the directory panel. An empty space blinked below the advertising area, and she touched the screen and spoke, "Coffee shops."

The screen blinked and then showed a number of choices within a few minutes. She chose one by the sound of its name and memorized the floor and location. Ten minutes later she arrived and picked a table by the false window, a view screen showed distant mountains.

She paused to consider what they did know about Haven, concluding it was very little. The Premier, that was what they called him, had indicated that they were the survivors of a single ship; apparently another two were destroyed by the Wave on a journey to a new world. Other than that, he was pretty closed mouth about Haven and its history. *So are there any records of the three ships that had left Earth together just before the Wave?*

Glora decided to type in her requests rather than vocalizing. She touched a function key on her tablet and a virtual keyboard appeared. The keys were semi-transparent, but as her fingers slipped through them, the letters reappeared on the screen. The keyboard took a bit to get use to, but she preferred it to the closely packed keys on the tablet's real keyboard. The screen then went blank for several seconds before coming up with too many choices. She thought for a moment. The Premier's name was Aaron Duggan. That implied the ships contained North American or European stock.

The choices were reduced to a dozen entries. She chose the first one and looked at the destination, a known planet, one that coincided with the initial inhabitation with the arrival time of the ships. Several other entries were the same, in others it was confirmed all three ships launched were destroyed. It seemed that either the ships avoided the Wave altogether by arriving at their destination first or were destroyed completely.

Near the end of her list, she came upon a launch of three ships that were hit by the Wave. Later search parties could only account for two of the ships; the last one had vanished. It had not arrived at the planned destination. The ships were leased by a religious order, by the name of the Starlight Collective, a Christian religion of some degree, according to the file. She pressed for more information. The Collective had ceased as a separate order, merging with a group called Leading with Brightness. They too, had merged with another order, the Children of Light. And they still existed. She touched her screen to go to their home page.

The Children of Light had an interesting entrance to their home page, flowing rivers of coloured lights spiralled towards a church door. The door swung open on its own accord, revealing a chamber filled with a choir of children singing hymns. The view carried forward, moving to the front of the church. There, glowing letters indicated choices a visitor could make, such as the history of the church, their beliefs, financial update, and so forth. She moved the pointer to a real time inquiry with a church member.

After a few minutes, she was able to converse with a smiling young man about the church. She couldn't tell yet if he was real or a computer generated image. She was fairly isolated in the coffee shop and decided she could use voice rather than the keyboard to have a dialogue with him. After a few pleasant exchanges, she identified herself and indicated she was seeking information on behalf of the Office of the Earth Overseeing Committee.

The young man looked surprised but did not waver from his smile. "That is interesting. How can the Church of the Children of Light be of assistance?"

"Before I go venture too far into an explanation can you tell me if you have access record to a religious order called the Starlight

Collective? Apparently they were merged with Leading with Brightness some two hundred years ago, which in turn merged with your order a few decades ago."

"Hmm. The Starlight Collective." He tapped on a few keys on a console, still smiling. "Well, there are some indications of records from that time. But I don't have access to them from this terminal."

"Are they classified?"

"Oh, no. Just that the information doesn't reside where I reach it from this terminal. I am going to confer for a moment off-line, please hold." He vanished, replaced by a choir of singing children.

A few minutes later, another smiling man replaced the singing children. This one was a bit older than his predecessor, and appeared to be in a more elaborate office.

"Hello, my name is Father Joseph. I have been told you need information about the Starlight Collective. Is that correct?"

"Yes. That is, I am interested in star ships that they launched. Specifically, the Mobridge, the Regal, and the Hood. These ships would have left Earth just before the Wave."

"I shall take a look." He typed a few keys and frowned. "Not much here I'm afraid. As you know, many computer records were lost from the effects of the Wave. I shall look in another file, however, that is useful for finding some of the older records." He touched some keys on the console and verbalized some additional commands. "Ah, here is something. Some of the records before the Wave were printed out on paper. Apparently, paper was used sometimes in place of view screens. Or perhaps as a sort of memory backup. At any rate, the written work was scanned back into the database in a compressed form. The processor has broken the key and is opening up the file. It looks quite substantial. What do you need to know?"

After almost an hour of extracting information, Glora had the data she needed. She thanked the Father for his time and efforts and donated a sum to their accounts, even though they assured her it was not necessary.

She wasn't finished yet. She contacted Universal Information Systems, paid a fee, and was launched into the glorified electronic encyclopaedia. A computer generated clerk waited patiently behind a desk, occasionally looking in a large book for some information.

Glora typed in her request. The clerk made a show of looking into his book again and responded with a written reply. The question and answer session proceeded for several minutes before she was finished. She took a break, and ordered a pastry and more tea and stared out at the artificial window. Between the data she obtained from the church and the speculative information she obtained from the encyclopaedia clerk, she could almost picture life on Haven. It would be a throw back to the twentieth century on Earth, more or less. No wonder the Premier didn't want to reveal too much about themselves, he may have guessed it could be devastating for Haven to come in contact with an advanced society.

After a bit more daydreaming, she finished off her report and headed back to the meeting room.

Dr. Reshew looked delighted with her report. "This is much more than I expected, even from you. We have quite a bit of time before the afternoon session begins so go and have some lunch."

Glora ate a small lunch and spent the rest of the time window-shopping. She had spent enough money on clothes already and decided to be a little more frugal for the rest of the trip.

The afternoon session was less heated than usual as there were not as many as controversial subjects on the agenda. This was good news for the chairman; he didn't have to intervene to stop disputes for most of the day.

"The next item on the agenda, Haven, is now open for discussion. I will remind the committee that this agenda item is for planning a course of action, and not to implement a policy. Starting with Dr. Schwartz, let us begin."

"My office has done some checks about Haven, but alas there seems to be little information forthcoming. The planet, as we know, is the second planet from a yellow dwarf, with roughly half land and half water. Other than that, there is little to be said about it. Perhaps someone else on the committee has a bit more information to offer."

The next four committee members agreed that there was little to say about the planet until the welcoming delegation could arrive. A new planet was normally the cause for some excitement, but there wasn't enough knowledge about it for debate yet.

"Dr. Reshew, do you have anything to add to what has already been said?"

"As a matter of fact, my assistant, Glora Bitmon, has managed to retrieve some valuable information about Haven. I have it in front of me, but I would prefer her to read the report this time. Ms Bitmon?"

Glora felt her stomach crash. Slowly she flipped her screen back to the beginning of the report and tried to remember her speech lessons of two years ago.

"When you are ready, Ms. Bitmon."

"Well, that is…Haven, as was mentioned earlier, is suitable to sustain human life without additional technological devices. The research I have done indicates that the Starlight Collective, a religious organization, launched a trio of ships just before the Wave. Two of these ships were destroyed but a third survived and discovered the planet Haven, not their original destination. Some of the records about people on the ship did survive, and some speculation about Haven can be made from them.

"First, the people on board usually were of North American descent, typically from the Midwest United States. For the most part, they belonged to the religious organization that had leased the ships, a type of Christianity. The ships themselves each held twenty-two thousand people, and if most of them survived the trip to the planet Haven, we can speculate on the character of the population there. Using Roger's Theorem on population growth, we can estimate the population is one and one quarter million, plus or minus two hundred thousand. This will be a conservative society that will not be as advanced in technology as the rest of the Alliance. At least that is the consensus of several social engineering textbook theorems."

Several questions were directed towards her, and she answered as well as she could. She noticed Rishew nodding at her with approval at the end of the questioning. In the end, the committee accepted her findings as a basis to start a database on Haven.

Later, Dr. Rishew complimented her. "You did wonderful, dear. You may well become our resident expert on the new planet. I suspect that there may be an opportunity for you to do more research in the future. No one else in the room had any data on Haven." Rishew smiled as she talked outside the meeting rooms. "Thursday's meeting convenes at ten o'clock, so you can sleep in. Go out and celebrate."

Glora hurried back to the hotel. She wanted to tell Robert in person about her day. Tonight they would celebrate. And they would have to find a place where she could wear her new orange dress.

Chapter Seven
Starship Constance

Cindy figured she had the men where she wanted them. Their tongues were loose from a few drinks and they were trying to outdo each other with fantastic tales. A few of them flirted with her to the point of putting a hand on her shoulder or leg but for the most part they were well behaved.

The stories were getting better as the evening went on, though so far there wasn't anything new, or exceptional. Corporal Willit Bushmar had hinted at a couple of other incidents, but was reluctant to tell too much. He apparently felt that it was to remain as a need to know for security reasons. The corporal was drinking like the rest of his men but was not showing any sign of the alcohol. *A pity*, she thought.

"Well, boys, we all have work to do tomorrow. You can stay longer if you want but make sure you're able to do your work." He stood up. "Ms. Lorncroft, it was a pleasure to meet you. I hope we have a chance to talk again."

He left the table. The rest of the men downed their drinks as well.

"Are all of you leaving too?"

"Afraid we must. The corporal is likely to work us real hard if he senses any of us stayed up too late or drank too much."

"But I was hoping for another interesting story." She gave a bit of a pout.

"Maybe another night." The speaker stood up and glanced at the others.

"Cindy, if you want a good story, you should talk to Steermaster Ravener, first class. He knows some dandies." The small, dark skinned man sitting across from her then downed his drink and stood up as well.

"Steermaster Ravener? Could you introduce me to him sometime?"

"Yeah, but sometimes he forgets passengers and crew shouldn't get too close."

"I can handle myself. When can I meet him?"

"He usually hangs out in the Amazon Lounge. But be careful."

It was too late to go over to the other bar now but she left feeling that she had accomplished something on the way to a story. She hoped Scotty hadn't had success yet.

* * * *

"So tell me this tale, Gerry."

"I might, Scotty. But you haven't told me the truth about yourself yet. You're not just passing time here, are you?"

He sighed. "I guess not exactly. You looked like a guy that knows a fair bit. Been around, as they say. I'm a reporter for a tabloid and I was looking for an interesting story."

"I see. I can provide you with a story." He took a drink while watching Scotty's eyes. "For a price."

"A price? How much are we talking about?"

"You get a commission on your work. Give, let's say, half."

"A half? You must be joking."

"Offer me a percentage then."

"Five percent."

"Now you must be the one joking. Let's strike a deal at ten percent and stop this haggling."

"It had better be a good story." He looked at his watch. "Why don't we meet here at eight tomorrow? If I'm going to use a story from you, I'll need details."

By the time Scotty had reached his cabin, he was feeling pretty good about his situation. He was positive Gerry was going to provide a story, his reporter's instincts were buzzing with anticipation. Cindy was already there, finishing up some notes on her pad.

"Hi. How was your evening?" Scotty noticed she barely glanced up at as he entered the cabin. *Fine, be cold. I can still act civilized. Probably piss her off even more.*

A few more seconds passed before she answered. "Fine. Yours?" She continued to work on her notes, her voice distant.

"Uneventful. Played some at the casino, but lost."

She finally looked up. "Scotty, what are we going to do about sleeping arrangements? Fake marriage or not, we have only one bed. I suggest you may want to try to be the gentleman and use the floor."

Scotty didn't like the way she put it, let alone the proposition. *She couldn't even bring herself to ask me nicely.* "I have another suggestion."

She sighed. "Which is?"

"That we take turns sleeping on the floor."

"Well that's one solution, I suppose." She didn't make it sound like she cared much for his idea.

"If you don't like that, I have another one as well."

"And what, pray tell, would that be?" She shut off her notebook and stared at him.

"How about a bet?"

"A bet. Like what?"

"This trip is three weeks long. A long time to keep switching sleeping positions. So I suggest that whoever comes up with the best story by Sunday wins."

"Wins what?"

"If you win I will sleep on the floor for the whole trip."

"And if you win?"

"We sleep in the same bed."

"I think I might prefer the floor."

"Whatever. Bet?"

"Okay." She extended her hand slowly at first, then quicker with more confidence.

* * * *

Cindy went to the Amazon Lounge, choosing a table where she could watch people coming in and leaving. She wore her blue dress that had a scooped neckline while a high slit showed off her leg that caught a few eyes as she walked. She ordered a drink and sat quietly, discretely looking at the other people in the lounge. No one looked like they were part of the ship's crew; she assumed that Steermaster Ravener would be dressed in an officer's uniform.

She didn't have to wait long. Dressed in the dark blue and white of the ship's uniform, a tall, thin man with an olive complexion strode into the Amazon and proceeded to the bar. He ordered two drinks, both a dark coloured liquid, and downed the first in a single gulp. The second drink sat on the bar a bit longer before it too disappeared. He then ordered two more of the same and carried them to a table. There he took off his cap revealing short salt and pepper hair.

She watched him carefully. No doubt he was an officer of some sort, but was he Ravener? The bar wasn't busy, and if this wasn't Ravener, he might still know a story or two. She stood up and walked to the restroom, moving past his table to make sure he saw her. After checking her makeup and hair, she left the restroom and approached his table. She watched his eyes move up from the slit in her dress, pause at her neckline, and then look at her face. He seemed surprised when he caught her gaze on him, looking a bit embarrassed for a moment. She continued to slow as she neared his table, coming to a stop in front of him.

"Hi. You must be one of the ship's officers."

"Un … yes I am."

"Well, I'm all by myself. Could I join you? Just to talk about the ship? I'm so bored and would love to have some company. That is, if you don't mind." She gave a shy smile.

"No, not at all." His answer was unnecessary, as she had already pulled out the adjoining chair and was lowering herself into it. "Be my guest." He half rose out of his chair as she sat down.

He signalled the waitress, dressed in a fake grass skirt and a top made of two large leaves, for drinks.

"My name is Troy Ravener, Steermaster first class, Ms …"

"Cindy … Adair." She decided against giving out her real name at the last moment, reverting to an alias she had used before. "Steermaster first class. That makes you pretty important on the ship, doesn't it?"

"I work next to the captain, Ms. Adair."

"Please, not so formal. Call me Cindy."

Their conversation drifted about on areas of the ship, Cindy trying to make him talk by acting to be fascinated with everything he said. In truth, he was not the talkative type. But she was sure he was holding a big story, if only he would stop talking about how he did his work. If he kept drinking, his tongue was bound to loosen if he didn't pass out first.

"Don't you ever come across something unusual? Something scary or weird?"

"You like unique things?"

"Yes, and strange stories. That sort of thing."

He leaned forward in his chair. "Well, my dear, I have been to almost every planet in the Empire, and I have a special collection of artefacts. Some of them actually predating the Charter." He whispered the last sentence as if she was part of a conspiracy.

"Wow, they must be something."

"Indeed they are. Would you like to view them?"

"Un … yes, perhaps later. Tell me some of stories you have come across."

"Well, the stories are best told in conjunction with the artefacts. Perhaps another time, when you are free. Would you care for another drink?"

"No, thank you. But how special are these artefacts? They're not illegal are they?"

"No, not really." He took another drink. "Illegal in some respects if they were used today. Some people would be shocked by them."

"Why don't we take a look at them?" She hoped her decision wasn't too hasty. But surely a ship's officer could be trusted.

A few minutes later, they walked to the lounge exit.

* * * *

Ravener's quarters covered two levels; the upstairs consisted of a bedroom, bath, and the kitchen. The lower level, where they sat, included in a small room that was primarily used for entertainment that included a video and sound system as well as a well stocked bar.

"Are you sure you want only tea? Perhaps a brandy?"

"Maybe later. The tea sounds good right now."

He sat next to her on the couch, drinking another rum. His hand rested on her thigh as he talked about how he obtained his collection.

Cindy held her mug of tea, deciding that if his hand should start moving up the slit in her dress too aggressively, she would accidentally spill the tea on his lap.

"Instead of just talking about these artefacts, can you show them to me?"

"'Course." He hiccupped. "They're in the next room. Shall we go and have a look?"

She stood up and turned towards a door.

"No, that's just a closet. This way please." Smiling, he gestured with both hands to another door.

The room was larger than the entertainment room and filled with objects displayed on various tables. It gave the appearance of a museum with its shelving and printed description in front of each item. She looked at some of them, not certain of their use. Ravener was silent, standing at the doorway.

"What is this?" She pointed at one of the items on display.

"It is called a pipe. It was used to smoke ground up tobacco leaves. That one there is over four hundred years old."

"And this?" She touched a hood with a screen in front.

"Oh, that is a themis. It was used on a planet called Jordan by people as protection against a hive insect called trites. Trites were not a food producing insect like bees, but protected another insect that did."

He explained several other objects. Some were interesting, but not enough so to generate a story. The gun collection was better for shock value and she wondered if it was legal for him to own such items.

She looked over to another table. "What are these things?"

"Ah. Those are restraining devices. This one was used by a police force on Terance to hold criminals."

"And this?" She held up some braided rope.

"That has a bit of a story behind it. You see on Cirbus Three they actually had a bit of a slave trade. There was a population problem there, and after a series of wars, the victors made the losers slaves. This was pre Charter, of course. Would you like to try it on?"

"No, I don't thing so. There isn't any slavery now is there?"

"No, but there are still some class problems. People, it is rumoured, are sometimes treated like a slave on that planet. Though to get around the Charter, they are paid for work after they serve a term. For example, a lump sum after three years of slave work."

He pointed to another group of items. "Now these restraints are more modern. On Praxton, all women wear collars given to them by their guardians. They also usually wear these cuffs as well. The females there consider them to be a sort of jewellery."

"How unusual." She looked at the one inch wide collar made of a gleaming white metal with a metal ring at the front. The cuffs were joined by a two foot long chain and matched the collar.

"Perhaps to some. Would you like to try them on as a demonstration?"

"No. That isn't necessary." She backed away and tried to turn his attention to some wooden bowls.

"Did you know that long ago on Earth, when they had ships that sailed the ocean, it was considered bad luck to have a woman on board?"

"No, I didn't." She took another step backward away from him and looked around quickly to see if there was a place she could run to, but he stood between her and the entrance. The counter blocked her other way.

He folded his hand on her arm. "They could get around that problem if the woman was nude, some of the sailing ships sported a carving of a naked woman on their bow for good luck."

"That is very interesting, but I really must be going." She could smell the liquor not only from his breath but also from his body.

"Oh no, That would bring bad luck." He increased his grip on her arm and pushed her against the counter. "Allow me to show you how things should be."

"Let me go!" She hit his arm that held her, but he didn't seem to notice and merely twisted her arm until she turned around.

She found herself pinned against the counter, bent slightly at her waist and her back to him. She kicked at him and tried to twist out of his grasp but couldn't break free. He didn't tear at her dress, but undid the buttons on the back and when they were undone, pulled the fabric off her shoulders. Now it became a wrestling contest, as he had to release her arm to allow the dress to slip off. Cindy tried to kick and punch him, but he used his body to pin her at the counter, freeing his hands to pull at the dress. A minute later, it lay on the floor. He held her hands together with one of his and picked up the cuffs. "These will be suitable for our demonstration."

She found her hands cuffed in front of her and then a thick collar was placed around her neck. She heard the click as collar and cuffs were closed, locking them into place. A small chain ran between her wrists and the collar that continued along to form a leash. After these were in place, he removed her underwear, leaving her naked and quite helpless.

"Let me go. Please."

"No, not now. How does the slave collar feel?"

"Awful. Please undo this." She started to shout.

He ignored her pleas and put his finger to his lips. "Shhh. Or else I will gag you."

She glared at him, but he only smiled and picked up the end of the chain attached to the collar and now led her around the room, pointing out other objects. "This is a branding iron. It was used to mark animals with a special mark. Not used on people, don't worry." He continued to show her the room, casual about her nakedness and restraints. "Are you thirsty? A drink perhaps?"

She took a drink of water, and then took a brandy as well at his insistence. She didn't wish to make him angry, for fear of some sort of punishment.

"There, now you've seen most of my artefacts. Plus you're able to wear one of them as well. What do you think of them?" He talked as he led her to the entertainment room, sitting down in a large chair.

"They're very interesting, but I should be going."

"Nonsense. Besides, you wouldn't want to bring bad luck to the ship by putting your clothes back on."

"I'll leave them off, if you will just take these collar and cuffs off."

He ignored her plea. "Sit on the floor beside me. I shall describe some of the duties of females on Praxton."

She didn't feel she had much choice. If he talked, perhaps eventually he would get bored and let her go. In any event, she was worried about some of the other devices he had shown her and didn't want to see their use demonstrated.

He chatted on their duties and then about his travels. For the next two hours and several more drinks, she sat listening to him. He acted as if it was a perfectly normal situation to have her restrained to his chair as he talked. She found herself taking mental notes on some of the tales and asking the odd question, the initial fear giving way to a reporter's curiosity.

"Well, I am getting tired. Perhaps it is time to turn in." He led her upstairs to his bedroom, the chain pulling her along. She applied a weak resistance, concerned that if she appeared too willing he would assume she had accepted him. On the other hand, too much resistance might mean other repercussions.

The bedroom was small, with a bed and a dresser and not much other space. He pointed to the far side of the bed.

"You may lie in the bed. As she did so, he secured the chain from the collar to the bedpost. She feared the worse and tried to prepare herself for him, hoping to blank out the last part of the attack. Instead, he undressed for bed, climbed in beside her and fell asleep. Eventually she fell asleep herself and woke up to Ravener leaving the bedroom.

He returned a few minutes later and undid her restraints, and told her to make use of the washroom. When she had finished, he instructed her to sit in the kitchen and gave her breakfast of cereal and toast.

As she finished her tea, he handed her dress back. She decided not to risk asking for her underwear as well, getting the dress back was good enough.

"You slept well, I trust? Breakfast satisfactory?"

"Fine. Can I go now?"

"Of course. Perhaps we can get together another time."

"Yeah, maybe." She slipped on her shoes, and quickly put on her dress. As far as her panties was concerned, if he wanted to add them to his collection, fine.

"Do you need help with the buttons on the back?"

"I can manage."

He showed her to the door and she walked quickly down the hall, glancing back to see if he was following her.

* * * *

Scotty was waiting for her when she made it back to her cabin. She grabbed him and cried for a minute, blurting out her story. "Scotty, it was awful. I didn't know if I was going to get out of there alive."

He didn't know what to think or do when she grabbed him. True, he was worried about her when she failed to return that night, but partly because he was concerned that she was his responsibility. The Dean would kill him if she got hurt. And he always was a sucker for a pretty girl. His resolve to be miserable to her disappeared and he patted her back. She continued to cry and blubber out her tale, which he found astonishing.

"Well, you're safe now. Do you want to see the authorities about pressing charges?"

"No. What good will that do? His word against mine. No sex. Fortunately. So there isn't any proof of anything wrong. Just another stupid woman in the Steermaster's cabin."

"Look, why don't you take a shower and then I'll take you for a drink or something. We'll get by this, okay?"

* * * *

As she showered, Scotty looked at his notes from the meeting with Gerry. There were several excellent stories. One was about a giant single cell animal that floats between stars, devouring organic molecules that it came by. Of course, the rumour was that an especially large specimen also swallowed a small ship as well. The crew apparently becoming part of the cell's food supply. The ship was discarded, and was later found as an empty shell punched by holes where the cell's digestive juices ate through it.

This type of story would normally be sent to the back pages of the tabloids except that Gerry supplied the name of the ship as well as the coordinates of the mishap. This might make the story more probable and move it up to the front. Another story was about a planet named Norety.

The population lived in the northern hemisphere, protected from the larger southern islands by force field fences. The south was home to large reptilian creatures, about half the size of Earth's extinct dinosaurs. It seems that the people of Norety would hunt some of the pseudo dinosaurs. They were not hunted for food; civilized people belonging to the Charter of Conduct didn't eat flesh anymore but hunted and killed animals just for recreation.

Occasionally, for a high enough price, outsiders from the planet were also allowed to hunt. Because the skulls were too large to carry, trophies were not taken, though there was little proof this was happening. If the authorities ever suspected this was occurring, the whole planetary government could be held accountable.

The Charter of Conduct provided severe penalties for such violations. This, if true, could prove to be a gem of a story. A final story involved a ship that had slipped into another universe for a full week. The physical laws of this second universe were extremely close to our own but for a few variances in the gravitational constant and the speed of light, both within one tenth of one percent. But those small changes made for an extreme difference between the two universes.

The stars were overly bright and intense, with small planets spinning rapidly around them. Galaxies were large misshapen clumps of stars. The ship somehow managed to reverse the mistake that sent them there and were able to return to our own universe.

The military refuses to talk about the incident but Gerry gave Scotty a bootleg copy of the ship's log. If true, this was a great story. But it could be a hoax, the difference between a story at the front to one hiding at the back of the tabloid. All in all some pretty good stories, any one of them would make home office happy.

They went for drink at the closest bar, feeling too cramped in their small cabin. Over drinks, she related details of her night.

"For crying out loud, Cindy, didn't anyone ever teach you not to trust strangers?"

'Sure, Scotty,' she reflected dryly. *Don't trust strangers but trust you instead? Scotty, the great 'skirt chaser'.* She let the thought drift away. "Of course, but he was a ship's officer. And I wanted a story. He was my best chance. A reporter has gotta take some chances."

"Yeah, some chances. But not where you risk your life. If you do something like that, tell someone what you're doing so they can go looking for you. I spent most of the night wandering around the ship searching for you."

"You did?" *I didn't think you cared about anything except money and sex.*

"Yeah, well, I couldn't sleep anyway." He took another drink, looking embarrassed at his revelation and signalled the waitress. "Did you get your story?"

"Only if you count a dumb girl being attacked in an officer's cabin."

"That might work. Change a couple of details. Make it Ravener's chamber of horrors where innocent young women are held captive. Could be a decent story there."

"You think so? What about you? Did you get a story?"

He was silent for a moment. "Naw. My source was a dud. I guess you win the bet. Let's go back to the cabin."

Chapter Eight
Oasis City, Haven, year 2596

Aaron Duggan checked his watch and sighed. He had used up most of the morning drinking coffee and reading the newspaper and now it was time to get some things done. He slipped on his favourite jacket, a black leather coat that was showing signs of wear, making it more comfortable than before.

He drove the truck down the highway, passing only a few vehicles on the road. He recognized many of the ranches he passed, having dealt with the owners a few times when he was ranching. A couple of hours later he arrived at his destination, the half-completed bridge that Roger Healy's construction company was working on. He knew it was pretty rare for the Premier to drive his own vehicle, a truck at that, but he felt keyed up and wanted to get away from the confines of his office.

"Hi Roger, how's it going?"

"You don't wanna know, Aaron. How's the drive up here? Much traffic?"

"No, not much at all." He looked at the half finished bridge and then pointed to the riverbank. "Is that what is causing all the trouble?"

"Yeah, the damn bank is too soft. It'll hold for a bit, but then it'll start eroding from the river. And the bridge will be unstable again."

"So you're suggesting carving out the bank and replacing it with concrete supports. Isn't that going to be expensive?"

"Yeah, some. But cheaper than doing it all over again in three years. Your choice. But I thought you should know why this bridge has to be rebuilt every four years. Whoever built this bridge last time should have told you."

"All right. Go ahead. I'll sign some papers to that effect next week."

"Fair enough. Hey, I noticed some red quest hooves here the other day. Good area for hunting."

"You might be right about that. But I'm not much into hunting. Fishing is a different matter. Use to fish about two miles upstream from here."

"You don't say. I might give that a try. Hunting is tougher on the body as you get older. Sitting in a boat and doing nothing appeals to me right about now." He kicked a rock with his steeled toed thickleathered boot and watched it sail down the muddy bank. "Appeals to me a lot, as a matter of fact."

* * * *

Glora Bitmon woke up with a start, cursing that she had over slept. Fortunately, she still had time to make it to work on time and she slid out of bed slowly, careful not to wake Robert. She jumped into the shower, dressed and looked at her orange dress on the floor. She picked it up and placed it on the chair. The dress, with its open back, was a hit at the nightclub last night. She wore it without anything underneath it; which made her feel erotic and nervous at the same time.

Robert stayed close to her the whole evening, and was pretty excited by the time they got back to their room. There were a couple of partial see-through dresses there as well but they didn't get as much attention as her dress. All in all it was a great evening but now it was time to hurry to work.

At work, the meeting was following its usual reserved procedures when the topic for Haven came up again. The issue was hard to define, as the planet hadn't been officially invited to join the Charter of Conduct yet. That did not stop several members from making long speeches about possible problems and solutions. Rishew didn't say much herself but did refer to Bitmon's report to make a point. The consensus was that there was not much information to go on, but that Rishew, for now, should head up the investigating committee of the Office of the Earth Overseeing Committee for the Charter of Conduct as she seemed to be in possession of the best information.

After the meeting, Dr. Margaret Rishew surprised Glora by appointing her head of the subcommittee to meet with representatives of Haven's branch of the Charter of Conduct, when and if they joined.

"Dr. Rishew, I'm surprised that you picked me to be a liaison officer to Haven. I mean I'm grateful for the appointment, but there are so many others that are senior to me." Glora spoke rapidly; she wasn't use to walking with Rishew after the meeting. Normally the head of the Earth delegation stayed behind to converse with her counterparts to smooth out the political waters, but this time she made a point of walking with Glora, suggesting that they go for a coffee.

"I have my reasons, Glora. And since we are outside formal office surroundings, you can address me as Margaret. I have had my eye on you for several months now. All your reports have been excellent and on time. You have shown an instinct for ferreting out information and making me look good as a result."

"Thank you." She sat down opposite Reshew in a quiet café.

"I decided to give you the liaison job because you don't have a built in prejudice of other worlds and cultures. Many of your colleagues do. My instincts tell me Haven is going to give us some surprises."

"Why do you say that?"

"You quoted, in your report on Haven, from some of the social textbooks on cultural diversification. I believed you implied a conservative society that held outmoded views. But because they are likely to be short of technology as well I think we are going to be shocked on their views of what is acceptable and unacceptable. And that, my dear, is why I choose you. We need someone who can be objective, and who can think outside of the printed words of the Charter of Conduct."

* * * *

Cindy looked at the sleeping form on the floor. Scotty had not once complained about sleeping on the floor since losing the bet. And Cindy did wonder if in fact she did win that bet. It was hard to believe Scotty couldn't come up with a story. For a guy that had a reputation as a womanizer, a drunk, someone that couldn't be relied on ... and the rumours why he was twice divorced ... he was acting quite different. And then there was story floating around the ship that a passenger had punched Steermaster Ravener in the nose, breaking it and causing quite a commotion. Apparently, Ravener had declined to press charges, claiming it was just a misunderstanding.

She later noticed the bruise on Scotty's hand and it wasn't hard to figure out who the passenger was. The why, she didn't understand. She smiled in the dark at him. Well, she would ask him when it was appropriate. In the meantime, they would be arriving at Haven in two days. She thought about getting even with Ravener and, if there were any way to make him pay for what he did, she would do it.

* * * *

Aaron Duggan sat by his desk in the dark. It was four in the morning and he couldn't sleep and ended up in his study. The expected arrival of the Sol Alliance Representatives in a few days had him upset and it wouldn't leave his mind. He thought of Haven and the small section of the planet the people had tamed on it. No real industries; farming, pulp, fishing had kept the civilization going. But what could they offer the rest of the galaxy? Nothing of value he could think of. Was this the end of Haven, a new beginning, or the end of the culture that defined Haven? He didn't like the odds.

PART TWO HAVEN

Chapter One
Sol Alliance Starship Monteith, year 2596

General Louis A. Burgess stalked around the bridge, his hands clasped behind his back. The crewmembers looked quickly away at his approach, doing their best to look busy at one task or another. The General's patience was wearing thin, and it wasn't normally any higher than his stature to begin with. His forehead turned pinked as he fumed, trying to understand what was taking so long in power engineering to repair a simple generator.

"Damn it to hell!" The crew collectively jumped. "That passenger ship is going to arrive at Haven before we do. A passenger ship, for God's sake, arriving before the Sol Alliance Representatives! Absolutely unacceptable! There will be consequences for this … this ineptness." He spoke loud enough for everyone on the bridge to hear, though to no one in particular. He stood glowering in front of a window size viewscreen on the wall that showed a host of stars that hung stationary around the ship.

An ensign walked quietly up to him a few moments later from her station, cleared her throat, and then waited for him to direct his unwelcome attention on her. She tried to make herself as small and inconspicuous as possible while still delivering a message. He finally noticed her and turned his head slightly to stare at her.

"General Burgess, sir, power engineering has an update on repair. Sir."

Burgess spun around and looked at the Ensign, Telli Parker. She stood five foot four, plus another inch with her shoes on. That made her three inches taller than him, and he took an immediate dislike to her.

"Well, what is it? Or am I suppose to read your mind?" His eyes became almost as dark as his hair; hair that required constant help from pills to keep it from disappearing. Unfortunately, for him, other pills were not as successful in growing a beard, leaving him with a pencil thin moustache that he would occasionally stroke with his fingers, pretending it was thicker than it was.

"No, sir. Power engineering said they would be finished by nineteen hundred tomorrow. Sir."

"Nineteen hundred tomorrow! Totally unacceptable!"

She flinched at his outburst, even though she half expected it.

"Inform power engineering that they are to be finished by oh six hundred tomorrow, otherwise, there will be an official reprimand. And you can inform them that I will make an official entry into their personnel files."

"Yes sir." She turned away and walked briskly back to her console, releasing her breath as she rolled her eyes upward.

That didn't escape the attention of Captain Lorraine Ellison who was watching the orders with interest. The General had stepped into her jurisdiction, and not just for the first time. It was unfortunate there wasn't much she could do about it. She felt sorry for the power engineering staff; she knew what was involved in repairing the generator and it certainly wasn't a simple task to calibrate and set one up. The reason it failed was because the General had ordered the ship to achieve a speed it wasn't designed to do for extended periods. She would make sure that she would add something to their files as well, a carefully worded entry that would help lessen the negative aspects of his opinion.

Between an arrogant diplomat and the equally boorish General Burgess, she had her hands full trying to keep her ship running smoothly. Another general would not have infringed on her commands. And if it was another general, she might have even made some noise about it. But not when it was the famous General Burgess, leading the Imperial Alliance to victories over the rebel government on Thomas, quelling the riots in New America and then in Taurus.

There were some military observers that questioned how difficult it was to defeat an enemy when you not only outnumbered them in terms of men and equipment, but also had the advantage of superior weaponry. Nevertheless, Burgess had risen to the highest rank and become one of the most powerful military men in the Imperial Alliance, partly because of those victories. As for Dr. Roger Beaumont, it was good thing there was a large supply of liquor on board and that the female crewmembers had been warned about him ahead of time. His favourite pastime was to use his tall, handsome features and diplomat's charm to try to seduce as many women as possible.

* * * *

In orbit around Haven

Scotty spent three hours on the ship's communication terminal talking to a bank representative on Haven. Oasis City was the capital, and where they were scheduled to land, providing the local airport could double as a spaceport. Scotty tried to arrange a transfer of galactic funds to the local currency. The bank official was reluctant to accept galactic funds on anything more than a fraction of their value to convert it to the Haven monetary system. Scotty expected that reaction and offered a combination of platinum and gems as security. The ship's captain, who was anxious to depart, helped arranged for the transfer of the collateral. The bank official looked pleased with negotiated exchange of Haven currency funds.

There was another reason the captain was anxious for Pearson and Lorncroft to depart, and that was the altercation between him and one of his officers. Pearson had walked up to him while on duty, established the officer's identity and then punched him in the nose, right outside the officer's dining lounge. With all the other officers present it caused quite a commotion. Security was called and it looked like things could get quite complicated. The captain was not anxious to fill out all the required reports concerning the incident and then work out the appropriate measure of discipline to the officer, if any.

As far as the passenger was concerned, that could be even more difficult. In a bit of a surprise the officer had declined to press charges and the captain was not sure exactly what had transpired earlier to cause the problem, though he had his suspicions. There were whispers and rumours concerning Ravener and his off duty time, though he was an otherwise excellent officer.

The captain decided he better vouch for the accuracy of the funds; not only was the negotiation using up time, he would also have to wait while the shuttlecraft dropped off the two passengers and then returned. The captain pointed out that there were going to be other visitors and there likely would be other financial trading done in the future. If the bank official was not prepared to bargain in good faith this time, the bank may not receive its fair share of business in the future.

"Are you ready, Cindy?"

"As ready as I can be. Pretty ugly dress, huh?" The light green dress was loose fitting with the hemline just above the knee.

"Well, we have to dress like the locals. Don't want to cause a scandal, do we?"

"That's easy for you to say. Men seem to wear the same style of clothes no matter where they go. I feel like I've borrowed my grandmother's clothes."

"Well, I guess you can't wear sexy clothes all the time."

"Hey, you don't know what I'm wearing for underwear. It might be sexy."

"I'll bet it is."

"And you're not going to find out." She grinned and headed to the shuttle, carrying an oversized handbag with her.

He watched her walk towards the exit with a bit of interest. She could put on the charm when she wanted to. He had noticed that she had thawed out considerably during the trip and was almost pleasant to him on several occasions. But he also recalled her attitude at the beginning of the trip and sensed that she was only being nice to him because he was there to support her after her crisis with Ravenor. He also remembered what she said to him on the shuttle; that her opinion of him hadn't changed since she first met him. While he could let that go, he was also aware she could swing back to being her old miserable self. No, he would keep cool towards her as much as possible. Besides, he also remembered the Dean's warning about any extracurricular activities with her. His job was more important to him than any fling with a moody, spoiled girl, whose rich daddy kept bailing her out.

* * * *

The shuttle landed without a problem at the airport that was suddenly converted to a spaceport. The shuttle was the largest vehicle on the runway, and what it lacked in wingspan it made up in length, looking like a huge tube with small wing tips along its body.

The airport was bursting with activity as Scotty and Cindy left the shuttle and entered a covered tunnel that was fortunate to be long enough to reach the exit doors. They were surprised at the crowd in the terminal that came to see them as they made their way into the arrival foyer. The couple smiled and waved at their greeters, feeling like celebrities. They stood in the small two-story terminal, looking around. The glass windows gave an appearance of openness that was startling after the time they spent aboard the ship. Their bags were picked up by airport personnel, several young men actually wrestled for the privilege of doing so. The manager of the airport herself led them through the terminal. She tried to be professional as she talked to them, but she giggled nervously as she asked them questions about their flight.

"… such a long journey, of course you do travel fast so it wouldn't take so long. Oh, dear, I just keep rambling on, don't I?"

Scotty smiled back at her. She had a fair complexion, blonde hair and was tall – taller than he was. He looked around and noticed everyone, including the ever-smiling baggage handlers who were tall and, for the most part, fair skinned. She also spoke with a heavy accent, not hard to understand, but with a pleasant sound to it.

She guided them towards the exit, then to a waiting taxi. The taxi driver was grinning away, standing in front of his just washed and waxed car. There were other taxis as well, but they were parked a bit further away and were not nearly as clean.

There was another small crowd waiting outside the terminal doors. The assembly was quiet and well mannered. Some held up signs welcoming the visitors, but most were content to look, wave and take pictures. They felt a bit foolish as they waved at them and returned their smiles. They both hesitated before stepping outside to the taxi. Neither of them had actually been outside a building on Earth in the past several years, though many buildings had interior parks with ceilings that gave the indication of being outside. With everyone watching them, they stepped boldly forward and gamely sat in the taxi.

Cindy giggled at the attention they were getting. The trip was a novelty for both of them. She had been in a personal ground transportation only once before, and that was on Mars. Scotty was a bit more worldly and had been in one three times, once on Mars and twice in Africa. But both of them were unprepared as the taxi drove down streets, stopping at intersections and moving along with other vehicles. Pearson noted there were traffic control devices in the form of lights and signs, but didn't try to decipher them. Most of the buildings looked to be made of stone or brick, averaging less than ten stories high. Both Scotty and Cindy were amazed to see people walking up and down the streets without the protective covering of a building.

The taxi pulled up to the curb in front of a large grey building proclaiming, "Haven National Bank" in gold coloured lettering above the double doors. Scotty stepped out of the cab and hesitated before leaving the edge of the sidewalk. He received a few glances from passers-by as he reached the doors. Cindy watched nervously from the cab as he stood in front of the doors, but they refused to open. A woman exiting from the bank held open one of the glass doors for him and he ducked inside. It suddenly became apparent to him that the doors were not powered, that he had to push them for them to open. He strolled slowly across the floor, looking around when a woman, wearing a conservative suit approached him.

"Hello, you must be Scott Pearson. My name is Patricia Simmons, I'm one of the managers here at Haven National Bank." She beamed at him, her smile straining to cover her large face. "Mr. Payne, the bank president will personally assist you with the financial arrangements." Smiling all the way she led him to a small office in the corner, where a tall, older man stood up to shake his hand. His voice was as thin as his neck that stuck out of a high-collared shirt. "Welcome, Mr. Pearson, welcome!"

Scotty wasn't sure he meant welcome to Haven or welcome to the bank, but he gave a return smile and thanked Payne with the same enthusiasm. The bank gave him two plastic cards, a book of cheques and some paper money. He had Scotty sign some documents and a few minutes later, he left the bank.

Scotty and Cindy were amused by the paper money and cheques, not too sure what the cheques were to be used for. The plastic cards were easier to figure out. While not as elaborate as the cards back home, they could use them without being puzzled. They also found out their tablets didn't function on Haven; the Internet didn't respond to any inquires and payment for merchandise couldn't be made through it either. When they reached their hotel, Pearson had trouble paying the driver; he simply didn't want to take his money. The driver tried to explain, in the strange dialect that was spoken on Haven, that it was an honour to drive them. Pearson eventually gave him some paper that passed for currency and the driver finally took it, but then insisted on autographs as well.

"Did you see how tall these people are? The men are all over six feet! The women are nearly as tall too. No fashion sense though," Cindy whispered to Scotty, who was doing a wide eyed search himself.

"Yeah, they're tall, that's for sure. Did you notice that they are all nearly white, you know, Caucasian? When was the last time you saw this many people of one race clumped together?"

As they entered the Oceanview Hotel, the odd feeling of being outside returned to them. Cindy looked straight ahead, scared of the open sky, and waited for Scotty to finish his nervous look at the clouds above them.

"Wow. Those view screens don't do the outside justice."

Several people waited at the hotel entrance, some were reporters, but others appeared to be ordinary citizens who wanted to see the first people from Earth. A little girl shyly came forward and presented Cindy with flowers and then ran back to hide behind her mother. The reporters recorded the scene but didn't approach the couple. Pearson wondered how a reporter could be so polite and stay working.

The Oceanview Hotel staff was obviously well prepared for them as well. Several staff members clustered around at the front desk as they signed in, the grins on their faces bursting forth when Scotty put down the pen. He noticed the manager pick up the pen and wrap it in a cloth before putting it in his pocket. A group of four staff members led them to their room, smiling away but too nervous to say much other than wishing them a pleasant stay.

They finally managed to leave the stares and smiles behind when they reached their hotel room, closing a door. Scotty thought the door looked remarkably like wood, and that the plastic fibre material had to be of top-notch quality. The luggage was placed by the bed and Scotty reached into his pocket to give them some of the paper money, not certain just how much five dollars was actually worth. Before he could separate the bills from one another, the bell boys were gone, quietly closing the door behind them.

"That was odd. Maybe they tip only when the guest is paying, out of the hotel bill."

Cindy sat down on the couch. "Wow, that was some greeting. Nice people, awful clothes."

"Come on, Cindy. You're still not on about their fashions are you? These are just conservative people. Decent size hotel room. Big bed, a couch, chairs and even a kitchenette."

"It is nice and big. Look at the size of the view screen."

He walked over to the window. "Hey, that's not a viewscreen; that is a real window."

"Oh, my gosh." She took a step back. "A real window. And look at the view! A lake with a beach."

"That's an ocean, not a lake. This might be a fun work assignment."

"Hey, Scotty, looks like you won't have to sleep on the floor."

"Yeah?"

She saw the hope in his eyes. "The couch folds out to a bed. You can have that, and I'll get the bed."

"That was mean."

"I know. Sorry. Hey, I'm hungry, let's go eat."

"Okay, do you want to order in?"

"No, let's go for a walk around outside and find a place. I want to try to get use to being outdoors." She thought for a moment. "It is safe to go outside, isn't it? Nothing bad will happen, will it?"

"Oh, we'll be fine. These people are outdoors all the time and it doesn't bother them." He spoke more confidently than he felt. He had felt dizzy when he looked at the open sky last time. He wondered if something could fall out of the sky. Without a building to protect them, perhaps there was a bit of danger. He remembered walking outside on Mars, and knew that was safe. Of course, on Mars a giant transparent bubble protected the whole city, so he really wasn't outside.

Chapter Two

The restaurant they chose was just a block away from the hotel, not far to walk. Even so, a number of the locals stopped them to say hello, ask them about Earth. Politely they answered with a quick response and went on their way. They finally stepped inside the restaurant and were led by a grinning hostess to a table.

"It's going to be tough to do undercover work. Everyone seems to know us on sight. Do you understand these menu items?" Cindy whispered across the table, her eyes flicking side to side to see who might be watching.

"Well, I don't think we have to do undercover work. I think the natives are more than willing to talk. Stories are going to be easy to come by. These menu items are a little different. The items on the bottom must be a type of fish or sea food." He looked at her, wondering if she was willing to eat fish. A good portion of the population on Earth now refused to eat fish, considering them to be too intelligent to be used for food. Several lobbyist groups were trying to get the majority of fish declared as being self-aware. The definition of being self-aware would mean to use fish as a food would require special permits of consumption. Some animals, such as pigs, monkeys and whales had an elevated status of not only self-awareness but also understanding life cycles. The definition of understanding life cycles a grey area, but once the Charter of Conduct Office passed them, that particular animal was protected from humans. "Do you eat fish?"

She looked embarrassed for a moment, then nodded. "Not too much, but I don't think fish, at least most of them, should be considered self-aware."

"I agree. But I want to know what some of the other items on this menu are." He waved over at the waiter who hurried over.

The waiter explained the different dishes for them.

"… and these are the different steaks we have available."

Cindy looked at where his finger pointed. "What do you make your steaks from?"

"Make them from? Oh, you mean from what animal. We use only grain fed cattle."

"You mean this steak comes from a real animal, not soybean or vegetable matter?"

"Well, yes." He looked puzzled. "But we do have other dishes besides steaks."

Scotty looked at her bewildered expression. "Give us a few minutes please."

"Certainly, sir." He turned and walked away.

"Scotty, they eat animals here!" She spoke in a hushed tone, looking around the room to see who might be in hearing distance.

Scotty felt she was acting as if she was in some cheap spy movie. "I know. Let's not make a scene though. There must be some safe stuff here we can eat. Let's order, let me see, this pasta dish. And there's this seafood thing as well. My Lord, I can't believe that this story just dropped into our laps like this!"

The food they ordered was good, though Cindy poked through her plate looking for suspicious items. Scotty was full from his meal but she ordered dessert as well, devouring the pastry dish.

They paid with the meal using one of the plastic credit cards and assured the waiter the meal was great. There was an awkward moment when Scotty decided he better ask what gratuity was expected, not wanting to either under or over tip.

"Gratuity, sir? I am afraid I don't quite understand. Are you referring to a sum paid in addition to the meal?"

"Yes. A tip. Say, for example, a percentage of the meal."

"That is very kind of you to offer, but you will find, with the possible exception of home delivery personnel, tipping isn't done here on Haven."

Slightly embarrassed Scotty thanked him and then followed Cindy outside.

"Now what, Scotty?" They walked down towards the waterfront, still receiving too much attention, but at least the inquiries were polite. "And by the way, stop ignoring me like we're strangers to each other. We're supposed to be on our honeymoon."

Cindy had been dreading the thought of spending an assignment with Scotty at one time. But so far he had paid little attention to her, far too little attention as a matter of fact. Being on a supposed honeymoon, he could have gotten away with a few grabs and sometimes a quick kiss, maybe even a smack on her bum. But he really was ignoring her, something she found quite annoying, even insulting. She had told him at the beginning of the trip that he better not touch her, to keep his wandering paws to himself. But she hadn't expected him to actually do that completely.

"Oh, right. Our cover." He slowed down and walked next to her.

"That looks better." She slipped her hand through his arm. She wondered again, why he hadn't made a move on her yet, content with sly comments and a few winks now and then. Maybe she just wasn't his type. She didn't have trouble attracting other men but was still annoyed at his indifference. She felt she should at least have the chance to reject his advances.

The waterfront was interesting, the smell of the ocean intoxicating. They walked down the pier, watching birds circle and then suddenly swoop down, usually carrying something back up. There were several boats and a couple of larger ships in the water. The larger ships caught their interest. These types of floating vessels had all but disappeared from Earth as they sat low in water. Most Earth ships stayed high in the water to avoid drag, using their high-powered fusion generators to provide lift and drive.

In all, several ships were moored just outside the pier. A sign on one of the large buildings that fronted the ocean proclaimed Captain Anderson Shipping.

They went along a paved sidewalk, not saying much except to point out another sight. Cindy continued to hold his arm, occasionally switching to his hand. It was a good deception; they acted like a newly married couple.

"Scotty, that small dock by the shed?"

"Yeah?"

"Is that real wood?"

"Real wood? But that would be an awfully expensive material for a dock. Let's take a closer look."

The dock was made of wood, weathered wood to be sure, but there was no mistaking this as a clever plastic fibre copy.

"Scotty, this means they use wood as a common building material! Does the Charter allow for using wood like this?"

"I don't know. Wait, there're special conditions in which trees may be harvested. But those are very rare conditions. And the wood is extremely expensive, certainly not for use in building a dock."

"Good afternoon."

The quiet voice behind them startled them and they turned quickly to see a young man approaching them wearing a coverall with several pockets plus a leather tool belt. There was an assortment of tools attached or hanging from the various pockets and clips, making a musical clinking sound as he walked.

"Best be careful, that old dock may have some loose boards."

Cindy looked him up and down, and then up and down again. Almost six feet tall, a well tanned complexion, handsome, well muscled, though perhaps just a bit on the heavy side. Her jaw dropped. She then felt her hand being squeezed tight by Scotty. *Ouch!*

"Oh, thank you. My wife and I were just taking a closer look at your dock."

"Not anyone's dock. It's not used much except to unload a rowboat or something like that." He shrugged his shoulders. Then suddenly recognition lit up his face. "You must be Mr. and Mrs. Pearson! Pleased to meet you!" He stuck out his hand after he wiped it on his pant leg. "My name is Christian Rossdale. I saw your pictures on the newscast."

Scotty found his grip strong and tried to counter as well as he could. Cindy had recovered her composure sufficiently and offered her hand as well, which he took gently.

Cindy listened to the two men talk about wood on the dock and then what Christian did for a living. He was a farm boy who decided to make a few dollars in the slow season as a handyman in the city. She thought about Scotty's reaction when she first saw him. Was the hand squeeze and 'my wife' bit to prevent her from acting foolishly, or was he in fact a bit jealous? He hadn't let go of her hand yet. Meanwhile she was impressed by how Scotty was talking about farming, woodworking and tools without, as far as she knew, the slightest clue about any of it.

"Well, I don't want to take up your time or anything. It was just an honour meeting our first guests from Earth."

"The pleasure is really ours. Fine people here, lovely city."

"Before you go, allow me to go get you something. I'll be right back."

He ran back up the walkway, tools jangling as he went. He disappeared and then he returned, carrying a folded piece of paper.

"This here is a map of Oasis City. On one side is a detail map of the streets and the like, but on the flip side is locations of the touristy places. Like parks, museums, shopping centers and the resting place of the Regal."

"Thank you very much. But this must be your map, we shouldn't take it."

"Oh, I don't need it no more. If I do, I know where to get another."

Cindy pointed at the opened map. "What are those yellow X's?"

"Oh, those are crosses that indicate where churches are."

"That is a lot of crosses."

"Yes, ma'am. But this is a big city, several hundred thousand people."

After saying good-bye to Christian, they made their way back again to the main sidewalk. Aware that anyone who saw the newscast would recognize them at once, they decided to use the map to walk back to their hotel in a round about fashion and avoid the busier streets.

They found the sidewalks, made out of rough concrete, peculiar compared to the smooth walks back on Earth. There was a lack of moving sidewalks and it looked like transportation was limited to vehicles and walking. Here they also had to watch out for vehicles when they crossed the street, but they soon found the vehicles would stop for them when they indicated that they were crossing. Another unique thing was the different styles of buildings that were lined up along the sidewalks. Scotty was amused that he could actually see the tops of the buildings. He wondered if people were allowed to go to the top and peer around.

"It's going to be hard to do undercover work if everyone knows us," Cindy said.

"That's true. Even though this is a medium size city, the people act like this is a small town. Notice the lack of policing, no garbage lying around. And quiet, no shouting or noise from a thousand people trying to go somewhere fast. But if we can't do undercover work, Cindy, then maybe the opposite will work to our advantage."

"What do you mean?"

"They know us, and it seems that they trust us. We can make that work to our advantage. They'll tell us what we need to know."

They made it back to their hotel without incident, but once in the lobby Scotty checked for messages, in case NightHawk was trying to get a hold of him. He knew it was unlikely since the planet hadn't established regular communication with the outside universe yet, just the basic radio and video with short range. He decided to check anyway when he saw the large message board with the wooden cubicles.

"Yes, Mr. Pearson. Several messages are here for you and your wife." The blonde hair girl smiled as she handed over the slips of paper.

"Thank you." His hand brushed hers as he took them. And then looked into her eyes and smiled. Scotty did this out of habit; if he was introduced to a pretty woman he did his flirtation routine automatically and then checked the results. She blushed as she turned her head away and then quickly glanced back. He turned away to read the first message and then saw a cold look from Cindy.

"Looks like there is someone waiting for us in the coffee shop, and another message for us to call someone in the government. Plus a request from two newspapers and a video-cast station for interviews."

"It looks as if fame has caught up to us." She said that in such a flat voice that he looked back at her, but she refused to return his stare and looked over at the coffee shop. "Let's check out this coffee shop person and then see what we have to do about those interviews." She walked over to the coffee shop without checking to see if he was following.

The gentleman in the coffee shop was of medium height of slender build. Dressed in black save for a white collar he stood up as they entered.

"Ah, Mr. and Mrs. Pearson. Thank you so much for coming to see me. I was going to just leave a message but decided that would lack any warmth. So I took a chance and waited here for a half hour or so. I do hope you don't mind my intrusion. Oh, my goodness, my manners. My name is Reverend Thomas Blanchett." He spoke rapidly, not pausing between sentences. Smiling with a mouthful of teeth, he extended both of his hands to them.

"Pleased to meet you, Reverend. This is Cindy, and my name is Scotty."

"Please sit down for a minute if you have time. I was wondering, since you are new to our world ..."

They listened to him patiently as he rambled on different topics, pausing to ask questions now and then. A waitress brought over two more cups so that they could share his teapot.

"But I know I must be keeping you from other things, so I shall come right out and request a favour from you."

"Certainly, if we are able ..."

"You are on your honeymoon?"

They nodded.

"Did you two have a large church wedding? Or was it less formal?"

"Well…" Scotty stammered. What was the agreed upon cover story?

"It was a small service, just close friends and relatives." Cindy kicked him hard on his shin to shut him up and took over.

"And that, of course, was on the mother Earth … how long ago?"

"Almost a month, Reverend."

"How very nice. Had you known each other long?"

"Over a year. We both worked in the same office."

"Well, it's so nice to meet two people such as yourselves. But I wanted to personally invite you to our service. Our church is one of the larger churches in the city and like many of the others, we are cross denomination. So regardless of your own church and beliefs on Earth we would try make you feel most welcome in ours."

"When would this service be, Reverend?"

Pearson looked at Cindy. 'Was she nuts? She should be trying to dissuade him, instead, she was agreeing to go to this church service.' He couldn't remember the last time he went to church and this certainly didn't seem to be the right place to start.

"This Sunday at nine. And this is a special service as well. It is the anniversary of the first wedding on Haven, a very important occasion."

"Well, I'm not sure how to get around …" Scotty finally was able to speak.

"That's not a problem at all. I would be happy to arrange transportation for you."

"Then we would be glad to attend, Reverend." Cindy smiled at him and then at Scotty as she replied.

"Excellent! I'm so glad that is settled. We'll have a car pick you up at half past eight."

They walked with the Reverend to the hotel lobby with Scotty trailing slightly behind the other two while slowly shaking his head.

After the Reverend left, Scotty and Cindy waited in silence in front of the elevators, and then Scotty jabbed the call button one more time.

"Cindy, what were you thinking of? Why did you accept this church service so easily? We should have discussed it first. A church service for crying out loud." He shook his head in disbelief.

"Come on, Scotty, it will be interesting. This will give us a chance to study another part of their culture; churches seem to be a big part of their lives. Another story might be hiding there."

"I rather doubt it." He was a bit miffed on what she had done but there was little he could do about it now. He decided to just let it go and try to smooth things out with her. "Maybe we better go over our cover story on how we met and then won a trip here. That was fast thinking about our wedding."

"Thanks, but someone had to plan for those questions and that sure wasn't going to be you, was it?" She turned and walked into the elevator.

Scotty wondered what she was talking about and why she was acting so upset. He sighed and walked in behind her. *Hell, it isn't a real marriage after all.*

Chapter Three
Toronto, Earth, year 2596

Glora lay on her back naked. After making love to Robert, she initially had felt tired and relaxed. But now, nagging thoughts were coming back to her. She propped herself up on one elbow and looked at him, equally naked but lying on his stomach, sleeping quietly.

Robert was well on his way to becoming a power engineer, and good marks were the norm for him now. His early struggles to grasp some concepts were long past and he was within the top ten percent of his class. The stars were his if he wanted them, and she didn't want to be the one that stood in his way.

The stars were coming sooner to her, however. In a few weeks she would be in Haven, to meet with their delegation regarding the Charter of Conduct. The Charter meetings were going to demand more and more of her time.

'Whatever.' She decided to play out this relationship with Robert as much as she could. It was going to end, she could see that. But not right away. She smiled at him. "We're going to have that ride a bit longer, my love." She gently slid on top of his back, closed her eyes and went to sleep.

* * * *

Oasis City, Haven

"So when did you leave that message at the hotel?"

Aaron Duggan was a bit nervous. Irene was definitely annoyed at him and did have a point after all. "About two in the afternoon."

"I'll wait for their return call in the office. But from now on, please don't do my job. Let me send out requests. There's a certain protocol to follow. Remember?"

"Of course. But it suddenly occurred to me while I was out of the office …"

"Then phone the office and get me to do it."

"Geez, you're tough."

She walked out of the office, wearing another of her interesting outfits, this time a conservative skirt but with a clinging top that accented her figure. Aaron had noticed that the criticism of her dress habits had slowly disappeared. In fact a recent newspaper article had praised women who were secure enough to wear what they pleased without being offensive about it and had mentioned Irene as an example; "The trend setting Premier's receptionist."

He was buried with paperwork when Irene returned to his office. He noticed that she looked like she was in a better mood at least.

"Your foreign guests phoned back and were delighted to meet you for dinner tomorrow," Her voice didn't hide the excitement in her voice. "I reserved a table at the King's Head for seven pm. By the way I told them the Premier's office would pick them up from their hotel and pay for dinner, of course."

"Did they ask why I wanted to meet them?"

"I only told them we wanted to properly greet our first visitors from Earth."

He raised his brow. "We?"

"Yes, we. Or didn't you want my company on Friday night?"

"Of course. I just didn't have the opportunity of planning an evening get together with you. This will be perfect."

She squinted her eyes at him. "Right."

* * * *

"Really, my dear," said Dr. Beaumont, "You shouldn't let everything the captain says control your every action. The captain, I am sure, has only the best of intentions, but it would be incorrect to assume she knows what is best for each crew member at all times."

"I'm not saying she knows everything, Dr. Beaumont. But she has always been truthful in the past about such things." The blonde ensign used her fingers to put a few of her long hairs into place.

"And well she should be, Terra. That is good, no?"

"Yes …"

"And does she not also ask the crew to think as a unit, but also as individuals?"

"Yes, she does. But that doesn't mean we should do just anything."

"This isn't just anything, is it? Ah, when I look into your lovely eyes I can see you agree with me. Come with me. Allow me to share a truly exotic drink with you."

"I don't know …"

"Please, I insist on you trying just one sip. And we'll leave the door to my quarters open. I only wish some conversation on this long journey. Do you realize how few intelligent people there are to discuss ideas with on this ship?" He smiled broadly as he gestured to his suite.

* * * *

General Burgess studied the map of Haven. He had already marked off areas of defence, government and communication. If it came to battle, it would be an extremely short one. Hell, a dozen craft could have this planet under control in two hours. Planet contact would be made in two days and Diplomat Beaumont better be prepared to lay out the law to these primitives. No more soft touches. The Charter was law!

* * * *

Terra watched as he dipped his finger in his drink, encircled her navel with the fluid and then licked it off. The drink was marvellous, a strange mixture of flavours and alcohol. And something else, too, though that ingredient was probably illegal.

"Roger, that's a funny name." She giggled. "Can I have a bottle of that drink?"

"It is very rare, I'm afraid." Beaumont smiled gently and then he leaned down to kiss her breast.

"It makes me feel so good."

"Yes, that is good, my sweet." He returned to kissing her breasts.

"Can I come back sometime for some more?"

"Hmm, perhaps. If you do, bring a friend with you."

She sat up slowly and wagged a finger at him. "Dr. Roger that would be a threesome. Very naughty, very bad. But I'll do it because I'm you're friend. And I know just the girl."

"Is she as pretty as you?"

"Very pretty. You'll like her. She has big boobs and a small waist."

"That's nice, my sweet. Now let's stop talking and let us use our lips for other things."

She laughed as he started to kiss her. "Hey, why don't you lick that liqueur off me again, that was fun."

* * * *

Oasis City, Haven

"What should we do about these interview requests?" Cindy plopped down on the couch next to Scotty.

"I don't know. Somehow it escaped the powers that be that our arrival before the official welcoming committee was going to cause a big splash."

"We can't ignore them, though. What we should do is have a press conference and get all those interviews done with."

"That's a good plan. Then we can say we're turning down future interviews because we're here on our honeymoon and need some privacy."

"Let's get our stories straight. I can't believe you couldn't remember any of our cover story. The Reverend must have wondered why you couldn't remember your wedding date of a month ago." She elbowed him for good measure.

"Yes, well, at least my tongue doesn't hang out when some young stud comes bouncing up to us to say hello."

"Oh, is that so? And you didn't flirt with the desk girl when you got our messages? How many women do you need to bed anyway?" *If only you would flirt with me a bit more you might get somewhere.*

"Come on, I wasn't really flirting. I was just being friendly. And for crying out loud it wasn't anything that would blow our cover. Look, it's going to be a long assignment. Let's try to keep an even keel and not let small issues become big ones."

"Fine. Let's just ignore problems then. Just try to remember who you're supposed to be married to." She got up and stomped off to the kitchenette.

Scotty watched her walk away and wondered what brought that about. He really didn't have time for an emotional partner that could very well blow their cover. He sighed, got up and went up behind her. She was standing in front of the empty fridge looking annoyed even from her back. He put his hands on her waist and she made a half-hearted effort to shake them off.

"Look, Cindy, I apologize if I haven't been paying attention but a lot of things are going on and I have to concentrate on them." He congratulated himself on his nice general apology that covered a lot of areas and while he still didn't know exactly what he was sorry for.

"I know." Her tone had softened. "But it's hard for me too."

"Of course. Look, we have a kitchen here and I noticed a food store a block or so away. Why don't we pick up some groceries and make a meal here? Get some wine and then we can go over our press conference thing."

"That would be nice." She turned around and started to reach for his waist to give a hug but then suddenly stopped, looking uncertain.

They walked hand in hand to the store, a small neighbourhood one that carried groceries as well as a few hardware items. Cindy started picking up out food and Scotty went to look for some wine. In his search, he noticed that they also rented video cartridges. Scotty inquired if he knew if their TV in the hotel room accepted these, and was informed they would.

"Well, I don't know any of these titles. What would you recommend?"

"What are you interested in?"

War movies. Naked women dancing. Action with fighting and women. "Maybe a romantic comedy. Action-romance if that exists. Something that my wife will like and not put me to sleep."

The clerk laughed. "I understand. Yeah, some of the movies women like can be pretty boring. Here, I've seen this one. It's got some action in it and my girlfriend liked it too. And this one is funny and has a good romance story to it. This, I haven't seen, but I heard it was good. A bit more on the serious side."

"I'll take those. Do you sell wine?"

"Yes, sir. One aisle over."

He looked at their selection, not having a clue what any of them were, then chose the four most expensive ones.

He found Cindy picking over some fruit. "How's it going?"

"Good. I got lots of stuff. But I'm not sure what any of it is, except that it isn't meat."

They left the store, carrying five bags between them.

"Cindy, you bought enough to feed the whole hotel."

"What about you? Four bottles of wine? The clerk must think we're alcoholics."

"Actually I am. You get one bottle, I get the other three."

Back in their room, Cindy started dinner while Scotty made calls to arrange the press conference. Then he joined her in the kitchen.

"Scotty, read the package. Don't just dump it in the water!"

"Ah, this pasta stuff is all the same. Where's the salt?"

All considered, the meal turned out pretty good. And the wine, once they got use to it, wasn't bad.

He settled back on the couch next to her and activated the TV. Moments later the rented video turned on and they watched the first movie.

It was not up to standards they were use to as far as video quality was concerned, plus it was only two dimensional on a small screen. The acting wasn't bad but there seemed to be limited resources in the budget. Still, it was a lot better than the normal TV programs they had found so far.

Cindy leaned into him as they munched on something like popcorn but closer to the taste of wheat.

"Scotty. Can I ask you a personal question?"

"Sure."

"You don't have to answer because it's not really any of my business, but what happened to your first two marriages?"

He was silent for several seconds. Then he seemed to make up his mind. "Well, the first one was one to a woman, I won't say lady, named Shelly. I married her because she was pregnant with my son. She wanted everything her way. Big apartment, expensive stuff. I worked my butt of to keep up with her tastes. I came home early sick one day and found evidence that someone else had been in my bed. She denied it and I couldn't prove it exactly. But I knew, I knew. From then on, it went from bad to worse. I started to drink, a lot, and didn't make as much money either. We lost our apartment, and she sued for divorce on grounds of neglect. I couldn't believe how the damn court sided with her. So I lost my kid and have to pay so much a month 'till he's eighteen. She moved with him across the continent and I have access rights only every third weekend. And he hates me. She and her new boyfriend have turned him completely against me. He's only eight years old so maybe he'll understand some day.

"Then I really started drinking, big time. I lost a couple of jobs and a lot of friends. I lost my self-respect too. So I didn't have much on the ball when I met Jodie. Jodie was a big, bossy woman. But she wasn't bad looking, so we kind of hustled each other. I was looking for some easy sex. She was looking for an easy husband. We both got what we wanted I suppose. One thing though, she got tired of was my drinking. She tried to get me to join the AA, but I wouldn't go. I didn't have a problem, or so I thought. So she tried the next best thing, motivational classes.

"You remember the fad of those 'Yes, you can be happy' seminars? Well it actually worked for me. She bribed me to go the first few classes by offering to buy me this really expensive scotch; I should have told you, this woman had some dough. So I went reluctantly at first but then started to understand some things about myself. So the end result was I obtained a liking for really expensive scotch and I realized I was too good to stay married to her. Compared to the first one, the second divorce was quick and, for me, painless.

"Today, I guess I still drink too much, I'm in danger of losing my job and I suppose I chase too many women. But that is a long sight better than a few years ago. As the program preaches, 'not all at once, just the right direction'."

"You have been through a lot."

"Yes, but as the program says 'Don't blame bad luck because of bad choices'."

"You can really quote that program, can't you?"

"It did stick with me. But let's drop this for now. Let's try this other movie. It got a four star rating."

The second movie was better that the first but after that they both felt tired.

"Scotty, I want to go shopping tomorrow for clothes. I have nothing to wear, and we have that press conference, the church service, and the dinner with the Premier."

"Sure, do you want me to come along?"

"Well, how about if we go to the shopping center together and then separate? You can poke through stuff you want to see while I get some clothes."

"Sure, sounds good." *Boring. I hope there's a bar close to the shopping center.*

Chapter Four

Aaron Duggan sat on the porch swing with Irene. The swing overlooked the acreage of the backyard, and in the daytime, he could see the work that had to be done soon before it became a state of too much disrepair. Time was becoming a luxury and he knew he might have to hire someone to do the work rather than let it go undone. Now, late at night, the work disappeared and they listened to the sound of insects chirping away.

"So you still haven't told me why you wanted to meet with the Pearsons."

"I find it odd that a couple would suddenly decide to come here on their honeymoon. That star ship had to make a special drop off for them and that had to be expensive. I thought a meeting with them would help clear this up."

"Do you think that they are spies?"

"Maybe. Maybe not. But I'm not really sold on this honeymoon thing."

They sat quietly again, listening to the sounds of birds and insects. Gradually his hand moved up her leg, pushing the dress away. She closed her eyes, enjoying his fingertips on her thighs, then felt his breath on her face and she turned to kiss him. The kiss was longer than usual, and she didn't resist this time when he slowly unbuttoned her dress and allowed the top to fall from her shoulders. The bra slipped off with equal ease as she played her fingertips on his chest. Then she slowly pushed him back.

"I have to be going soon."

"It's still early."

She laughed. "It's one in the morning. Early for what?" She stood up and did up her dress, stuffing the bra in her handbag.

"All right. I'll walk you to your car."

He was surprised how the evening went. She had dropped by his place to give him some documents he had left in the office, stayed for dinner, and now this. This was as far as they'd gone so far, the first time he had managed to remove her top. It had taken four months but he was slowly seducing her.

* * * *

"Good morning," Cindy said as she entered the living room where Scotty slept on the hide-a-bed. "I made the local equivalent of coffee. Want some?" She offered the cup to him.

Scotty was still in bed, sleeping uneasily through most of the night but then sleeping in past his planned eight o'clock. He took the offered cup and sat up. "What time is it?"

"Almost nine. You had set your alarm for six in the morning, God knows why. It was bleeping away, so I turned it off."

"Oh. Well, I guess I must have needed the sleep. Hard work and all that."

"Right." She sat on the side of the hide-a-bed. "Scotty, I was wondering if I could ask you a favour?"

Oh, why not. After I babbled my past life to you last night, I'm capable of other stupidities as well. "Sure, what is it? This is not very good coffee, no matter what you call it."

"Hey, don't blame me. I only followed the directions. This might be as good as it gets. Anyway, I was looking at my story this morning. You know, the one about being kidnapped by Ravener. And I think it needs some help. I figure if I get it published, it will make his life a lot more difficult. I really want to get even with him."

"No problem. Show it to me. I'll see what you've got."

"Okay. But be honest with me, please. I know there is something I'm doing wrong because all my articles and stories end up in the back pages."

Scotty sipped at the pseudo-coffee as he read her tablet. The coffee got better after the initial taste, not so bad after all. The story didn't get much better as he read on. It was rather obvious why her stories, even when collaborating with someone else ended up in the last section of the paper.

"Well, what do you think?"

"First, you are a good writer, technically. Good sentence structure, grammar, spelling. It's all there. But the combination lacks punch. You're forgetting your audience. This would be a writing style for a respected magazine, or a family daily. But NightHawk's readers might not lack intelligence but they're after something else when they read the tabloid."

"So I have to spice it up?"

"Well, let me show you…take this part, for example:

'The entertainment room was done in soft greens, the soft couch and chair boasting a large print of yellow and black. Inside there was a self-contained bar as well as a large video screen. Ravener smiled as he handed me a drink.'

"Now if we write this, instead, I think you will see what I mean by appealing to our readers:

'The entertainment room was painted in jungle greens with the furniture decorated in animal skins. The self-contained bar held various drinks and other stimulants; a large screen showed naked bodies intertwined with each other.'

"Do you see the difference?" he asked.

"Yeah, sure. More descriptive. And you bent the truth a bit."

"Sure, but also lead the reader to expect something is about to happen. Something's wrong, devious perhaps. And Ravener won't be able to refute some of the things you are saying unless he invites an inspection."

"I see. Okay, I'll rewrite this piece. Will you check it again?"

"Sure. Don't be afraid to exaggerate and make up a few facts."

Later, at the shopping center, a small one, at least by Earth standards, Cindy and Scott split company and agreed to meet three hours later for a late lunch in the food court. The mall appeared to be a group of independent businesses that later on decided to add a roof over their common area. The stores themselves looked a bit odd, some with a brick front and others with a wood face. A couple of the shops even supported a second level accessible only through the store itself.

People pointed and stared at them, speaking in hushed tones when they saw them. They weren't approached and other than a warm smile when they did come in contact with others, they could do their shopping without interference. Scotty breezed through the shopping complex in an hour, picking up only a few small items. He noticed that the shops rarely specialized in any one item, often mixing clothing with a bit of furniture. There were some brand names but a lot of the goods had a homemade or simplistic manufactured look to them. Some of the hardware items looked interesting but he had little use for a rawhide stitcher and the like. Then he went in search of a bar.

Cindy received more attention as she went shopping, "This is a nice outfit. It would work for church, as well."

"Yes it would. But if you are going to this Sunday's service, I recommend this one here," the saleswoman said.

"White?"

"Yes, the service allows married couples to renew their vows. Several selected couples will go to the front and repeat their vows. Those in the congregation will also repeat them. Because the service is dedicated to the institution of marriage many women who are married will wear white."

"I see. What type of vows?"

"Oh, nothing elaborate. Just a promise of love and devotion, that sort of thing. It's very nice. You and your husband will enjoy it so soon after your wedding. It helps keep our wedding promises fresh."

"Well, I better take a look at those white dresses then."

Cindy also managed to find a formal outfit for their press conference, and then picked out several more casual clothes. The shoes she didn't care for as much; she felt she needed a higher heel being so much shorter than the rest of the population on Haven. Besides, she felt the higher heel made her legs look longer as well.

"Most women prefer a lower heel here."

"I understand that. But if these shoes are going to be worn back on Earth, then I need something a little different. These will do, but I was hoping for a bit more height, I feel so short here."

The saleswoman smiled. "Well I shouldn't say this, but the Premier's receptionist likes that sort of thing as well and she does shop at Doreen's."

"She does? Where's Doreen's?"

Doreen's was located at the corner of the shopping complex, out of the way of the main shopping area. Cindy was impressed by its decor, much more open than the smaller shops. It carried shoes and jewellery, as well as clothes on its two levels.

Cindy described what she was looking for and was shown a better selection of high-heeled shoes, located upstairs where the more risqué fashions were kept. They were also more expensive, but money was not a problem according to what Scotty had told her.

"And I was also looking for a dress, a more formal occasion."

"Well, we have these. And there's also this style here."

"Hmm. Well, to tell you the truth, on Earth this would be considered a very conservative dress. Do you have something a little more daring?"

There was a moment of silence as the salesclerk thought about what she was told. "Of course. We don't normally show these designs unless someone asks for them. Some people get offended by the newer fashions and make a bit of a fuss when they see them. This is still a rather conservative society. How about this?"

"That's better. What is a good length for a formal dress here?"

"For you, just at around the knee. But a slit could go much higher."

"Okay. Let's hold onto that thought. I kind of like this one, but is there something like it with a bare back?"

The salesclerk dropped her jaw.

* * * *

Scotty found a lounge just outside the shopping center and ordered a beer. It was better than he expected, strong in taste and high in alcohol content. On Earth, and other Charter of Conduct worlds, beer was restricted to a maximum of 3%. Other beverages had similar restrictions. This was to help people live more healthy lives; the alcohol content was part of the regulations concerning food and drinks. Many foods were also required to include certain minerals and vitamins and before any new food or drink was allowed on the market, it was required to show health benefits. Liquor was given special consideration due to the public's demand for it but the permitted alcohol content was slowly being reduced to cut down on its harmful effects.

Scotty ate some munchies as well, not wanting to wait to lunchtime to eat. He engaged in small talk with the bartender who was unaware of who Scotty was. Apparently, when he and Cindy were separated as a couple, Scotty could pass as a native to Haven, perhaps on the short side, but his manner of dress wasn't odd enough to warrant special notice. After consuming a couple of glasses, he headed back inside the shopping center and to the food courts.

Cindy was waiting for him when he arrived, looking extremely happy.

"Hi. You weren't waiting long, were you?"

"Oh, no. Just got here. Shopping went really well. I got lots of stuff."

"Where is all of it?"

"I'm having it sent back to the hotel. Too much to carry."

"Good. I'm just glad that it wasn't my money you spent. Fortunately, the NightHawk can afford it. Let's find a place to eat."

Back at the hotel they discussed what their cover story was again, and who should answer what questions so they wouldn't be contradicting each other.

"Okay, I guess that covers that. We have a couple of hours before we have to get ready for dinner with the Premier, so I'll work on my story."

"More than a couple of hours. But I have lots of work to do. Lots of stories have surfaced so far. I'm going to make a mint if half of this stuff is published."

Two hours later Cindy poked him in the shoulder. "Hey, it's time for me to get ready. But I rewrote it. Would you check it again for me, please?"

"Sure. But it's only five-thirty. We don't get picked up for an hour."

"I know. I need the time. And you better shave again."

He read her story, made a couple of notes, and added a couple of line while she dressed in the bathroom. He then checked it again. He looked at the bathroom door where she was still shut in and decided to get out his best suit. He brushed it off, the wrinkles fading out to nothing and then he selected a shirt. He changed and she still wasn't out.

"Cindy, what are you doing in there? Putting on a dress or making one?"

"Just a couple of more minutes. Now stop bothering me."

Cindy did eventually emerge from the bathroom. Scotty looked up from his tablet, and sat staring at her.

"Well, what do you think?" She spun slowly around and fixed a look at him.

His eyes ran from her high heels to the new waves in her hair and to the blue dress that fit her rather tightly. The dress itself started from just above her knees with a slit along the side and ended with spaghetti straps. In between, he took in the low cut front and a half bare back.

"Well?"

"Very nice. Great dress. And you did something with your hair." *Always comment on the hair if a woman asks you how she looks.*

"You like my hair like this?"

"Un huh. Everything looks great. You'll be the hit of the evening."

"My dress. Is it all right? Most of the dresses were so conservative. This one looked okay, but I had their seamstress do some modifications, except it's a little on the tight side."

"Naw. Fits you perfectly. Hold still for a minute."

"Why?"

"I want to take your picture." He got up, rummaged through a bag and pulled out a slim grey rectangular box. He pulled out the sides of the box and unfolded them so they extended out over a foot.

"Don't be silly. I don't want my picture taken," she protested.

"Stand by the window. This will take only a minute. Besides what kind of honeymoon would it be if we didn't have any pictures to show?" He punched a couple of buttons and she saw a flicker of light go between the sides of the camera and then a quick flash from the center.

"There, that looks good. Give me a couple of poses, turn a bit."

Cindy did as he asked. "Come on. We're going to be late. You can take pictures of me another time." She tried to sound annoyed but was flattered he wanted to take pictures of her. "That's one of those holographic cameras, isn't it?"

"Partial holographic. The ends sit out just far enough to allow some rotation of the subject. I usually use this in its folded up form but I thought I would increase the picture quality this way."

"Show them to me later. We better get going. Hey, didn't you shave yet?"

"You were hogging the bathroom, how could I?"

"Well, hurry up. If we're late it'll be all your fault."

Scott started to shave, pulling on his face as he ran the razor over the evening shadow. Cindy stood watching him through the open bathroom door.

"Scotty, what did you think of my reworked story?"

"Much better. I made the odd correction and left some notes with it for you to read, just some suggestions."

"So do you think NightHawk will accept it?"

"Well that's always hard to say; it often depends on the editor's mood more than anything. I would think it'll make it easily to the back pages of the tabloid, but more likely in the middle." Scott looked over at her as he finished shaving. She didn't look too pleased. "Hey, what's the matter? I'm sure the story will be fine if we work out a few parts."

"Thanks. But I really wanted this to go in near the front. It would be my first solo story that would be at the front. Just my name under the headline. But I also wanted to get even with that creep, Ravener. I want the story to be up near the front so that he would be embarrassed to show his face to anyone. I guess I had my hopes too high."

"Really important to you?"

"Yeah, really important." She sounded rather glum.

"Well, there's a way to send your story to the front."

"Really, how?"

"Pictures."

She looked at him puzzled.

"I know you didn't get any pictures when you were there but we can shoot some pictures here, doctor them up, and then attach them to your story as photos taken by a hidden camera. Pictures always grab attention, especially of the ones that happened to the writer."

"Those pictures would be of me … being attacked by Ravener? I'm not sure I would want … to be seen that way in the NightHawk."

"You wrote about it. So you don't mind people hearing about it. But our photos won't show anything. We don't have Ravener in the pictures either, but people will believe it's his room. Think about it. No sweat either way. If we take the pictures you can still change your mind about putting them in."

"Okay, I'll give it some thought."

* * * *

Aaron Duggan was a patient man. He sat quietly reading a magazine as Irene finished dressing. Normally she was on time, but this meeting with the new visitors had her nervous.

"Okay, how do I look?"

"Nice dress, you look great." And she did with a long black dress with a small front slit. The neckline was high but the back was quite low, dropping several inches below her shoulders.

"Thanks. But what about my hair? Does it look good this way?"

He hadn't really noticed much of a difference in the way her hair looked but saying that would be a mistake. "Of course. You must have gone to the hair salon after work. It really suits you."

"Are you just saying that? Oh, come on, we'll be late if you don't hurry."

"Me? And here I thought I was waiting for you."

The dinner was served in a private room in the restaurant and the two couples greeted each other warmly. Over wine they searched out topics to discuss that which were of non-serious issue. The men seemed a little more comfortable than the ladies who stared at each other's dresses, and made the appropriate compliments before slowly joining in the conversation.

Aaron was doing his best to ignore Cindy's dress and the exposed skin. He thought Irene's dress was daring but the foreigner's dress left her half-naked and she couldn't have been wearing a bra either. *Was this how Earth women dressed now?* He could only guess what was going through Irene's mind. "So, Scott, what type of work do you do?"

"I work in the security field. We help set secure sites for clients, protect against invasion of privacy."

"Would that be like a private police force?"

"Not exactly. This is more protection from electronic surveillance. Eavesdropping, that sort of thing. Here's one of my business cards." He passed over a plastic card that advertised 'Roland Securities'. The card included an actual phone number and web site. The company, set up by NightHawk, was strictly to protect their reporters by giving them a fake employer. It also provided a ready excuse if they were caught snooping around. Roland Securities had an actual receptionist and a couple of staff members in case someone called their bluff in asking for an estimate to secure their business.

"Interesting card. Is plastic a common material for business cards?"

"The only material. I noticed Haven uses paper products as well as wood. Not on Earth, or the rest of the Imperial Alliance for that matter. Plastic is used pretty extensively in its place; it's even made into sheets for writing rather than paper."

"Well, that's different. So your newspapers are actually news-plastics?"

Scotty returned his laugh. "Actually, our newspapers aren't even that. Magazines and newspapers are simply downloaded into our tablets. We read it off the screen and then delete it, or save it if we want to."

"Those tablets are pretty impressive."

"Well, one couldn't function without it. Besides acting as a computer, it can also tap into the Web, serve as a videophone that uses a camera and, as I mentioned, for reading and writing."

"That sort of technology is way beyond us on Haven and may always be."

"Why do you say that?"

"The Regal, and her sister ships the Hood and the Mobridge, were hit by a space abnormality on their journey to a new world, a planet called Candida Pax. The Regal, and it was a miracle it made it to Haven, virtually crash landed here." Aaron shifted position slightly and leaned on the table. "What I'm trying to say in a round-about way is that the people of Haven are reluctant to embrace technology because of that disaster in space. We do have cell phones, computers, electronic devices of various sorts but we just don't allow our lives to become too dependent on them. I suppose we are fearful the same thing could happen again."

The first course arrived, an orange and green leaf salad that was served with dark bread, followed by mushroom soup.

Scotty thought over what he had said. Fear of technology had showed up many times in human history. These people, however, had a very valid reason for it. "This space abnormality you mentioned. On Earth, we called it the Wave, with a capital W. It was generated near the center of our galaxy; scientists speculate that it was caused by a massive black hole that suddenly tried to absorb too much mass. I never really followed the scientific explanation for what happened but apparently this caused the black hole to become unstable, vibrating within itself that caused a wave of something to propagate outward."

"The Wave? Good, concise name. You called it something; don't they know what it was?"

Scotty shrugged and smiled. "Sorry, not my area of expertise. I have heard it being called something like dark energy or some other exotic form of particles. But they now know how to protect against it or at least they say they do. You can buy products that claim to be Wave proof and I'm not sure how valid those claims are, but they're really pricey."

"So has Earth reverted back to using technology that may suddenly become unusable if the Wave strikes again?"

"Earth and the rest of the worlds." Scotty rubbed his hand over his face. "It's not that simple, Aaron. It's not that we decided to use this electronic gear because we love toys. We have eighteen billion people living on Sol alone. When the Wave hit, billions perished because we have too many people. Consider that there are buildings on Earth that are five hundred stories high to house the population, where would those live if it was decided we shouldn't depend on high technology? It wouldn't be a pretty sight."

"You're quite right, we have a choice here. I didn't mean to sound lofty. It sounds like a precarious situation at times on Earth."

Irene sensed the conversation needed to be changed before it got too depressing. "Some more wine? I'm not sure what wine is like on

Earth, but this wine is made near the interior of our continent and I'm told follows the same process used on Earth to produce it."

"It is excellent. It has a bigger kick than that on Earth. Health laws require wine to be less than five percent, and I notice this seems to be a bit higher."

Aaron checked the label. "Hmm, you're right about that, this is twelve percent. By the way, we understand that you two don't eat meat so this meal will consist of vegetables and fish only. I hope that will be agreeable to you both, if not please let us know."

Cindy and Scott felt relief. They weren't sure what they would have done if a slab of bloody flesh were placed in front of them.

The rest of the meal went without incident. Dessert was interesting. Ice cream was something no longer used on Earth but it tasted much the same as the substitute now used, except a bit richer. Cindy thought it was strange to eat something that came from the inside of a cow but she buried the thought and finished her dessert.

"Liqueur?" Aaron held up the green bottle.

"Please." Scott wasn't sure if he could put much more in his stomach but a shot of liqueur wouldn't take up much room.

"I would too, if you could tell me where the washrooms are." Cindy was glad she had slowed down on the wine after feeling the effect of just one glass.

"I'll show you. I have to go there myself." Irene stood up and led the way.

When the ladies returned, Scotty and Aaron were getting along quite well and had made some plans to get together in a few days. Irene and Cindy were laughing about something and Aaron was suspicious by how Cindy looked at him.

Aaron looked across at Scotty's tablet. "Would it be possible to take a closer look at that?"

"Sure." He touched a couple of buttons on the keyboard and slid it over.

Cindy looked amused. "Can't men ever stop playing with toys?"

"That must be one of many their flaws in the genetic makeup." Irene nodded in agreement.

Aaron played with a few keys, going through the screen's menu. He found it fairly easy to navigate and was impressed by how quickly it flashed to new tasks.

"You can use the miniature keyboard to type in information or you can write with a stylus on that dark pad on the base if you prefer.

The tablet will convert the writing to printed text." Scotty watched Aaron study the tablet carefully; looking worried about touching any of the symbols. "Go ahead. You can't cause any damage."

With a bit of hesitation, Aaron touched a couple of icons on the screen and then typed in an inquiry. "Interesting."

Irene looked over. "What?"

"I typed in Candida Pax and you know what it said?"

"Tell us."

"Candida Pax. One of failed pioneer worlds. The soil and climate was unable to sustain agriculture. Uninhabited except for scientific research teams." He looked up. "So it looks as if the best thing that happened to the people on the Regal was the Wave throwing them off course."

Chapter Five
Toronto, Earth

Robert sat by his desk and finished up with his assignment. It wasn't difficult to wrap up but his heart sure wasn't in it. It was a week of fun in Denver and now this. He checked his watch. Glora was late, though that wasn't unusual. But he was looking forward to seeing her and the extra minutes seemed to take longer.

A few minutes later, she came through the door, carrying a pizza. "Hi, thought you might be hungry. Did you finally finish that report?"

"Of course. Was there any doubt? What type of pizza?"

"Greek Island."

After they finished, she sat on the edge of the bed. "Robert, I need to talk to you."

"Sure, what's up?"

"Robert, my promotion ..."

"Yeah, I'm really proud of you. You deserve it."

"Thanks, but this promotion is going to send me to that new planet, Haven, for a while. I leave in three days, and, well, I'm not sure when I'll be back."

He looked crestfallen. "Damn. That's not good news at all."

"I know, but I can't turn this down. You understand don't you?"

"Yeah, I do. I'm happy you found something like this. It's what you deserve."

They tried to say the correct things to each other but the words just didn't sound right. Then they sat for a few minutes in silence holding hands.

"Look, I know this is difficult but don't wait for me. You have a life to live." That wasn't what she wanted to say, but the words were stumbling out, not tied to her thoughts very well.

"Thanks, but let's not talk about that right now. We still have a couple of days together."

* * * *

A few days later, they stood together in the busy spaceport.

"Study hard and make those grades. You only have a few months left."

"Sure. And you do your Charter thing."

"I'm going to miss you. I'll think of you, a lot."

"Me too. You never know how things are going to work out; I have a feeling we'll cross paths again."

"That would be nice. I hope so."

"Well, it looks like it's boarding time."

"Give me a kiss to remember you by."

He did and after a final hug, she turned to go.

"Bye, Glora. You better go to the gate. And don't turn around. Just go straight in. It'll be easier that way."

Glora walked through the gate without looking back but that didn't seem to make it much easier.

* * * *

On the Sol Alliance Starship Monteith orbiting Haven

Dr. Beaumont thought of the previous night. Looking at Haven from the viewing lounge, he wondered what the women on the planet were like. They couldn't be much wilder than the ship's crew. Despite the captain's warning, several young ladies had taken up with his company. That was certainly true last night of the two young ladies. That secret ingredient he added to the liquor last night certainly caused for some interesting events.

But now it was time to review his agenda for the meeting in two days time. Haven was dragging its feet concerning the meeting arrangements. They refused to come up to the ship for the initial introductions, which was not unexpected. But a simple meeting on their planet surface was also difficult to arrange. Monday was the first day, local time, they would meet him, claiming Friday and Saturday was too soon. And Sunday was out of the question, claiming it was the Lord's Day and business was not to be conducted. He decided to decline their offer for him to attend one of the churches thinking that had the potential of putting him in an awkward position. He sighed. This would not be a noteworthy welcoming to the Imperial Alliance; a small, under populated world stuck far from the main trade routes. In fact, he suspected it might be a rather boring event, a small ceremony to invite a backward planet destined to be always near the bottom of habitable worlds.

* * * *

The press conference was noisy, the small room over filled from the various media. Scotty and Glora tried to answer the questions the best they could without revealing too much about themselves.

"What made you choose to come to Haven for your honeymoon?"

"We won a contest that promised a round trip to any of the human inhabited planets," Scotty said. "Right after we won the contest, it was announced that Haven had been discovered. Both of us thought going to Haven on our honeymoon would be something to tell our children – that we were two of the first visitors to a new planet – our claim to fame. The contest organizers balked at first to send us here because of the expense but we won out because of the way the contest rules read. Next question."

And so it went for over an hour. At the end they were tired but happy they got through their ordeal.

Back in their hotel room they made plans on how to spend the afternoon.

"Look, I think it would be best if we stayed together to keep up the appearances of being married. I have arranged for a car and a driver to pick us up after lunch. I need to take some pictures of Oasis city and the surrounding area. I think we should have the bulk of our stories done by Monday. That's when all hell should break loose."

"Sure, that would be fine. When are we due to leave? Friday or is it Saturday?"

"Saturday. One week from today."

"Oh, Scotty, that church service tomorrow?"

"What about it?"

"It is a special service and it may be a little more complicated than the Reverend let on."

"So be it. It will take only a couple of hours, not a lifetime."

Glora opened her mouth to say something, but then changed her mind. She had tried to warn him after all.

* * * *

The driver picked them up from the hotel and drove where they requested. The whine of the electric motor in the small van was subdued compared to the blare of the radio. Scotty and Cindy weren't sure how to define the music except as bad country, though the driver seemed to enjoy it as she tapped her fingers on the steering wheel.

They stopped at a number of places, including the docks again, a park and the museum. The museum was larger than they expected and they saw only a portion of it, deciding they would check out the rest of it if they had time. The Regal was a good picture taking spot for tourists. The size of the ship was enormous, stretching for over two miles. The oval shaped cylinder was two city blocks wide. Scotty and Cindy knew present passenger ships were not normally made this large although there were military ships that would rival the Regal in size. In space, the enormous ships also looked smaller.

"The Regal was heavily damaged when it landed and although the ship was repaired later they say the structure is too weak to ever lift off the ground." The driver, a middle aged woman named Rita, recited the facts from memory. She continued, "For a number of years the ship served as living quarters for Haven and power engineering supplied power for Oasis City. The generators aren't used anymore, due to the need of repair. Unfortunately we don't have the necessary knowledge and parts to get them up and running but apparently there isn't much wrong with them. The ship is still used for conventions, parties, weddings and things like that. The founders wanted the Regal to be a living memory and anyone can take a tour and see the ship. It takes a long time to see the whole ship. There are rumours of ghosts that guard the ship against those who would do it harm. My brother was a guide for the Regal a few years ago and he told me several strange tales."

They drove to a couple of more spots; the driver had shut off the radio to give them a running commentary of whatever they passed. She told them about how the original settlers put the first buildings near the Regal and showed them the preserved wooden structures. They passed Elliot Park where a statue of Jason Elliot stood.

"Jason Elliot and Elaine Trestle were also the first couple married on Haven and this week we celebrate the anniversary of the wedding in our churches."

Cindy looked at Scotty to see if he understood what that implied, but he continued to watch outside the vehicle, taking pictures of the structures. As they moved away from the center of town, they saw some rather old looking buildings, including several streets that contained only one or two story shops made only of wood and stone. Most of the buildings were closed, or operated as part of a museum, but others were still operated by small proprietors.

As they drove out towards the edge of the city, the buildings became taller and more modern looking and the material used in construction changed to something other than wood. Besides apartments, Pearson and Lorncroft were surprised at the number of individual dwellings for families, something that had disappeared except for the very rich in much of Earth. As more streets and avenues rolled past them, they moved into more open areas, less business and more homes. Eventually they reached farm and ranch lands. Cindy and Scott were amazed at seeing a ranch, taking photos of the cattle, horses and the fields of grain.

"This is incredible, Scotty. Such a huge open space and all these animals walking about in it." They walked gingerly along the side of the road, touching the plants that grew along there.

"This must be what Earth looked like a few hundred years ago."

"If you two like this, hop back in the van. I can give you a better view."

They drove for about fifteen minutes and then started up a long climb with the motor whining a high-pitched scream. The van eventually stopped off the road on a rocky ledge.

"Take a look. You can see the how far the foothills extend. The hilly areas are where we raise cattle and horses and as the land smoothes out you can see where grain is grown."

The sight was fascinating for them. The vastness of it was startling and they both held their breath for a moment as they stood by the van.

Scotty took a deep breath and without thinking slipped his arm around Cindy's waist. "Unbelievable. I've see whole worlds from space and parts of it from shuttles, but this is different. You don't realize how shut in we are on Earth until you see the openness of this."

"Excuse me. If you will show me how to use your camera I'll take your picture." Rita held up Scotty's camera with a big smile.

"Evening is coming up so I guess we better had back to our hotel. You've been great, Rita."

"Thanks. But have you two made dinner plans yet?"

"No, not yet. Why?"

"How would you like to have dinner at one of those farms you were looking at? It would be a real privilege to have you folks for supper."

They looked at each other. Scotty shrugged, a message to Cindy that it was up to her.

"Sure, we'd love to," Cindy said. "As long as we're not imposing."

"Don't be silly. We'll be glad to have you." Rita picked up her mobile and punched in a number. "Mom? Could you set a couple of more plates for dinner? Yeah, that's right, them. About ten minutes."

The van returned down the hilly road, drove a while longer, and then turned into a farmyard as the sun slowly went down. Two large dogs came bounding up to greet the vehicle.

"Down, Simon. Down, Shadow. Don't mind them, they just want to sniff you and check out who you are."

Scott and Cindy were hesitant about leaving the safety of the van. The dogs seemed huge when they stood on their hind legs and Scott had to endure a lick on his face. He gently pushed the dogs down and kept between them and Cindy as much as he could. They made the short distance to the house without serious problems as Rita not so gently shoved the dogs back.

They were introduced to the residents of the house. Dawn and Darren Bishop were the parents with Rita being the oldest of their five children. Marty, Randy and Stewart still lived at home. In addition two of their grandchildren were also visiting.

"Quite a household you have here, Dawn." Scott was trying to remember all the names as he looked about; trying to picture people living in self-contained houses instead of apartments. It felt strange.

"Shucks, this is nothing. About ten times a year we have about twenty people over for supper."

The dinner table was set and both Cindy and Scott looked at the various dishes.

"Dig in, help yourself," Dawn said. "There's a lot more where that came from. Everything is from the farm and there's no shortage of food."

They took what they perceived to be vegetables and food that didn't come from an animal. The others at the table didn't comment but put steaks on their own plates. Conversation was several people talking at once. Questions came about Earth and how they liked Haven was expected. But they didn't stick on that topic and talked on a variety of subjects.

The food was good, and Scotty looked at the meat again. He wondered about its taste and if it was like the soybean substitute.

"I see you eyeing the steaks. Try a piece. If you don't like it, just spit it out. Can't expect you to like everything on the planet we make." Darren lifted up the plate and passed to him.

Now what do I do? With a bit of hesitation Scott took the smallest piece. Cindy watched him with her eyes wide. Cutting off a small piece, he placed it carefully in his mouth. The taste was similar to the soybean substitute, but the texture completely different. "Not bad. Very good, as a matter of fact."

He realized everyone was watching him so he made a bit of pretence chewing on the meat. He noticed Cindy watching him with a studied look.

"Give me a piece to try. Just a small one, please."

He cut his steak in half and gave it to her. She did the same thing as he did, slowly trying a small slice first. She tried to put the thought of it being the flesh of an animal out of her mind and concentrated on the taste. It was different, but certainly not unpleasant.

After dinner they walked outside, surveying the barn, the tool shed and other buildings. Scotty noticed that Cindy reached for his hand as Rita showed them around and when he looked at her, gave his hand a squeeze.

They continued to hold hands as Rita led them from one building to another showing them various types of machinery, including an impressive looking tractor. The wheels stood two feet higher than themselves.

"It's powered by an oil and gas mixture, unlike my van and other city vehicles. The electric motors aren't strong enough to drive this thing."

Scotty looked at the engine, and then at the exhaust pipe above it, the top covered in soot. "Doesn't this thing pollute the air?"

She shrugged. "Some, I reckon. Not much and most of that is either water vapour or carbon. We don't have much choice until we can come with better types of motors. A few decades ago all we had was these types of motors then someone discovered, or rather rediscovered from our old data resources in the library, how to make batteries that can hold a high charge. That is what drives our electric motors in the city vehicles."

Scott looked at his watch. "Well, Rita, this has been great but we better be heading back to the hotel."

"Sure. I'll just let the others know we're leaving." She disappeared into the house.

Scott turned and looked at Cindy, their eyes locked and he slowly moved closer to her. She started to close her eyes, her head tilted, when a door slammed closed and he jerked his head in the direction of the voices as the house emptied of the occupants.

Good-byes were exchanged and then they entered the van, which headed back to Oasis.

Scotty felt her lean into him, her hand searching out his. As he carried on a conversation with Rita, as his mind sought out what to do next. Cindy had warmed to him remarkably, as the trip went on and now she was telling him she was ready for them to establish a relationship. But he also remembered the warning from the Dean; if you have sex with her, consider yourself fired. Would he find out? Likely. Would he really fire him over this? Very likely. *Damn, this isn't good, not good at all.*

The conversation died out as they traveled through the city and he watched the city streets as they passed by.

"Scotty?" Her voice was low. "Those pictures you suggested for my story? Let's do them."

"Okay. When?"

"Tonight, while my mind is still made up."

Scotty moved some items around in the hotel room, turned on different lights and checked their effects.

"What should I wear? Will this dress do?" She held up a blue dress.

"Hmm, try a blouse and skirt instead, something you'd have worn on the ship."

She went to the bathroom to change while he set up his camera on a tripod, extending the sides of the camera to their maximum. Then he opened up a bottle of wine.

"Okay, I'm ready as soon as I have a drink. Where should I stand?"

"By the table. Put your hands at your sides and push against the table. I'm going to take a series of shots. So I want you to try to look frightened and twist your body side to side, as if you are struggling."

She did as he asked. Occasionally he moved the camera a bit and changed a light.

"Good, now undo some of the buttons on your blouse and keep doing the same thing."

She repeated her movements from before.

"Good."

"How is this going to look for the story?"

"Fine. I am going to fix the photos so they look like they came from a low resolution hidden camera and then I'm going to add some scenery from the museum we went to today to make it look like it came from Ravener's room."

Scotty took several more pictures of different angles, watching her face as he worked. She did seem to enjoy having her picture taken and he reminded her to look a bit more frightened and angry.

"Okay, that's it. You can relax now. I'll show you the results in a minute."

Twenty minutes later, she looked at the finished results.

"See, I changed your pose here a bit by rotating the image and substituted these shelves and tables from some archive photos I have. I also used a couple of pictures of the museum we went to today in the background. Next, I blurred the image slightly and added some shadows. Here I made it appear that there is a dark figure of a man standing between a hidden camera and you."

"That's really good. Hardly any detail but gives the impression of myself being attacked."

"I'm glad you like it."

"And will this put the story near the front?"

"Absolutely. That story with photos will be a winner. Ravener will know the photos are fake, but no one else will. His reputation will be ruined."

"That's wonderful. Say do you have the picture of me in that blue dress available? I would like to see that now."

"Sure, I'll pull it up."

The computer screen changed to show Cindy in her blue dress.

"That's pretty good. You do good work."

"Good subject. You're photogenic."

"You think so? I really like those pictures."

"The camera is still set up. Would you like a few more taken?"

"Well, maybe a couple. Where should stand? Should I wear this?"

"Depends on what type of pictures you want."

"How about you decide? You pick out how I should pose and what I should wear."

He was aware she was handing him control of what she should be doing. "Okay. Go to the bed and lie down on your side."

She went to the bed and propped herself up on one elbow. "Now what?"

"Relax and smile. Undo some buttons of your blouse."

The camera made a quiet humming sound as it took pictures.

"What else would you like me to do?"

"How about undoing some more buttons?"

"Okay, you're the expert." She unbuttoned a few buttons at the top and said, "Is this okay?" She struck a pose.

"Fine." He took several pictures. Gradually she removed some of her clothing under his suggestions.

She followed his direction, looking relaxed on the bed. She did several poses, including raising her leg up at the knee that lifted the skirt high.

Her skirt continued its upward journey and he decided it was now barely covering anything. "Would you feel comfortable taking off your skirt?"

"I suppose so." She shyly undid her skirt and then dropped it off the side of the bed and followed his suggestions on some more poses.

As he took more photos, his nervousness increased, while she appeared to be increasingly relaxed.

He shot several more photos and then stopped. "Well, I guess that's everything. You can get dressed again."

He turned back to his camera, pushing the save button and then looked back at her. She was still on the bed, lying almost naked on it, her head propped up by her arm.

"Scotty, maybe I don't need to get dressed. I'm here without hardly any clothes on and I don't know if I can make it any more obvious than this. And unless you really want me to get dressed I think you should come over here. I would really prefer it if you would just join me in bed right now."

Scotty thought about the Dean's warning again but realized he was already undoing his shirt. Oh well, maybe there were other jobs on Earth.

She held her hands in front of her. "Was it that hard a decision? I feel a little bit insulted."

* * * *

The next morning he woke up with her in his arms. He wondered how the events of last night transpired for this to happen, but his head still felt too foggy. But then he wondered if she'd planned the evening all along or whether it was something that just happened.

"Hey, wake up, Cindy. We have to get ready for church."

"Church? Oh my gosh, that's right. We better hurry."

She got in the bathroom before he did which meant he had to wait too long for his chance to get ready. When she came out, he was impressed with her white dress, remarking how good it looked on her.

She actually blushed which made him wonder a bit about the dress and the church service.

They were picked up right on time from the front of the hotel, and fifteen minutes later they arrived at a huge church, reminiscent of the old cathedrals on Earth.

"Mr. and Mrs. Pearson. How nice you could make it. Allow Brother Bailey to escort you to your seats. I was hoping you two would do the honour of being one of the special couples to come forth during our special service?" Blanchett made it sound a question and a statement.

"Well, we're not familiar with your customs, Reverend," Scotty said.

"Quite all right. Just follow the lead of the other couples and the process will be as clear as day."

"Very well, I guess we could." Scotty felt Cindy squeeze his hand. She looked pleased. He felt troubled.

The service went as he expected many sermons would go, preaching against sin and about the gifts from God. Scotty allowed his attention to wander over the decorations in the church such as the stained glass and carvings that adorned the walls when he felt a poke in his ribs from Cindy.

Two other couples had risen and were walking to the front. He noticed the other women were wearing white also. As a matter of fact, many women were wearing white in the church. The men were dressed like him, in dark suits.

He followed the other couples to the front and stood with them as the Reverend Thomas Blanchett spoke about marriage and its commitment.

Scotty was getting a very uneasy feeling.

"…and so let us pledge our love for each other once again. Ladies, if you will join me?" All the women wearing white repeated his words. "…to love and to cherish from this day forth…"

Cindy looked in his eyes and she spoke the words to him.

Oh my Lord, am I getting married? Can this be happening? This can't be legal. We didn't sign any papers. This doesn't mean anything. So why is she looking at me like this?

"And gentlemen, if you will…"

Scotty repeated the same verse of commitment to Cindy. Not exactly smiling as he did so and certainly with less convection.

"And so with the power invested to me by the Council of Haven, I pronounce you husband and wife. Please kiss each other to seal your love."

Cindy and Scotty kissed, though he thought her kiss a little too enthusiastic.

This can't be good. Not good at all. What if this turns out to be legal? Cindy looks happy, radiant even. Beautiful, in fact. But this isn't in my plans, and I hope it wasn't in hers either.

Back in the car, he sat looking straight ahead, pondering on what occurred in the church. She was still smiling away, not disturbed by the latest events.

"Scotty, lighten up," she whispered into his ear. "This isn't a legal marriage. I checked, there is a requirement for paperwork and other legal necessities."

Fine, he thought. *I just won't sign anything until I'm back on Earth.*

Chapter Six
Airport, Oasis City, Haven

Aaron Duggan, along with several other officials, stood in the observation lounge. He had just been given word that the 'welcoming committee' was scheduled to land within ten minutes. All incoming air traffic was cancelled for the next hour while the air/space port was prepared to receive their guests.

"Shouldn't they be here by now?" Irene looked up at Aaron, who looked uncomfortable in his suit. She herself felt quite comfortable in her long dress, enjoying occasions when she could wear formal clothes and could dress up. Aaron only dressed up when he had to and complained that lately he found too many instances when he had to.

"Any minute now. I suspect they are a little miffed that we kept postponing meeting them. Maybe they think they are getting even with us." He looked back at her and gave her a smile. "Don't worry; they'll be here soon enough."

A few minutes later a half dozen black dots appeared in the sky. They hung there for several seconds before suddenly dropping to hang just above the concrete runways. The low rumble of their engines vibrated inside the building. The six black Imperial Forces fighter ships now ringed the air/space port; each ship was 300 feet long and bristled with arms and other devices. Each ship contained 80 Elite Storm Troopers, though today they wore their dress uniforms.

The black ships hovered for a full minute before a blue Diplomat Ship arrived, half the size of the fighter ships. It sank slowly through the center of the other ships, coming to rest on the tarmac. After it landed two of the black ships touched down as well, but they did so with a rush that caused a cloud of dust to fly around, bouncing on the ground as the shock absorbers were tested. Through the noise and smoke, an honour guard of the black dressed Elite Storm Troopers emerged from the ships and stood by the exit doors of the Diplomat Ship.

"What are they trying to prove by that?" The edge in Aaron's voice echoed the thoughts of those around him.

"Maybe that's how they do things in the Imperial Forces." One of the councillors peered at the diplomat ship as the doors opened and the first of the welcoming committee emerged.

"No, I don't think so. That's showing off, plain and simple. They must be annoyed we wouldn't see them right away. So they come in with a lot of bluster."

"I guess we should head out and meet them." Irene looked up at Aaron, waiting for him to lead the delegation towards the exit doors.

"We will, in a minute. If they think we are going to be intimidated by that display, well, let's let them stand out there for a moment or so wondering where we are."

* * * *

Dr. Roger Beaumont breathed in the fresh air; it was so much better that the stuffy air of the space ships. 'Wonderful. Bright sun, blue skies. Lovely planet.' He stood there with the other officials. He looked around. *Now where the devil is the delegation to meet us?*

"General, we have landed at the right place, haven't we?"

General Burgess looked annoyed at the speaker. "Of course this is the right place! Do you take us for fools? The bloody idiots are probably scared to show their heads, that's all."

The group stood by the blue diplomat ship, shuffling their feet and looking around. The Elite Forces Honour guard stood at attention, their black masks hiding their expression, though the slight movement of their heads indicated they were discretely looking around.

The moments dragged on until finally the doors to the terminal opened and out came Haven's delegation. They walked to within a few feet of the Welcoming Committee and there the two groups eyed each other.

"Welcome to Haven, ladies and gentlemen. I am Premier Aaron Duggan and it is my privilege to invite you to our home." The words came out flat, sounding almost like a challenge.

Beaumont looked up at the tall leader, and then glanced at the rest of the delegation. They were all tall, ranging from five feet six for one of the women to six feet eight for the men. They were also all white, unlike the mix of colors of their own committee. His own height of five feet eight was tall on Earth, but he felt undersized next to the new group. He wondered how Burgess was reacting. The powerful general hated being short and this was going to make him feel even more so.

"Premier Duggan, my name is Dr. Roger Beaumont. It is an honour to meet you and your people. Thank you for your kind invitation to your home and welcome to the Imperial Worlds." His diplomatic training came through, his words sounding like they held warmth and convection.

The rest of the two groups shook hands and exchanged names and titles. Beaumont noticed the General acted stiffly, annoyed at the height of the people he had just met. This was not a good start. He was not surprised by the locals' reaction to their entrance; he had not approved of the General's decision to arrive in such force; it made his own job more difficult.

The two groups moved to inside the spaceport, where refreshments were served in one of the lounge areas. Small talk and polite conversation replaced the earlier reserved greetings. Beaumont, in particular, worked hard to restore trust, feeling privately that General Burgess was looking for an excuse to flex the military muscle of the Alliance. Afterwards the newcomers were driven to the best hotel in Haven, the same one that housed Scotty and Cindy.

* * * *

Scotty wasn't far from the reception. Without trying to look too obvious, he photographed the various leaders talking and shaking hands. The earlier tension seemed to have evaporated. Cindy monitored the local news media from their hotel room, trying to piece together Haven's reaction.

"Scotty?"

Scotty answered on his new phone. The tablet viewphones didn't work on Haven, so he invested in a pair of the local mobile phones. They worked fine but did not have the capabilities of video. "Yes, Cindy?"

"Scotty, the Welcoming Committee is going to stay at the same hotel we're in."

"Damn. I should have thought of that. Look, grab a few personal items and the reports we made, the memory sticks should be all together in the black case, and get the hell out of there fast. I'll meet you at Samson's Diner."

Two hours later found Cindy and Scotty finishing off their pizza.

"Look, I just don't trust them at all," Scotty said. "Beaumont is okay. But that mighty mite, Burgess, is nothing but trouble. He brought along his henchmen, Rolland, Travitt, and Bergot."

"Do you think they'll look for us?"

"Absolutely. They're probably pissed off we arrived here first."

"So what do we do now? When do we go back to the hotel?"

"Well, I'm not sure when we can go back, if ever. We'll have to find another place."

"Another hotel?"

"Maybe, it depends on how badly they want to find us. Burgess will have his men doing some checks; probably they've already broken into the computer network here. It wouldn't take long for them to find us in a new hotel, especially with the lack of security around here."

"So we sleep in the streets?"

He shrugged his shoulders. "We'll think of something."

Cindy pulled out her phone and punched in a few digits.

"Who are you calling?"

She held up a hand. "Hello, Irene? This is Cindy Pearson."

Scott listened to the conversation that seemed to stretch on a fair bit of time. Bored, he got up to pay the bill. When he got back, she had just put down the phone.

"What was that all about?"

"That was Irene. She has an acreage just outside of town and has lots of room for us to stay."

"Hmm. Did you tell her why we needed a place?"

"I told her we would explain when we saw her."

"Okay. So how do we get there?"

* * * *

Twenty minutes later a red car stopped in front of the café. Cindy jumped in the front, while Scotty climbed in the back. The car turned eventually on an expressway after navigating through the streets of the city. Scotty was getting used to personal vehicles and was tempted to try driving one, something that would have been impossible back on Earth. The whine of the electric motor increased as the car picked up speed and Scotty's mind drifted to other things. He noticed the women in the front were talking about clothes and ceased paying attention shortly after.

The acreage was well lit up as they pulled into a garage. They walked straight into the house through the attached garage.

"I'll give you a wake up call tomorrow, and you can explain everything then. It's late now and I'm sure you could use some rest. Unless you want coffee or a drink first I'll show you to the guest room."

"No, thank you. We're both tired and I'm sure you are too."

* * * *

In the morning, Cindy and Scotty walked into the kitchen where they were greeted by both Irene and Aaron. Breakfast consisted of pancakes and coffee and polite questions on how they slept. After that, the plates were cleared and there was a silence at the table.

"Well, I guess it's time that you learned the truth about Cindy and myself. We're not, as you may have guessed, husband and wife on a honeymoon. We're reporters for a magazine on Earth and our assignment was to find stories of interest to our readers. We meant no harm and I hope you will forgive our deception. But if the people here knew we were reporters our assignment would be more difficult, if not impossible."

"Are these stories going to project Haven in a bad way?"

"To be honest, to a degree. Our tabloid is geared towards scandals and the barely believable. It really depends on the editor – on which stories he wishes to use – and the editing of the stories afterward. We have written a number of positive things about Haven as well so it's hard to say what the final stories will be like."

"And the reason you have left your hotel in such a hurry?" Aaron didn't look or act annoyed. He kept a poker face throughout the revelation. Irene sat quietly as well, crossing her arms when they talked about the tabloid. She did look miffed however. Her eyes had a hard look to them.

"Those people from Earth that are staying in the hotel are part of General Burgess's special security. They're not good to be close to. Because they want to learn about Haven, if they found us, they would try to get information from us. Their methods could be most unpleasant."

"But you're on Haven. They don't have jurisdiction here." Irene poured more coffee as she spoke.

"They don't recognize any authority accept their own. And they would be discrete enough not to alarm the local police."

"I see. We'll have to be careful as well then."

"That's not half of it. Look, I like you people and your world. I don't know if you have heard of the Charter of Conduct but the Welcoming Committee will expect you to sign it. If you don't, it means you are hiding something and the General will use force to protect the population of Haven from the corrupt government. And if you do sign, well, you're not likely to meet its conditions and will give the Imperial Alliance reason to take over administration of

Haven. It is a no win situation. I don't like what is going to happen to this world and I wish I could help."

Several more questions and answers followed and the information all pointed to same conclusion; Haven was about to be taken over by the Imperial Alliance.

Chapter Seven
Premier's office, Oasis City, Haven

"As you can see the Charter of Conduct is simply a document to protect the population of all Imperial Alliance members," Diplomat Beaumont said.

Aaron Duggan picked up the Charter of Conduct. "Quite a number of pages here."

"The Charter is designed to be complete and not to leave issues open to different interpretations. We wish to be exact on all matters."

"And if we study this document and find some parts we do not agree with Mr. Ambassador?"

"Well, the Charter is modified only by a vote of the Imperial Alliance Parliament. All of the worlds live by its conditions and we would expect Haven to do so as well. If there is an issue you disagree with you may present this matter to Parliament for a vote. If the vote agrees with you, it will be changed. To be frank there will always be some parts some of our member worlds disagree with. But to keep the Imperial Alliance strong and with the understanding all people should be treated as equals there is an acceptance to follow the Charter for the common good."

"And if we choose not to sign? What then?"

"I suggest that you study the document first. If you have specific questions about some of the clauses, I will be glad to go into detail about them. If you, and I assume Haven as well as you as the representative, still do not wish to sign then I will discuss that matter with you at that time. Let's not look ahead to obstacles until they materialize. Let us work towards the spirit of cooperation and allow the chance of being one people guide our actions.

"There is also the matter of becoming members of the Imperial Alliance. To be members, as I understand it, requires signing of the Charter of Conduct as well as the payment of funds to the Imperial government. These payments are quite steep and would be quite prohibitive to a planet of the size of Haven. It would seem that if we sign the Charter we would be without representation."

"There is a price to pay for to be part of the Imperial Alliance. Unfortunately, the Imperial Alliance cannot run on space alone and it is fair that all worlds give monetary support. This is pro-rated according to size of the world and considering the benefits Haven would receive from the Alliance it is of good value to your planet. If Haven decides against such an investment, a proxy would be appointed for you. This proxy would reside on Mars and would keep your government informed of the ongoing activities of the Representatives and would advance your needs as the occasion arises."

"That proxy would not be under our control nor would it be obligated to present our concerns, would it?"

"I see you have read much of the Charter already. You must have received an advanced copy of it." Beaumont paused to look at Aaron but received only a straight face in return. He was impressed how this small world politician could show only what he wanted to show. "Yes, you are quite correct. The proxy has no obligation but to keep communication open between Haven and the Imperial government. Though it will, and has done so in the past, advanced issues pertinent to worlds that cannot afford their own representatives."

After the meeting was over, Aaron thought back to when he first read the Charter of Conduct on Scotty's tablet. The initial preamble to the Charter sounded good; a document to protect the rights of all people; that all people came from Earth and must act as one people. Good stuff. No fighting; we are all brothers and sisters. But to act as one people the Charter put severe restrictions on how worlds could set up laws. Customs were secondary to the wants of the Alliance. In theory a person on Titan would feel just as at home on Haven because the laws and customs would be the same; a harmonized society.

He picked up the phone. "Irene, I need to see Cindy and Scotty right away. We have problems. Big problems."

* * * *

"Scotty, I have read this Charter and from what I can see our laws are not going to conform to the Imperial Alliance," Aaron Duggan said. "And our customs are not going to go over very well. Am I right?"

"Well, I'm not an expert. But I would say that's true enough."

"Scotty, tell him more. Tell him what we discussed." Cindy looked between the two men. She sat on the couch with Scotty while Irene and Aaron sat on two armchairs in the living room of the acreage.

"We tried to think of some examples to help explain some of changes the Charter will impose. For one they wouldn't want you to have businesses closed on Sundays. It wouldn't be fair to those who don't support that religion. Another might be the lack of your police presence. You may not need additional police but some people on some worlds would find it uncomfortable if there wasn't the constant presence of security. Haven would have to establish nude beaches, other worlds have been required to so, apparently you cannot infringe on the rights of some people to go around naked if they want to. The harvesting of trees is not permitted on most worlds and I'm not sure what would be said about your use of wood and paper products here. And the eating of meat is, well, considered barbaric and would almost certainly be banned. There is more but I believe you can understand some of the situations."

"Aaron, this is terrible. What are we going to do? We can't sign such a document." Irene stood up, looking horrified.

"If you don't," Scotty continued, "I will guarantee that within a month the Imperial Forces will take over Haven on some pretence of human rights violation. They will send you and other government leaders to Earth for trial, and then set up a provincial government of their own choosing. And Haven will be ruthlessly transformed to the Imperial Alliance ideal. The end result will be a very poor planet but with all the correct laws and customs."

"What do you suggest? Aaron looked between Cindy and Scotty."

"Stall. Tell them you are studying the Charter and need to consider this carefully. Point out that Haven has such a small population that it takes longer to go through the document because of the lack of experts in this area."

"Well, we can stall. But to what end?"

"Well, Cindy and I are leaving for Earth on Saturday. We won't arrive for three weeks but will be able to send an advance communication to the NightHawk. Obviously, most of it will be our reports about Haven but I'll also try and obtain the services of the company's high priced lawyers. I'll attempt to get them working on your problem and they might be able to come up with some sort of solution." Scotty paused for a moment. "I said try and attempt, but I believe I'll be able to get some advice from our lawyers. I've talked to them in the past on other issues and I don't think that would be a problem to get help on what to do next."

Privately Scotty wondered how cooperative the lawyers will be if he gets fired for having a relationship with Cindy. But he had dug out some excellent stories and it wasn't likely NightHawk would fire anyone who was bringing in top stories.

"Thank you for that." Aaron sighed. "That's not much of a solution but so far our only one. Stalling can't hurt in any event."

"There is one other thing. We need to get back into our hotel room to get the rest of our things. Could you get us an escort of some sort?" Scotty asked. "We don't trust the rest of the guests in the hotel."

* * * *

The two police officers escorted Cindy, Scotty and Irene to the hotel room. The door didn't show any signs of being forced open but when they walked inside two Imperial agents were waiting for them. The agents matched eyes with the police officers and then looked at the others.

Irene spoke up first. "I represent the government of Haven. You are trespassing and are without permission to be outside of your hotel rooms. If you are not out of here in thirty seconds, you will be charged accordingly."

One agent spoke rapidly into a small phone while the other opened his jacket to reveal a weapon. The agent speaking on the phone put it back in his pocket. "Very well, Ms, as you wish. We will return to our rooms. We were merely checking to make sure the citizens of the Imperial Alliance were safe. They were gone for several days and we were worried." They walked past the officers and out of the room. The last one paused at the door. "Nice pictures, by the way. Very interesting." He looked at Cindy, his eyes going up and down as he smirked.

Scotty looked outraged, but Cindy put her hand on his arm, halting him until the agents left. "Don't, it's okay. If I didn't want anyone ever to see those pictures I wouldn't have had you take them in the first place. I thought I looked pretty good in them. I'm not embarrassed they saw them so don't fret about it. Now let's just get packed and get out of here."

"Yeah, all right. But I had everything under a code. A good one."

"A code wouldn't stop those guys. Hey! They went through my underwear, those creeps."

Irene looked amused as she helped stuff articles into containers. "Men are attracted to the strangest things, aren't they?"

"Men are strange period sometimes."

The police officers continued to look on. They weren't happy about the confrontation that just took place. Having the Imperial agents show off their weapons caused one of them to quietly unclip his own gun from its holster though he appeared relieved the situation did not escalate after that. Other than target practice he had never used his weapon.

The two women were the last to leave the room, the police officers and Scotty headed out first, Scotty grumbling about being a packhorse.

"Irene, those pictures. I don't want you to get the wrong impression. But they were of me somewhat undressed. It was my idea, not Scotty's. And they really were in good taste."

"You don't have to explain, but there's nothing wrong with posing for your husband, or for someone special. If you really like the pictures, show them to me sometime. Someday I would like to get some photos done." She added to herself. *Though with my clothes on.*

* * * *

Farmland near Oasis City

The black ship dropped silently – to human ears – to the ground. Against the night sky it was hard to see unless one knew where to look exactly. The radar and sonic absorbing surface made it invisible to active probes while an inside protective layer prevented heat and other radiation from escaping.

A few seconds after the ship landed a half dozen elite guards jumped out and immediately the ship disappeared into the night again. The four men and two women wore dark, sound absorbing clothing. They wore special gloves that protected their hands as well as containing sensors that allowed their fingers to transmit infrared and ultraviolet radiation to a computer. A special air breathable fabric covered their faces and, in addition, goggles that also could see infrared and ultraviolet protected their eyes. Between the gloves and the goggles very little escaped the attention of the soldiers. On command, special microphones could also be turned on that allowed each soldier to pick up low-level audio.

On this assignment, the soldiers were required to meet exactly five miles north in three hours. They were to avoid detection by Haven defence forces and report any unusual activities. The whole point of the exercise was to test any possible reaction by Haven to them. If they were detected they were to surrender immediately as the Alliance knew it would look bad to have a military skirmish with a world they were inviting to join. It would be embarrassing to be caught but nothing compared to having weapons fired.

An hour later, the Alliance soldiers had made their way across the farm pasture and now took a rest behind a grove of trees near the edge of the field. They spoke quietly and took small drinks of the water they carried.

The silence was broken by the sound of a vehicle driving up, followed by two dogs that were barking. The headlights of the truck momentarily blinded them and then a single figure walked up carrying a rifle and a flashlight.

"What's going on here? Is somebody in trouble?"

* * * *

The commander on the Alliance ship was not pleased. "What the hell happened down there?"

"Hard to say exactly, sir. A local farmer discovered them seventy-two minutes into the operation. Apparently, the dogs heard the high-pitched sound of the ship when it landed and the farmer decided to investigate. The dogs apparently also were able to smell out their hiding spot."

"Oh, for crying out loud. A dog was able to find them in a location that is hidden from even our technology?"

"Yes sir."

"Shit. Where are they now? Are they being detained by their police or armed forces?"

"No. They're having pie and coffee at the farm house."

* * * *

"So we wait?" General Burgess crossed his arms. Waiting was not one of his strong suits.

"Yes General. They claimed they need time to study the Charter and we must give them that time. They are stalling, that much is obvious. But it will eventually come down to Haven signing the Charter of Conduct. Not to sign will be worse and they know it. They will plead they didn't understand all of the clauses and the Council will give them more time to make corrections. But in the end they will not meet all of the conditions and then there might be a need for your armed forces." Beaumont relaxed in a swivel chair in one of the view lounges. He found the General's eagerness for battle tiresome.

"I can hardly wait. Those damn giants. I will teach them who to look up to."

The ambassador nodded agreeably. But in his own mind he wondered how the General had become so paranoid about another person's height. Had he become so powerful because of that burning resentment or in spite of it?

"Yes, of course. However, I need to bring up a related topic. Your entourage has been in a few situations involving the local population. I think it is important for them to understand that we are guests on this world and for them to be seen spying is not what we need right now."

"Very well, I will have them curtail their fact finding activities."

"Excellent. And please tell them that it would be prudent not to flaunt their weapons either. There was most unfortunate incident regarding government officials in a hotel room."

* * * *

The trip was a bit delayed but Aaron picked up Scotty from Irene's place and headed out towards the distant mountains. The truck was a well used one and the cab had various pieces of junk in it, as Aaron called it, when he apologized for the mess. The back of the pickup was loaded with gear plus more of the junk. Aaron would have liked to have left early in the morning, around six, but a few last minute work problems showed up and it was seven thirty before they left. That was just fine by Scotty who continued to yawn as they walked from the yard, slurping on his coffee with his eyes half closed.

"How's the coffee, Scott?" Aaron held up the thermos. "Need a refill?"

"Yeah, I think so. This is pretty good coffee. A lot better than the stuff we had in the hotel."

"Well we do grow coffee on Haven, the climate supports it, but the beans may be a bit different from those used on Earth. The secret here is to put in a pinch of salt when you're brewing the coffee; gets rid of the bitter taste."

"Whatever works. Have you ever drunk this stuff with whisky?"

Chapter Eight

An hour later Scotty was awake enough to appreciate the countryside. The morning sun left enough shadows that he could see the contours of the land. He also noticed the paved road had disappeared in favour of a gravel one and the occasional bump jarred him from relaxing too much. Aaron pointed out different types of trees and plants as they went by and spotted some of the wildlife.

"So where exactly are we going?" Scotty asked.

"About half way to those mountains," Aaron said. "There's a lake there that is fed by runoff from those mountains and has some of the best fishing there is. I have what you may generously call a cabin there. I keep some supplies there, nothing much, and a boat."

Scotty looked ahead at the distant mountains, it was hard to gauge how far they were away. The fact they looked a greyish purple probably meant they had to quite distant indeed. "How long is it going to take to get there?"

"Oh, in about another two hours we should have the boat in the water."

The mention of the boat brought back the nervousness Scotty felt. It was bad enough that he would be fishing, pulling some poor wiggling creature out of the water; killing them he found harder still to take. But the thought of the boat, now that scared him. He couldn't swim, which wasn't unusual on Earth, and the image of being in a small vessel bouncing up and down on a huge lake caused more than a little apprehension.

"We wouldn't be going by a place that has a restroom, would we?"

Aaron looked at him, wondering if he was joking at first. For quite some time now, they had only passed trees and rolling hills. "No, but that's not a problem out here." He slowed down and then angled towards the edge of the road. "Here's as a good spot as any."

Scotty was a little bit dismayed by what he was doing, taking a leak behind a tree. If he was to do this on Earth, providing he went to the trouble to get to the great outdoors, he would no doubt be arrested and his name plastered in the media for committing some ecology violation. To make it even more bizarre, the Premier of Haven was doing the same thing a few feet away. This was truly a strange world he'd fallen into.

The journey continued and they passed only the occasional vehicle going the opposite way. Most of those were pickup trucks similar to the one they were in and in each case Aaron waved at them as they went by. The other driver waved as well in a strange type of salute.

"Do you know those other drivers?"

"No, not really. Recognized a couple."

"Why did you wave at them if you didn't know them?"

Aaron appeared to consider the question for a moment. "I dunno really. People just do that on lonely roads here. Kinsmen mentality, I suppose. Out here if something happened to your truck you could be out here a long time. Just makes sense to be as friendly as possible to anyone traveling along here."

"I see. You know, back on Earth there are always some people moving about wherever you go. Get in trouble and you just yell help and some security firm will come running up. Though come to think of it, I was once going down this tunnel that was under construction. I thought I was alone. It was pretty late when I came across some worker walking the opposite away. We spotted each other the same time and kind of eyed each other. Then he and I both kind of smiled and waved at the same time."

"Maybe Earth and Haven have more in common than you first thought."

"Yeah, that might be right." The silence continued for another minute and then Scotty became curious about something else. "I have to ask you, is that coat you are wearing really made from animal skins?"

"Animal skin? Well, I suppose so. We call it leather. This is made from cow hide."

"Isn't that kind of strange to wear the skin from an animal?"

Aaron thought about Scotty's question for a moment. "Maybe. But we try to make full use of the cow, the leather being one of them. We try not to waste anything and leather is an excellent material."

Scotty felt the leather with his fingers, and then shook his head. Some things were just too strange on this world.

* * * *

They arrived at the rustic cabin, built out tree trunks and some prefabricated material. A fireplace provided heat. Cooling was provided by opening windows and a trap door on the roof. Aaron swept out the place, sending dirt, insects and a dead rodent out the door.

"Scotty, now to enjoy a time honoured tradition in fishing. Let's open the beer." The two men sat on old tree stumps set by the front of the cabin and opened the bottles of beer.

"You know, Aaron, we have beer back at home, of course. But it sure lacks the punch of this stuff. And glass bottles! Unbelievable." He laughed.

"What does your beer come in?"

"Plastic. Plastic cans that you pull a tab to open."

After each had a couple of bottles, they finished setting up the cabin and then Aaron pulled a tarp off an old boat.

"There she is. The queen of Lake Moses."

Scotty looked at the fibreglass hull and shook his head. *This is going to hold two men afloat in water?*

They each grabbed a side of the boat and carried it to a dock made up of timber and old tires. They carefully slid the boat into the water and Aaron tied a rope from the bow to the dock.

An hour later Scotty slowly let go of the dock and gingerly sat in the middle of the front seat.

Aaron laughed. "Have you ever been in a boat before?" He handed over an orange life vest.

"No. And I'm not sure if I want to a second time."

"Relax, there isn't any danger at all."

"Then why the life vest?"

The small motor moved the boat towards the middle of the lake before turning to follow the shoreline. At some point determined by Aaron, they stopped.

He handed Scotty another beer, took another for himself and then put the rest in a net that he dropped off the side. "Keeps them cold that way," he announced to Scotty's unspoken question. "The water comes from mountain runoff and is pretty cold at this time of year."

Aaron showed him how to put bait on his fishing line and then Scotty tried to follow how to cast the line. He gave up quickly and was content to allow his line to drift behind the boat.

Aaron tossed Scotty an old hat and a small plastic bottle.

"What's this?"

The hat is to protect your head and the bottle contains sun block. Wipe it on your skin. The sun here can give a nasty sunburn."

Scotty did what he was told but was dubious about the danger. He did notice Aaron also wore a hat so there might be some truth to it. But the hats did look silly, especially Aaron's which had small bits of something attached to it.

"Would I be right in guessing that fishing on Earth is not common anymore?"

"You got it." Scotty noticed Aaron was still leaning back in the rear of the boat, barely holding on to his fishing pole, waiting for him to continue. "You see the problem is we have so many damn people on Earth. The only way we can feed and house everyone is for everyone to live in these huge interconnected buildings. Some of these buildings are hundreds of stories high, they contain apartments, retail shops, restaurants, parks, offices, schools and recreation facilities." Scotty took another drink of his beer. "A city on Earth would have several of these monster structures and they would be interconnected by pedways. Outside of these buildings would be acres of land devoted only to growing plants, they're generically called soybeans but can be a number of different plants that can be converted to other foods."

"So there are just buildings and soybean type plants?"

"Oh no. By concentrating all the people and food plants in small areas, the rest of the land will hopefully, return to its natural state. People need a special permit to go to those reserves, and there certainly wouldn't be any fishing or hunting allowed."

"You mean you need a permit to take a walk in the woods?"

"Well, yeah. But they're not hard to get. It's just so that there aren't too many people out there all at once."

Aaron shook his head. "That's hard to imagine, all those people cooped up in buildings. What about the oceans?"

"They're protected too, though if you have enough money you can use sailboats. Cruises on the ocean are popular but outrageously expensive. There are a few eccentric, rich people, who have these huge floating homes. What you have to keep in mind is that the environmental laws of Earth are strict, enforced vigorously and encompass just about every area of our lives. If it wasn't for the environmental laws Earth might be a dead planet."

Irene had made some sandwiches for them and they munched on them when they got hungry. A few hours and a few bottles of beer later they headed back to shore, about the same time Scotty was starting to enjoy the quiet and gentle rolling of the boat in the water. He was pleased he didn't catch any fish but was amazed how Aaron managed to catch several.

Aaron got busy after they had returned the boat to its dry land resting place by first building a fire in an old fire pit and then preparing the fish. Scotty flinched as Aaron took a large knife and then quickly cut open the fish.

"Don't get me wrong, but if you did this on Earth, you'd be arrested."

"For cleaning the fish?"

"For one. The knife would have to be registered with the police, you have a fire which is large enough to cause the fire department to investigate, and you are burning wood, another crime. The fish itself is partly protected and you would need a special permit to catch them and afterward you would need to prove they didn't suffer. These would all be serious crimes against the environment. On Earth there is a constant awareness of what people are doing to the environment."

"Interesting." Aaron looked up and then around him, taking in the fire, the lake and his cabin. "Here on Haven, we consider people to be part of the environment. The eating of fish, burning dead wood and living here is just part of a natural order."

Scotty watched Aaron toss the fish into a pan with some cut up potato – the pan parked precariously above the fire. "I'm not saying you're wrong, please don't misunderstand me. But this …" He swept his hand in an arc around him. "… is special. Haven and its people have something very unique. Nowhere else in human space could you find this. A regular Garden of Eden."

The fish was excellent. Scotty forgot about his earlier misgivings about eating a fish that he had seen alive only a few hours ago.

"I do wish something like this could be found on Earth. I guess the problem is our population is just too big not to have a serious impact on the environment. And the other planets are just following Charter Laws and therefore aren't allowed to invade areas outside the city. Pity, there is something to this."

"Well, Scotty, if you ever get the urge, there's lots of room out here."

"You mean to live?"

"Sure, why not? As you pointed out, you can't buy this on Earth."

Scotty couldn't think of a reason why not, though he dismissed that to having too many bottles of beer.

While Aaron and Scotty sat outside around the fire, Irene and Cindy sat in Irene's living room in front of a fireplace. Irene earlier had taken Cindy to a neighbour's ranch where horses were raised. It was a mixture of dread and excitement that Cindy felt as she climbed on a horse and was allowed to take it for a supervised ride. Now that they were back relaxing with a glass of wine, Cindy was able to get Irene to talk a little more about Haven. Irene usually let Aaron lead the conversation when they were together, though Cindy wasn't sure if that was just because Aaron was the political leader and therefore should be the one to take charge.

"So most of the population is around Oasis City?"

"Yes. In the beginning, the settlers of Haven didn't want the cities to become too big and so other towns and cities were developed, but not too far away. They also wanted to stay close to one another for security reasons and practical ones as well, such as travel time to ship goods. With one exception."

"Which was?"

"St. John. About ten years ago, it was decided that in the event of some local disaster, it might be good to have at least a portion of the human population some distance away. St John is located nearly on the opposite side of the continent and has a population of about three hundred thousand. We keep close ties with them and we hope that someday we can have some cities in between the two areas."

"I noticed most of your cities have religious types of names. Religion is pretty strong here."

"You can say that again. The Regal was made up of many people from a church, the Starlight. It was one of the three ships that left Earth as a group and was the only one to have survived. People took it as a sign that God was looking after them and made some of the first pilgrims extremely religious. Also, they were guilt-torn, as many of them lost friends and family on the other ships. The "why was I spared" syndrome, I suppose. The whole of Haven suffered collective guilt for a whole generation. So it's not too surprising the strength of the church here and also why some people still fear the wrath of God if they sin."

"So how do the people feel about coming into contact with Earth?"

"Depends on who you listen to. But, and this is a bit interesting, it was prophesied by a John Gibson long ago that Earth and Haven would come in contact again after the eighth generation on Haven. That Haven was kept purposely out of sight of Earth until such time that Earth needed help. It's been about ten generations so some people claim this was all predicted long ago by the Gibson Prophesies. Of course, they have been saying this is the year we'd re-establish contact with Earth for twenty years now so you might want to take that with a grain of salt. Aaron would never admit to believing anything about this but there are whispers that he is suppose to be the one who will save Earth and all humans from themselves. The new messiah."

Cindy took in the information. She would have to see if there were any record of those prophesies in Haven's libraries. "So tell me, what is it like to be the girlfriend of the new messiah?"

Irene laughed. "He can lead a whole country but can't make a commitment. I'm not in a hurry to get married but I wish he would take our relationship a little more serious. How about you and Scotty?"

Cindy took a drink of her wine before answering. "I don't really care. If he wants to get closer, fine. If not, well, there are lots of other guys I'm interested in."

Irene stared for a few seconds. "Even you don't believe that. You're sleeping with him and you don't care if the relationship goes further? He's no spring chicken. He should be glad to have a pretty girl like you."

"Thanks. But he's been married twice before and may be a little shy about another go at marriage."

"Married twice?! Two divorces here in Haven and you're black listed. Still, maybe he just got into the wrong situation before. My advice is for you to lay it on the line with him. Find out where you stand before you get back to Earth so you aren't wasting time with a hopeless situation."

"Yeah, maybe you're right. How about you and Aaron? Are you going to force the issue?"

"Not for a while. Like a lot of women in Oasis City I had a crush on him the first time he ran for office, back as a councillor. I don't want to scare him off; there are just too many others willing to take my place. He'll come around, I'm sure."

"I have another question for you. How come everyone seems to know the history of everything here? Names and dates of this and that."

"Oh that. Our great school system. Everyone is taught about the history of Haven to a point of overkill. We were also taught about Earth, as it was a few hundred years ago no less. And then we have to find time to teach them about math and science."

Chapter Nine

On the Starship Monteith orbiting Haven

Beaumont sat at the opposite end of the long table from Glora Bitmon. He filled her in on the latest details of the Charter situation, including the final time line for Haven to sign it. Though she was quite young to be in such a high position with the Overseeing Committee, he was learning why she had been fast tracked to be a liaison officer representing Earth. She was well prepared about Haven, seemed to understand their culture and was not taken back by their reluctance to sign.

Glora had quickly picked up on the current situation and asked some in depth questions. She had however, refused his opening gambit to get to know her better. The women of Haven had also been reluctant to be entertained by him and he been forced to go back to the ship's crew for social activities.

"I'm afraid that we haven't been able to convince them to even come up to our ship. I doubt there is much else we can do to get them to sign the Charter; I believe I have explored all possible avenues and they remain stubbornly fixed to the notion that they will be left alone if they don't sign," Beaumont said, disgusted.

"You have explained what will happen if they don't sign? What exactly did you express to them?"

"Well, to be precise, the refusal to sign was not the main topic of most of our conversations. I wanted to accent the positive nature of signing the Charter and not bring in too many negative topics. I did not wish to make them feel threatened."

Glora sat looking at the Diplomat for several seconds, considering his reply. "So how long do they have?"

"That is still open to the President's Council for consideration."

She looked annoyed and spoke in a more stern voice. "How long do they have?"

"Well, to hazard a guess, possibly a week, maybe two."

She sighed. "Thank you for your information. I think it'd be best if I went down to the planet surface and tried to contact them myself."

"That would be of little use. I have had many dialogues with them, to no avail, and I am a highly skilled diplomat. What could you possibly hope to accomplish?"

She stood up. "I would think whatever a highly skilled diplomat could not."

* * * *

"Aaron, there is another call from Imperial Alliance for you."

"Tell him I'm in a meeting. I'll call back later."

"It's a her, and she sounds different than the rest of them. You may want to give her a listen."

He was getting tired of the meetings with the Alliance, especially with Roger Beaumont. The diplomat could spend hours saying nothing. But Irene was a good judge of character and he reconsidered. "All right. Patch her through."

"Premier Duggan, my name is Glora Bitmon. I'm the liaison officer from Earth. I'm hoping that I can convince you to meet with me as I think that I have some additional information concerning the Charter of Conduct."

"Well, Dr. Beaumont has met with us several times."

"Does that mean that you are satisfied with the information he has given you?"

He laughed. "Not really. I'm not certain what he has said at times."

She laughed back. "If it makes you feel any better, I've met him only once and wasn't sure just what he meant and we are supposed to be on the same side of the negotiations. How about if I meet with you and see if I can straighten out some of this. It would be to both our benefit."

"All right. You sound sincere. When?"

"Tomorrow morning?"

"Fine. Ten o'clock okay?"

Irene stood at the doorway listening. "You sure changed your mind about meeting her."

"I liked her attitude. She sounded a lot different than that Beaumont character. Maybe she'll actually tell us something."

* * * *

"Ms. Bitmon, are you aware of Dr. Beaumont's directive concerning dress when meeting the locals?" The executive secretary to the diplomat stood at the hotel doorway with his hands on his hips, ending his question with a big sigh.

"No, and I'm not sure I care."

"To make you aware, Dr. Beaumont wants us to dress in similar fashion as the locals so that they are more at ease in our presence. I should think what you are wearing hardly qualifies in that regard." This was said in a rather annoyed tone and he glared at her outfit, a dark blue suit. The top was fitted while the skirt was loose with the hemline high on her legs.

"Fine, now I'm aware." She stepped around him. "Now if you'll excuse me I have a meeting to attend."

The car dropped her at the government offices and she slid out of the back seat. "Don't wait; I'll call when I need a ride back."

She walked up to front doors, trying to keep her confidence up. Was this the right thing to do? This meeting; her dress? What if she blew everything?

Glora knocked on the door and a pretty woman answered.

"Hello, Ms Bitmon. I'm Mr. Duggan's assistant. I'll let Mr. Duggan you're here.

Glora saw the woman take a quick glance at what she was wearing but made an effort not to show any reaction.

"Allow me to show you to the meeting room," Irene offered.

Irene led Glora to a room with a large table that had half a dozen chairs around it. She was still nervous but at least the receptionist was friendly towards her. And she didn't frown at what she was wearing. Glora had decided to wear what she was use to wearing on Earth. To copy what the people on Haven wore and trying to pass it off as her own normal attire she felt was dishonest. She thought they would see through that deception and were not impressed by the cover-up. She wanted them to understand that she was going to be honest with them.

* * * *

Aaron entered the room to find her standing near the center of the room. She looked nervous, but not unsure of herself. Then he noticed what she was wearing. The top accented her figure while her skirt hid little of her legs that sported high-heeled shoes. Now he understood what Irene meant when she told him she was in the meeting room dressed in a rather interesting fashion. She had said that with a raised eyebrow.

"Pleased to meet you in person, Ms. Bitmon."

"Premier Duggan. It is an honour to meet you." She extended her hand. He impressed her; he gave off an impression of strength while extending a feeling of caring and warmth. The strength part was easy. He was big, both in height and in the shoulders.

He took her hand in his own. "Please, have a seat."

They exchanged formal pleasantries and made polite comments for several minutes.

"Premier Duggan …"

"Please. This is rather formal for such a small meeting. Call me Aaron."

"All right, Aaron. And you can call me Glora. And I forgot what I was going to say exactly." She laughed.

"How about a coffee?" He rose and walked to the door, opened it and signalled Irene.

"Sure, that sounds good." She watched him as he walked back to his chair. He was rather easy on the eyes, she thought. With his height, he could dominate a room rather easily.

"Without trying to put you on the spot you indicated that you had a different perspective on the signing of the Charter of Conduct."

"That is true. What do you understand about the signing of the Charter?"

Irene entered the room carrying a tray of coffee and pastries as Aaron started to answer.

"The Charter seems to restrict rather harshly what a world can and can not do. There seems to be a regulation for just about each aspect of laws and culture." He looked up at Irene. "Thanks for the coffee, Irene."

Irene wanted to stay and listen to what the young woman had to say, she looked so young to be one of so much responsibilities, but quietly left the room.

"That is correct, in simple terms. The Charter is meant to protect, though I can tell you don't believe how it can. I'm not saying I'm a great fan of everything in the Charter either but the official line is this; the cause of many of the wars and society's problems in the past were due to clashes of different cultures. The Charter is designed to reduce and eliminate differences on all human worlds by enforcing common laws, customs and rights to citizens. It also will require these world governments to ensure their citizens behave in a fashion common to the rest of the Imperial Alliance. What is not spelled out, but implied, is that they want all worlds to act like a society on Earth. Furthermore, the theory is that anyone on any of the worlds will feel comfortable on any of the other worlds because there will be little cultural and language differences."

"A homogenized society."

"Perhaps. The supposed proof is that there are no longer conflicts between worlds. The reality is that Earth enforces peace with armed force. A planet would be foolish to cause problems with Earth carrying the big stick."

"Well, you certainly laid out the Charter of Conduct's intent, in a fraction of the time Dr. Beaumont took. Can you just as quickly tell me why I should sign this thing?"

Glora picked up a pastry and took a bite. "These are good. Sure, but you won't like the answer. If you refuse to sign, Sol, which is in reality Earth, will use less diplomatic action. They will discover that human rights have been violated on Haven and to protect the people they will take over the planet, by force if necessary. This will be done with great reluctance of course, but will be carried out for the greater good. The head of government, that's you, will be arrested and sent to Earth to face various charges. A temporary government under the President's Council will be set up to straighten things out here. Temporary governments can last a generation or more."

Aaron looked straight at her, trying to read her expression as she spoke. Was she telling the truth? "Beaumont mentioned nothing of this."

"I suspected he hadn't. He told me he wanted only to stress the positives of signing the Charter. I wish I could have told you better news but you need to know the actual situation, not the one painted by our esteemed diplomat."

"Well, that certainly puts a new light on the problem. Looks like I am running out of options."

"Can I offer a bit of advice?"

"Sure. I need some help right now."

"Not signing is one option and if you were to resign as Premier, they would not be able to arrest you as leader. Likely you wouldn't have any repercussions when the new government is appointed by Sol."

"That wouldn't be right. To leave Haven at a time like this would be irresponsible and wrong."

She looked pleased at his answer. "You are a voter's dream." *Especially a woman voter.* "If you decide to sign, you have a choice also of being part of the Alliance or not. The advantage of being in the Alliance is helpful. They will pay for a communication network to the rest of the Alliance; provide technical support in building spacecraft and other high-level devices. They will ensure that Haven cannot be taken over by any other member, including Earth, and you will have special legal help to fight against implication of all Charter conditions."

"Sounds interesting, but the cost of membership is high; too high for Haven. We have nothing to pay the Alliance with."

"The dues are not payable until the next election, fourteen of your months from now. At that time, you can simply decide to withdraw from the Alliance without owing a dime. In the meantime, you can use all the benefits of the membership. But don't tell anyone I said this. I'm not sure of the protocol of such disclosure."

"Are you sure about this payment schedule?"

"Yes, as a member of Earth's Charter committee we came across that situation a couple of times." She thought a moment. "It's in the section of 'Requirements of notice to withdraw membership', under prorated fees. You should look it up if you really want to know the fine details. Bottom line is that if you withdraw before the next Representative elections, no cost. And you get to keep the communication network."

"I will have to check that out."

"Your world is not poor, by the way. Did you know your planet is one of the very few worlds where trees suitable for wood products grow? On other planets that do, it is illegal to cut them down; Charter of Conduct environmental regulations. But Haven is so under populated, you may well get an exception. Wood is priced so high everywhere, you are sitting on a highly valued resource. You should see our people in your hotel trying to steal the wooden furniture, even the doors."

Irene opened the door. "Lunch anyone?"

Aaron looked at her. "Are you hungry? I am."

"I am a bit."

"Good. What would you like? We can order in anything."

"Well, I noticed a restaurant a couple of blocks away, with a sign advertising pizza. That sounded good, I haven't had any since I left Earth."

Irene sounded enthused. "Great pizza. Lots of cheese. They're a tad slow on delivery, but worth the wait."

"Could we walk down there? I haven't had a chance to do any walking for the past few weeks and it isn't far." She suddenly looked embarrassed. "I guess that isn't normal protocol for liaison officers when meeting a head of state. I'm sorry."

"Don't be. A walk would be nice. And please don't worry about protocol around here. We're a mite on the relaxed side of doing business here usually."

The walk was interesting, and Irene had wedged herself next to Glora when they started out. Aaron initially thought she wanted to prevent him from getting too close to the rather exposed young woman and Glora certainly attracted a lot of stares from those who passed by. A few people actually stopped to watch her. It turned out Irene was more intrigued in the fashions on Earth than worrying about Aaron's interest in Glora. Aaron caught part of the conversation as Glora told her about clothes, body coloring, and makeup. He noticed Glora didn't seem to be too concerned that she was attracting a lot of attention with her outfit; no one had worn such a short skirt before as far as he knew. Maybe there was something to say for Earth's customs after all.

A table was produced for them immediately and they ordered two pizzas to share. Glora stayed with the vegetarian. She remarked on the cheese, telling them it was the first real cheese she had ever eaten. She also told them about her former boyfriend that she had to break up with because of this assignment. The conversation flowed easily and they stayed longer, well into the afternoon.

"This was great. Say, I understand that you haven't gone up to the spaceship yet. Why not?"

"I would like to, it really sounds fascinating, but that basically meant being with Beaumont the whole time. Besides I didn't want him to think he was gaining any ground with me."

"Come up as my guest, both of you. It has a fantastic view of Haven. He may want to say some sort of greeting but there doesn't have to be a meeting of any sort."

"Well, I'll have to think about it."

"Aaron, it'll be fun. I know I want to go."

He gave Irene a look. Her enthusiasm wasn't making it easy for him to negotiate any advantage in agreeing to go up to the ship.

"Look, I don't want to be putting you on the spot but if you come up, at least it will look like some negotiations are underway and will give you more time to study the Charter."

Aaron looked at Irene's smiling face and knew he wasn't going to fool Glora about his reluctance to visit. "All right. Why don't we work out a time?"

* * * *

Dr. Roger Beaumont was visibly upset. The Premier of Haven and his girlfriend/receptionist had finally come aboard the ship and with barely a handshake and a hello had disappeared with that Bitmon woman. That was insulting enough but when Duggan had announced that he would be signing the Charter of Conduct because of her it was turning into the diplomat's nightmare. Not to mention those damn reporters running around, obtaining more information about Haven than his spies. He was going to lose considerable face and prestige over this one. He paced his room, but ended up without a means to deflect her influence or triumph. Perhaps, however, a bit of revenge was in order. *Yes, that's it; I will have a talk with that fool General. I shall inform the President's Council that there are some problems on Haven. I'll get the General to send in reports about some of the more unusual activities by the locals. And perhaps I can convince some of his friends on Earth for help in dealing with Haven. That should ensure some corrective action by the Alliance.*

Chapter Ten
On the Starship Fitzgerald, Earth bound

"Scotty, how is that last report coming?"

"Finished, just doing a final proof read."

"This one on the fishing trip?"

"Right. They'll get this story this afternoon, a week before we arrive at Earth. They probably have already printed some of the reports although we won't find out which ones until we get near Sol. Did you know that Haven has been declared a danger zone and that we were the only reporters that landed on the planet? Every news media in the Alliance wants to buy stories from NightHawk."

"That's good for us, isn't it?"

"Cindy, we are going to be rich. Our reports are going to be worth a lot."

"That's nice."

"You don't sound that enthused."

"I am, but I was thinking about something else as well."

"Which is…?" He hated to be pulling this out of her bit by bit. Especially since he suspected what she was thinking. Now she remained quiet and looked away. He finished the answer for her. "Which is about us?"

"About us. Are we together after we arrive on Earth? Or was this just another fling? Please, I can take it if you want us to go our separate ways afterward. Just be honest with me."

"Cindy, this wasn't just a fling."

"Then what was it?"

"Cindy, I don't want to define what we have as any particular relationship. Let's just continue it on and see where it goes. How you feel about me now may change once we get back to Earth."

"And yours as well? Okay, I can take the hint." She got up and walked out of the room leaving Scotty to wonder just what was going on.

Women, he thought, *always wanting the next stage whatever that may be*. The problem was that he really cared about her but the difficulty was that the next stage might be marriage. Was he ready for a third marriage? A real one this time to a woman considerable younger than he was. This was a question he couldn't answer yet.

* * * *

On the Starship, returning from Earth

Steermaster Ravener walked down the hallway to his room, whistling through his teeth. As he approached his room, his quick pace slowed. The door to his room was open and the cleaning lady was not due until Tuesday. Curious, he looked past the door and stepped inside.

"Steermaster Ravener, first class?"

Ravener recognized at once the Captain's second, Joyce Watson. He didn't like the sound of her voice, nor the two security officers by her. "Yes, Lieutenant Watson? What is this all about?" Technically, his rank was higher than hers was but this was not a time to exert authority.

"The captain wishes to have your explanation on this article copied from the NightHawk." She handed him a hard copy of the story.

He took the copy slowly and scanned the article. "Lies! This is a complete fabrication. We should launch a lawsuit against them and this woman who wrote it!"

"This woman, Cindy Lorncroft, never came to your room? These events never transpired? The photographs are fake?" The lack of creditability Ravener had could be heard in her questions.

"Well, she came to my room on her own accord. But everything that happened was on her urging. She insisted on staying the night. And those photos have to be fakes."

Watson looked at him as if to add additional questions but changed her mind. Instead, she looked him in the eye. "Steermaster Ravener, we also have testimony of other women who have experienced similar problems when they came to your room. We are prepared to have these women, plus Cindy Lorncroft, testify in court. The court will follow the guidelines set forth by the Alliance Space Conduct. Therefore, the court will be held on ship and testimony can be given by video link from Ms. Lorncroft. The other women are either on board this ship now or could also use video link. Do you understand this?"

Ravener looked shocked as he nodded his head.

"You have a choice. You can proceed with this court case if you feel you are indeed innocent of all allegations. Or you can resign from your commission, effective immediately. I will advise you that if you refuse to resign criminal proceedings will take place. The charge of abduction is a serious one and you will be in danger of not only losing your job but also serving time in corrective custody. If you choose to resign, we will agree to a stay of criminal proceedings. In either case, you will have new quarters set up in the third class passenger section. You have one hour to make your decision. Gentlemen, make sure he does not leave this room. His museum is strictly off limits." She walked out of the room, leaving Ravener to stare at the grim faced security officers.

"Well, at least the bar isn't off limits." He reached for a tumbler and poured a large drink. "Damn women. Always bad luck to have them aboard a ship."

An hour later, he was still drinking, this time in a third class cabin, having turned in his resignation.

* * * *

Toronto, Earth

Robert read the news article and then reread it. There was no doubt about it. Glora had scored a major coup. The writer on the editorial page was a bit more blunt, asking what we needed diplomats for if a mere liaison officer could do a better job. It went on to lambaste on political strategies for sticking only to textbook diplomacy instead of approaching each situation with an open mind.

He was quite proud of Glora. He also knew that there was no way she was coming back to Earth in the near future. Haven was going to be her home for the next several years, except for the few business trips home.

He sighed and then went back to his studies. One last exam on geometric field theory and he was done, ready to become a certified power engineer. Already the job offers were pouring in, thanks to being in the top ten percent of the class.

* * * *

Oasis City, Haven

Aaron Duggan read the letter twice, but it was not unexpected. The letter delivered by the diplomat Beaumont was on a plastic sheet and carried the Alliance stamp, a logo showing all the worlds embracing a common center. There wasn't much of a surprise in its arrival, Bitmon had indicated when it might arrive and her timetable was not far off. He understood the content of the letter well enough the first time, the second reading was just to understand the implications of the letter.

Premier R. Duggan, recognized leader of the planet Haven:

After a thorough and careful investigation of the laws, cultural and social activities on the planet Haven, we have concluded that there is serious breach of the guidelines and in the spirit of the Charter of Conduct. The Charter of Conduct was signed by you and became effective on that date, July 7/2597 on Haven. It is with regret that we must press charges to maintain the Charter of Conduct as the guiding force in human space.

Therefore you, or your duly appointed representative, must appear in the Alliance Court of Human Conduct in Amsterdam on November 5/2598. The exact time and courtroom will be given to you at the appropriate time. We recommend that you obtain proper legal council and if you require, legal help can be requested through the Alliance World Government body.

Claims of not fully understanding the nature of the Charter of Conduct, nor having sufficient time to make amendments to conform to the guideline, will not be entertained as an excuse.

Further details of the charges and penalties will follow.

James Gault

Enforcement Officer, Charter of Conduct

Aaron put the document down and considered it was time to launch their defence to maintain life on Haven. He had enjoyed politics much more than he had expected; the debates and trying to convince others that he were right was second nature to him. Now was the moment to see if he could carry that ability to the next step. He had no doubt this court case was more political than legal. If so, he felt he had a fighting chance.

* * * *

Starship Fitzgerald

Scotty was wondering where Cindy went off to. She had been gone since lunch time and now it was getting on to five o'clock. He didn't know what he was going to do about their situation but wished he had more time to sort things out, like another month or two after they got back home.

The door to their suite opened and he turned, expecting to see Cindy, perhaps with red eyes, but at least with a chance to make up with her. Instead, two men entered. One was wearing a sports jacket, the other dressed in more casual clothes. Both were in their thirties and were slightly bigger than Scotty was.

"Hey, what the hell are you doing in here?"

The casually dressed stranger walked up to him quickly and delivered a punch to the solar plexus. Scotty buckled over and then fell to floor from a fist between his shoulder blades.

"We'll ask the fucking questions here Pearson."

Scotty curled up on the floor, unable to grab his breath. He heard them rifle through the desk, their suitcases and anything in the room that could be opened.

"Here's his tablet. Too bad the woman took hers along."

Scotty raised his head to see the man with the jacket slide a memory stick into his tablet. A few seconds later, he was pushing a few keys on the tablet and then he withdrew the memory stick.

"Okay, I got it." He tossed the tablet on the floor.

The other man grabbed Scotty by the hair. "Now listen good. You didn't see us. We'll come back if you talk to anyone about us and there isn't anywhere we can't find you. Understood?"

Scotty tried to nod. "Why are you doing this?"

"Because Haven needs to be taught a little lesson, wise guy." He took his other hand and belted Scotty across the mouth. "Now shut up, stupid."

"Let's go." The two men disappeared out the door.

Scotty slowly got up from his knees and looked around at the mess. He picked up his tablet and looked at the screen. *Damn. They went through my security like it wasn't even there. Probably copied everything I have. Shit.* Burgess has his people after Haven.

He just finished cleaning up when Cindy returned. She didn't say much to him and he decided against telling her in case they were eavesdropping on them. She hadn't really looked at him and didn't notice the bruise on his chin and if she ignored the few items still lying around the room he figured it was best he kept the visit a secret. Scotty was looking forward to Earth more than ever.

PART THREE—EARTH
Chapter One
Toronto, Earth

Robert read the news articles on Haven with increasing interest as the newly discovered planet continued to generate a lot of publicity. Reporters were anxiously awaiting clearance to visit the newest member of the Alliance but Haven, citing the need to prepare facilities for them, was withholding permission now. It sounded suspicious, which made them all the more eager to investigate.

So far only two reporters had managed to get on the planet itself; and all types of media were reprinting their reports. Originally, the stories were exclusive to the NightHawk, but now that information was being sold to at a rather high price to the other news media. Of course, each newsmagazine reworded the stories and interpreted the information differently, or gleaned a missing fact or two from the data. Still, the source was the same, and Robert thought those two reporters were making a tidy sum along with the NightHawk.

He searched the news for information on Haven, hoping to learn what Glora was doing. Since she had left, he had felt miserable, cutting out a lot of his social life and just concentrating on his studies. His marks improved but that was about the only thing he felt good about lately. He scanned some of the stories on Haven; occasionally stories from different tabloids were almost word for word with each other. Then his eyes lighted on an article from one of the more respectable newspapers. He read carefully, excited with his find.

National Post-Times: Secrecy Surrounds Haven

The recently discovered planet Haven has generated controversy by the refusal of allowing accredited news media to visit the planet surface. Citing the need to improve accommodation, Oasis City officials refused to give an indication when permits would be issued. The Professional Guild of News Media believes the Charter of Conduct is being ignored concerning free and easy access and PGN wants officials to investigate. The office of liaison officer, Glora Bitmon, refused comment other than negotiations are continuing in many areas with Haven and that as of yet there has been no evidence that the Charter is being violated.

There, no doubt about it; she was making her name known. First with getting the Charter signed in the first place and now she was the Liaison Officer they were quoting from. Liaison officers from other planets, including from Sol, were only just arriving and were still being shut out of most of the negotiations. Apparently the officials of Haven preferred to negotiate only with small groups and with Glora at the table. His interest in Haven stemmed mostly from trying to find how Glora was doing; personal emails were low priority in the communications being sent to and from the planet and her replies were short due to her busy schedule. However, he was beginning to find the planet interesting by itself. He pulled down a menu on his tablet and asked for a search on the news media about Haven.

Hutler Times Magazine
Haven Destroying Trees?

Reliable sources have revealed there appears to be evidence of trees being cut down on Haven. The forests apparently have been used as raw material for furniture, building supplies and as a heating source. Recent observations have indicated that atmospheric analysis shows that there are smoke particles that could only have come from the burning of wood, some of which that could not have come from natural sources.

Marc Secomb, an official at Environmental Sol, stated the cutting of forests could also lead to other ecological problems, including the loss of natural habitat for birds, animals, other plants and also climate changes.

More: Extinction of lesser known species// Trees; A century of growth, a minute of death// Building materials, Then and Now.

Boston Globe-Times
Haven's Population Armed

The news media spokesman for General Burgess admitted that there are concerns about the availability of weapons on Haven.

"It appears the general population have access to guns. This raises the concerns for the safety of both our armed forces and to Alliance visitors to the planet. We do not know if there is hostile intent but we will be taking precautions."

When questioned if this was a violation of the Charter of Conduct the spokesman refused comment. However, an unidentified corporal of the Elite troops indicated that having the general population armed with guns was a grey area in the Charter, but "if common sense prevails guns will be only in the hands of soldiers who know how to use them."

In a related story, Anna Shovail, the president of Safeguarding Our Animal's Rights (SOAR), reacted angrily to reports that hunting takes place on Haven as a source of recreation and food. "I cannot believe in this day and age that we still allow this barbaric activity. This is a clear violation of the Charter, and SOAR demands immediate action take place to save these animals."

Professor Jarvis Blake of Meadowlands College denied that eating meat of animals was poisonous as asserted by SOAR. "I am not saying it is morally right to eat flesh, of course, but it is not harmful to people in small amounts."

* * * *

MidNight View- America's News Source
Haven's Captive Animals!

Exclusive evidence to MidNight View proves that the inhabitants of Haven keep animals locked in pens. MidNight View has also found that many of these animals are later murdered and then cooked for food. It is suspected that the use of the animals as a food involves special feeding and preparation. MidNight View determined that the actual killing of the animals was done as a mass production, the animals crying out in fear before their final moments. The Premier of Haven, Aaron Duggan, refused to discuss the matter with MidNight View.

The stories were interesting but he wasn't sure of their accuracy. Still, there seemed to be a common ground to their direction. He wasn't sure what they exactly indicated but after a few minutes of thought phoned a friend who was studying modern social sciences. Carlos Lugo was more of a drinking buddy, though they had met in one of those forgettable courses in their freshmen year. Carlos agreed to meet at small bar the next night.

* * * *

"Hey Carlos, don't you ever tire of reading?" Robert approached the table where Carlos was absorbed with his tablet.

"Not of this literature." He turned his tablet around, revealing an undressed woman promoting a breath mint. It was an interesting short video but not over the top as far as the commercial censors was concerned. The brand's name floated above critical areas of her body.

"Ah, the icy-cool but warm lips breath girl."

They exchanged a round of beers before Robert asked for his opinion on Haven.

"Oh, that new planet? Yeah, interesting. I read some of the stories. My prof in Social Climate talked a bit about it."

"Can you tell me what the experts think? Here, I downloaded some of the news stories."

Carlos took a look at Robert's tablet, looking at the earlier stories and then some of the additional ones that he had found.

MidNight View-America's News Source
Haven's Gruesome Eating Rituals

In an exclusive interview with MidNight View, acclaimed Professor Furuta Noriyuki of Boston Elite College gave a valuable insight in a religious feast ceremony on Haven. "It appears that some of the ceremony was adopted from ancient rituals done on Earth. While it is hard to establish the exact details because such events are done in secrecy it is possible recreate much of the ceremony from what we know early people did on Earth." Professor Noriyuki has written several articles on culture in the Americas before the Wave. The exclusive interview with MidNight View also revealed other details. "First, the carcass of the dead animal is coated with special oils. Sometimes the whole animal is treated this way, other times only part of is cut up and then coated. What the religious significance of this is not clear, perhaps some parts of the animal represent certain strengths or medicine the participants wish to receive. Next, the flesh is placed over a fire to cook. During this time the religious order drink intoxicants, dance special dances and occasionally undress as the ceremony reaches a fever pitch. When the chief decides the flesh has been properly cooked, the rest of the tribe joins in devouring the food. The name on Haven of this ritual is unclear, but on Earth it was called the Beech Barr Bee U."

RICHES TO BURN ON HAVEN
Scott Pearson/Cindy Lorncroft exclusive

The newly discovered planet Haven has such a wealth of natural wood that they burn it for amusement. The wood comes from trees that had their origin from Earth, such as oak, maple, fir, birch and evergreens. Haven also had trees that are native to it, but like on many other planets the wood does not lend itself well to looks or as a building material. However, the Earth developed trees thrived extremely well on Haven, to the point where it threatened to take over completely natural habitant. Thus to keep the forests in check, a number of trees have to be cut down on a regular schedule. In fact, there is more wood to be had than can be used as a building material, and the excess is burned, usually in what people of Haven call campfires.

NightHawk
HAVEN CLAIMS HELP FROM GOD
Scott Pearson/Cindy Lorncroft exclusive

On the outskirts of the Oasis City, the capital of Haven, lies the remains of the pilgrim ship Regal. The citizens of Haven have carefully preserved the giant spaceship because they believe God guided it to its present resting place. The ship was lost in space without navigation when the captain of the Regal led a prayer asking for help to find a new home. Less than 48 hours later, they found Haven. Astronomer William Housley of the Argentina Observatory calculated the odds of finding a planet without navigation "as less than winning the national lottery four times in a row. And that doesn't include it being habitual." Was it luck or God? The people of Haven decided it was God, and Haven has 22 times more churches per hundred thousand people than the Alliance average.

"Hmm," Carlos said, "at first glance there seems to be a rather negative aspect to the reporting of Haven, like they are trying to portray it as a primitive world, barbaric or something like that. I would discount what MidNight View has to say; they're rather sensational in their stories. And their experts sometimes don't even exist. But most media is doing hostile reporting and there could be a couple of reasons for that. One, it could be true that Haven is a world where the people have lost their civilized behaviour, and have degenerated into our less redeeming qualities. Perhaps the stories are merely reflecting that."

"Or?" Robert replied.

"Or, this could be part of a setup. My prof mentioned it could be something like this; that General Burgess and that crook Diplomat Beaumont might have been pissed off the way the Haven government greeted them. You know that story, that the liaison officer … Hey! That was your lady friend, wasn't it? I'm so bloody dense at times. That is why you are so curious! Shit, I couldn't figure that out earlier. That's why the interest!" Carlos grinned at his discovery.

"Right. That's one reason all right. But I'm kind of hooked on Haven after reading so much about it. But you were saying something about Beaumont and Burgess?"

"Right. Well, one or both are pissed off. So one of them decides to use his influence to get the publishers of various news medias to write unfriendly stories. He might leak a few tips to some reporters, or even have a quiet talk to an editor or two. Nothing heavy, like trying to get certain people elected, but a gentle persuasion for a slant on the stories. Nothing unusual there, lots of things like that happen in those circles. Like Beaumont would say, if you would like a hot tip on the next appointment for this or that, print a story about them, like Haven doing some un-Charter activities. Now suddenly Haven looks like a world that is going against the Charter. Send in the troops! We better save them while we can."

"So you think this is a set up to the world being taken over and the Alliance setting up a government of their own?"

"Well, take a look at the stories written by those two reporters that actually were allowed on the planet surface. Their stories weren't negative, just described a different culture. They even seem to indicate the planet is well administered. Judging by what I read, Haven is a lot like us, two hundred years ago maybe, but not likely doing evil things. But as my prof pointed out, chances are that Haven is going to lose its right as a free planet. Someone powerful has decided to teach them a lesson and the wheels have been set in motion."

* * * *

Chicago, Earth

Scotty walked into the offices of NightHawk News. The receptionist seemed quite happy to see him for a change, apparently there was nothing like success to change people's opinion.

"Scotty! Welcome back. I hear you did really well out in Haven."

"Thanks, Shelly. Is the Dean in?"

"He sure is. I'll page him right away. I'm positive he'll want to congratulate you on your reports." Smiling away at him, she touched a button on her console. "Mr. Rosedale, Mr. Pearson is in. Shall I send him up to your office?" She received his reply by her earpiece. "Go right on in, Scotty. And congratulations."

Dean Rosedale wasn't sure if he was more surprised Scotty was in the office early in the morning or that he was clean-shaven and wearing clean clothes. "Scotty, you really pulled off the big one! I can't believe the quality of those reports and how the readership has picked up on anything about Haven. You did us all proud here at NightHawk News. Well done!" He shook Scotty's hand and kept his hand on his shoulder as he heaped praise on him.

"Thank you for your sentiments, sir. I do have some concerns, however. I was wondering if we could discuss them?"

"Certainly, anything you want. Are you dissatisfied with your commission? We can renegotiate your salary if you like."

"No, no, nothing like that." *Though I'll keep that in mind for later.* "I have some reservations on what is happening on Haven and some of the reports concerning it."

Rosedale looked concerned and a little puzzled.

"You see I received a visit from two rather nasty individuals." He went on to describe the incident to Rosedale, including the dire warning afterward. "This place is as secure as it gets and I felt I had to tell someone in case something else happens. I haven't told Cindy about it yet. They have me a bit nervous."

"I don't blame you."

"And I'm also a bit pissed off. If they think they can just barge in on me, steal my notes and then think it's done with, well, I would like to get a little bit of revenge."

"Scotty, let it rest. You don't want to fight these guys."

"I know, I know. I'm not that dumb."

"Good."

"But I was thinking." He stopped as Rosedale heaved a big sigh. "Just hear me out. Look, we've made a lot of money on Haven and the sales are still coming in. I would bet there are lots of more interesting stories to be had there, especially for a newspaper that is in good standing with the government of Haven."

"And that newspaper could be us?" Rosedale shook his head. "I'm not sure they are very happy with us right now. We did kind of help expose their lifestyles."

"Trust me on this. They're not really upset with us, at least not completely. So I was thinking about a win, win, lose situation. I know of a way for us to get into Haven's good books so we get more exclusive stories, help Haven at the same time, and screw whoever was behind that little visit I received."

"Okay, that sounds all right. How do we do this win, win, and lose situation?"

"We pay for the best lawyers in town to handle their case, namely the NightHawk lawyers."

"Our lawyers?"

"Yeah, they're the best there is. They sure have saved our bacon often enough. They're already on our payroll, so it shouldn't be a big deal. Right?"

"Well, they're not actually on our payroll, more like a retainer. Still, I guess we could help them out. It's, I suppose, the right thing to do. Do you really think there are a few more stories to be had out there?"

* * * *

Scotty was pleased with the outcome from his meeting and a little surprised Rosedale agreed to cover the costs of the lawyers. It wasn't going to have a big impact on NightHawk's budget, and might pay a few dividends. Now it was time for meeting number two.

He approached the desk where Cindy was working. She barely looked up.

"Hi Cindy."

"Hi." Her voice was directed towards her desk where she sat hunched over.

"Do you have time for a coffee?"

She shrugged. "I suppose so." She finally looked up at him. "New duds?"

"Yeah, I'm trying my best to impress someone. Come on, I know a place that makes coffee just like on Haven."

Chapter Two
Oasis City, Haven

"Thanks for taking my call, Glora, I have a few questions about this up coming court case."

"Of course, Premier. I imagined there would be. I also received a couple messages I was to pass on to you."

"Please, you can call me Aaron? I was wondering about the location of the court. Mars is the Capital, but the court is in Amsterdam on Earth?"

"That's correct. Mars does have the courts for Free Space infractions but Earth has court for the Imperial Alliance. Also for trade disputes, Sol regulations and has the highest courts for Earth laws as well. You would not believe the amount of buildings devoted to the justice department."

"I am sure it'll be impressive. I have another question on the travel to Earth. How long does the space ship take to arrive to Earth?"

"The ship travels at a fairly high speed so there is a difference between the travel time and subjective time. It's about six weeks ship time and about four weeks subjective time."

"I see. And has accommodation been arranged or do I have to do that?"

"I will be doing that. I have half a dozen rooms reserved for you. They can be arranged as sleeping quarters or as office space. I can change those requirements as you see fit. If you want more rooms, just let me know."

"That sounds fine. Legal council. How do I go about getting a good lawyer?"

"I will help you with that as well. However, those two reporters that were on Haven, Scott Pearson and Cindy Lorncroft?"

"Yes?"

"Well, they have arranged for this lawyer to help you. He is tied in with the NightHawk News but judging by his business page he is very high priced. The message I'm to pass on to you is that NightHawk News is sorry for any trouble they may have caused and that this lawyer, Shannon Crouts', services are available to you at their costs. News media do not normally do this sort of thing and I suspect this is the doing of those reporters as a way of making things up."

"And they're willing to pay for this lawyer?"

"Well, judging by what I have read, NightHawk News and those reporters are making a lot of money on those stories. Exclusive rights and that sort of thing."

"Interesting. A question off the wall. How do you manage faster than light communications?"

"Actually, they discovered faster than light travel before they learned how to send messages faster than light. But to tell you the truth, I don't know. I'll ask my boyfriend, that is my former boyfriend, to give me a quick explanation. He would know; he's studying power engineering."

"Power engineering. Sounds like an important field."

"It is. The working of field generators is what he is leaning towards as a major, basically, the power plants of spaceships. Also the physics of faster than light communication."

"Sounds like a smart guy."

"Yeah, he is."

Aaron detected a bit of wistfulness in her voice.

Aaron discussed the conversation with Irene. She agreed with Aaron that using the NightHawk lawyer would the best thing to do, at least at first until they were certain of their plan of action. They weren't certain Alliance appointed lawyers would be working entirely in Haven's best interest. They also talked about who else should go to Earth from Haven. The problem was that there was a risk of anyone going to Earth representing the Haven government was liable to be kept there in prison, or forced confinement, as it was more prone to be called. However, as they learned from Glora, it might be better if they indicated that only Aaron was responsible for Haven's laws and customs, that the councillors themselves did not have a large influence. This would allow, if Haven was found guilty, to probably retain the present councillors and part of the government, regardless of what happened to Aaron. Irene disagreed with him that it was dangerous for her to accompany him, declaring she would be there to make sure that he did not get into too much trouble and that she was not going to miss the shopping chance of the century.

* * * *

The spaceship Galileo left Haven with three passengers, Aaron, Irene and Glora. Aaron was hoping that Irene would share his cabin but she told him that they were not sleeping together on Haven and they were not about to start on this trip.

Both Aaron and Irene were amazed the spaceship could have so much in it. They wandered about, thinking that it seemed more like a small city than something that flew between stars. Glora was amused at their wide-eyed reaction to some of gadgets the shops sold and to the various fashions that people wore. The fashions were certainly not something that would have been seen on Haven, though Glora did point out that most of the people were on vacation and were wearing their casual clothes. Aaron found the sight of the women's clothing rather distracting as they walked about, the skirts and shorts too tight and too revealing. Of course he tried to be discrete about it but he found Irene glaring at him a couple of times.

"Would you rather be by yourself? That way you can do all your girl watching you want without my interference."

"Wait a minute, Irene." He hurried after her as she stalked off.

Glora smiled as she followed them down the concourse. The truth was it might be hard for Aaron to suddenly adjust to the women walking around in rather revealing clothes. On the other hand, Aaron at six foot four was attracting lots of attention along with some rather obvious flirts from the ladies. Considering Irene was still wearing the conservative fashions of Haven it was no wonder she was feeling left out from his attention. She decided that she better help smooth out the situation, and that included cancelling the trip to the ship's beach section. The beach area included additional artificial lighting that imitated the heat from a strong sun, a wave pool, and a large sandy beach section. Most of the women also went with just the bottom part of their suit on and she thought that might make Aaron's visit there a little too anxious.

"Irene, I was wondering if you wanted to go shopping with me. I need some new clothes, and perhaps we could make a day out of it."

"Thanks, Glora, but we are on a rather strict budget. Haven doesn't have much in the way of Alliance funds."

"That's not a problem. As a Liaison Officer I have a budget allowance that can cover those expenses. In fact my boss would be pretty upset with me if you didn't take up on my offer and showed up on Earth without new clothes."

The expression on Irene's face changed from anger to a big grin when Aaron quickly nodded his agreement.

* * * *

"So you two are having fun it seems." The three talked over lunch in a Polynesian restaurant. "Oh, by the way, I got that answer to your question about faster than light communications." She passed over her tablet. "Better you read this than have me try to repeat it. It may get muddled in the translation."

There are actually two different methods of faster than light communication. One method is similar to the one we use for spaceship travel. First, a null point is generated by field generators near the ship. But instead of having the fields envelop the ship with a focus just outside the ship the field stays collapsed and the focus is set towards infinity. The signal, which is actually a carrier that contains the coded data, is directed through the null point and is sent in a straight line only, much like a laser beam. The signal can arrive at the destination station, where the retrieved data is decoded almost instantly. Unfortunately, as we know, null points are only stable outside high gravitation fields. Therefore this communication is only available between star systems. Inside the solar systems, light speed can be rather limiting, several hours in some cases from the outer edges to habitable planets.

The second method is dependent on rather basic laws of physics. First, let us consider ordinary light. If you add more energy to it, it will not go faster, but rather increase in frequency. For example, it will shift from infrared to ultraviolet. But if you put this light in the form of a laser beam and increase its energy inside the laser, it cannot change its frequency to a higher range. A laser requires light to be synchronized in a common frequency, and if you increase its energy, then it adds more photons to use up the energy and becomes stronger that way, a more intense beam. Now suppose that as the light leaves the laser, we add more energy to the photons. It cannot change its frequency because the nature of a laser prevents this; it cannot get brighter because the number of photons is fixed. The excess energy must be used somehow, and the result is a quantum leap in speed, several times the normal speed of light thru the higher dimensions. The device that adds the extra energy is a gravity field generator, gravity being an energy source that cannot be turned into photons, at least directly. I hope that explains things well enough Glora. I can send additional technical information if you require it.

Love Robert.

"Wow, that is interesting. Thanks Glora." Aaron handed back the tablet.

Irene looked at Glora. "Looks like Robert still has some feelings for you."

Glora sighed. "Well, so do I for him. I wished things had worked out better. Him in school and me on another planet."

"At least you will have a chance to see him on Earth."

"I hope so. But I'll be in Holland with you and he lives in the States. That's quite a distance to be jumping back and forth. Besides, he's just finishing up his school year and may not have much time."

Aaron and Irene looked up Glora several times during the trip to Earth, asking her questions about the planet and its culture. Glora was happy to help them and to that end took them to several different types of restaurants and the occasional lounge to experience the Imperial way of life. Irene seemed to enjoy trying out the new foods more so than Aaron, who complained about the lack of meat. The soybean imitation was not close enough for him, finding the texture wrong and the flavour off. He also complained about the potatoes being too starchy and the women decided at that point he was being just too fussy.

"The food is fine. Do you want to try some of these string beans?

He pulled a face. "I'll stick to the potatoes, thank you."

* * * *

"Tell me, Glora, what and where is the exciting entertainment on this ship that the literature promises?" Irene was now shopping for shoes with Glora and the two had stopped for lunch at a small bistro. "I don't believe those lounges you took us to are what they're talking about." This she said with a smile as she added a fork of dessert into her mouth. Irene was now in a much better disposition since she went shopping with Glora. She was wearing fashions more in line with what people wore on the ship and no longer felt like she was being ignored by Aaron. Glora wasn't sure if she knew she was doing a small amount of subtle flirting herself. Aaron was doing much less of his obvious stares when a woman wearing one of the revealing outfits walked by. Of course how he was acting when Irene and Glora were not around was a matter of speculation.

"Oh, those lounges are quiet. Some dancing and some real bad live entertainment but there is more."

"Such as?"

"Hmm. Well, there're some places that specialize in entertainment for men, and others for gambling and that sort of thing. Some places are geared towards young, single people, loud music with flashing lights and dancing holograms. You may have noticed that a lot of lounges also have underdressed waitresses on the pretence of some theme or another."

"Those waitresses would have been arrested back home. Haven is pretty conservative and I haven't had much of a chance to be inside the less than reputable establishments being the Premier's secretary, but I doubt even the women there would be as exposed as those waitresses. But I was wondering what some of those entertainment lounges were like; I'm just kind of curious to see what goes on behind those doors."

"Well, I know of one lounge that seems to be geared more for men but a lot of couples go to as well. If you would like to try it we can go tonight. I take it that Aaron would be coming as well?"

Irene smiled. "I'm sure he will. If not we can go alone."

Aaron tagged behind the two women. It wasn't that he didn't want to go, or at least have a look. It was just he wasn't sure it was appropriate to take a woman to such a place that Glora describe as a bit risqué. Irene had no such reservations and made it plain she was going with or without him. The women had also chosen to wear somewhat revealing clothes themselves; Glora wore an orange dress that exposed her back while Irene wore a tight pair of multi-coloured pants that hung low at her hips and a blue sweater that hung lower one side than another, exposing a good portion of her side in the process. The ladies insisted that this was acceptable eveningwear and there was little he could say that would change their minds.

The entrance to Tarzan's Jungle was done in fake bamboo that led to a hostess dressed in a grass skirt and several oversized necklaces that covered her top. They paid the cover charge, and as Glora suggested earlier, gave the hostess a tip to get a good table.

Their table was close to the stage at the front, which consisted of a jungle backdrop that included several hanging vines. All the tables were done in fake wood and the floor itself appeared to be grass with stone pathways. Waitresses, all named Jane, attended the tables. Each waitress wore leopard outfits that varied in style from one girl to another. The Jane serving their table wore a two-piece leopard skin and as soon as they sat down started to serve them. She openly flirted with Aaron that caused him to feel a bit nervous with Irene being present.

"Have you been to Tarzan's before?" Jane was a petite brunet that smiled easily.

"No, this is our first time." Irene answered for them all.

"You'll enjoy the experience. There are several small plays or skits that are done throughout the evening. Besides Tarzan and a few extras in the back, each waitress is in at least one play. As a matter of fact, the Janes think many of the skits up. I designed the play I'm in." She went off to get their drinks at the back.

Aaron looked around as the women talked. The whole room was done in the jungle theme. Plants and bamboo walls separated some of the tables and the sound of birds and animals could be heard. The high ceiling was dark, but included several vines that hung down. The place was nearly full and there seemed to be an equal number of men and women, with the Janes all hurrying to keep up with the customers' orders. Suddenly the lights dimmed and the stage was spot lighted. Drums could be heard as birdcalls and animal shriek sounds increased.

From behind the tables a woman ran up to the stage dressed in a white safari outfit, though this one consisted of a tight white top, matching shorts and high-heeled boots. She brandished a shotgun and waved it around as she stared around wild-eyed.

"Help me! Someone help me!" She swung the gun around and fired; the noise not overly loud but managed to produce a bit of smoke from the barrel. She stood on the stage for a minute looking around when a net was dropped on her from above. She fell to the ground, tangling herself in the net as two tribesmen appeared, each wearing a loincloth with their chests painted in red and yellow symbols.

They rushed towards her and took away her gun, and then pulled her out of the net. As she struggled with them her shirt and shorts were removed, leaving her only with her underwear and boots. Her arms were soon tied above her to the dangling vines and there she struggled uselessly. The tribesmen stood holding spears at her sides making threatening gestures at her. They also yelled at the crowd asking for suggestions what to do with the great white hunter. The audience began to get into the play and shouted out suggestions, the most common one was to remove the rest of her clothing. This suggestion was greeted by the hostage with a vigorous shake of her head.

The warriors were still debating what to do to her when a yodel was heard and Tarzan, a young muscular blond man wearing the traditional Tarzan costume, swung down on the group from a vine. He quickly subdued the men, freed the hunter and carried her to safety via the same vine upon which he arrived.

"They sure aren't shy about their bodies, are they." Aaron voiced it as fact rather than a question.

"I think that's good. There is nothing wrong with that, is there? We could learn some things from Earth, right Aaron?" Irene was smiling as she said so, testing his reaction.

He wasn't about to be snared in an argument here, however. "Of course. Earth and its culture have much to offer." He smiled at her with a 'nice try' look in his eyes.

She looked back at him and then shook her head. "You're too much of a politician."

After a while, their Jane came by with new drinks and asked them how they enjoyed the show.

They gave her compliments on the show and relaxed when the lights dimmed for the next act. This consisted of an overweight man with grey hair wearing a leopard wrap. He stood by a tree, holding a vine and claimed to be Tarzan, but the years had taken their toll. He proceeded to tell hilarious stories of his earlier life in the jungle.

The next play started with a loud argument in the restaurant area. After some discussions, a well-dressed couple was escorted at spear point to the stage. A pot bellied chief, the same man who played the over-age Tarzan as a comedian, sat in a chair and pounded a spear on the floor for attention. Apparently the couple was refusing to pay for their drinks, claiming poor service. The crowd booed.

"What should we do with them?" the chief asked in a loud voice. The audience shouted answers and he listened to their suggestions. But the man had a suggestion. He offered to give up his wife in payment. This was greeted by boos and cheers.

"Well, this woman has a sharp tongue," the chief said. "But I would like to see if she meets my qualifications in other ways. Remove her clothing and let us have a look at her."

She yelled a protest at the chief and cursed her husband. The dress she wore was a shimmering silver dress that was partially transparent under the strong stage lights. It was more expensive than the regular costumes and was removed carefully. She stood in her panties and bare feet on stage, protesting her innocence.

"Young lady, one more outburst and I will have you gagged and bound."

She looked annoyed but remained quiet.

"This man. Should we let him go? Does he need to be punished? We could just keep his wife as payment."

The audience reacted. Voices, mostly women urged punishment. Calls for stripping him as well could be heard.

"It seems that you are not going to get away from your crime. Your wife is insufficient payment, not worth the cost of the drinks."

"Hey! What do you mean I'm not worth the drinks? That's insulting! How dare you, you oversized rat."

"That is enough!" The chief pounded his spear on the floor. "Gag her and tie her up." The woman was quickly gagged and her wrists tied behind her back. This led to loud cheers.

"Now back to him." He pointed a finger at him. "Remove his clothing, and then we will decide on what else is in store for him." He was stripped to his underwear, and then he stood before the chief.

The male captive had his hands tied above him to a vine, and now he was positioned towards the front of the stage.

"What should we do with him? Let him go?"

The crowd was negative to that.

"Hmm. Well, he gave me his wife. So perhaps he needs a new one. Just as well. We have another wife in mind. Tarzan's sister as a matter of fact. Lucy! Come out here and get your husband!"

Aaron looked on as a person dressed as an ape came out, and by the huge sagging breasts and bright red lipstick was obviously supposed to be female. He couldn't decide whether the person inside the costume was male or female. Lucy waddled up to the man, poked a finger at his chest, then released his hands from the vine and put him over her shoulder. She turned towards the stage and patted his backside affectionately before heading offstage.

"Now what do we do with her?" the chief said.

The gagged woman stamped her foot in frustration.

Aaron listened to crowd yell their suggestions but found his mind drifting. The people of Haven would be shocked by the fashions, the music, the drinking, and even by their leader being present in this establishment. He went to church on every Sunday and wondered if coming here qualified as something that had to be confessed.

He returned his attention back to the stage where the woman was bent over a bar stool and spanked with a palm leaf. Aaron wondered how the palm leaf was supposed to inflict any pain but the woman reacted to each blow. After several strikes, she was released to applause and after acknowledging the crowd disappeared behind a curtain.

The next act consisted of topless women dancing around men dressed as warriors. The music wasn't something normally heard in a jungle but the dancers showed great zeal and energy.

Glora looked at Aaron. "What's wrong? You don't look happy."

"I'm trying to decide if it's wrong for these women, and men in some cases, to show off their bodies so much. It seems almost every type of entertainment I've seen so far, whether it was those TV shows or live entertainment, usually involve nudity, sex or violence."

"It's just entertainment. It's not how people actually live on Alliance Worlds."

"I know that. But I wonder if the entertainment is a substitute for an otherwise well behaved society or if it mirrors it. The fact is that Haven was being effectively charged with non-conformance to behaviour that Sol deems reasonable worries me. To me Haven is a well behaved society and if Earth finds fault with them then maybe the problem is with Earth and its cultural values."

"You may be right but that will be tough to convince the courts of that."

Chapter Three
On orbit around Earth

Aaron and Irene had an hour before they were to board the shuttle that was to take them to Earth. They choose a lounge that offered a view of Earth and sat nursing their drinks and stared at the blue and white globe by their side. They watched a little too intently and didn't perceive the arrival of the captain of the Galileo, who had to make a small coughing noise to attract their attention.

Aaron started to rise from his chair as soon as he recognized the uniform but the captain held up his hand.

"Please, there is no need to get up, sir. I do not wish to disturb you two. However, I would be remiss if I did not take this opportunity." He smiled as he swung his eyes between Irene and Aaron.

"Opportunity?" Aaron returned his smile. He then noticed that there was a semi-circle of the ship's crew and passengers behind him.

"Since you are the leader and representative of Haven, and I am the captain of the Galileo, I would like to express to you, and to all of Haven, welcome home!" This statement was greeted by applause by those behind him.

The spur of the moment ceremony touched Aaron. "Thank you. It is good to be back."

Touchdown was breathtaking for Aaron and Irene; they stared out of the windows as the shuttle flew them from the ship down to the ground. The government plane went straight from the Galileo to Amsterdam's Alliance Spaceport, designated for government and military officials only. They were spared having to wade through a throng of news media when they landed, and again when they went to the hotel. In fact they didn't even have to check in at the hotel front desk; being a head of state, prior arrangements had been made.

The ride over from the air terminal was by a shuttle that flew over the huge buildings, each structure connected to its neighbour either by sharing a common wall or by multiple pedestrian crossings. It was an interesting sight from the air, skyscrapers over four hundred stories high connected by glass-covered tubes. The tubes themselves were located on multiple levels, and were often wider than they were long, sometimes as broad as three hundred feet. From the air dot sized people could be seen being transported along moving belts, the inside tracks moving the fastest.

The hotel room offered a breath taking view of the ocean; the Imperial Alliance Government section was on a platform that extended from the famous dykes out to the ocean. The government section of Amsterdam also included a security zone of an additional fifty miles of the ocean, which made Amsterdam technically one of the largest cities on Earth in terms of area. The window could also be converted to a view screen that could show, in real time, many other views of Holland. The rest of the hotel room was equally impressive, furniture and decor that was carefully selected to establish an early nineteenth century look. One part was a fully stocked kitchen that containing both food and liquor.

When Glora dropped in to see them she was met with a sea of questions and she calmly explained as much as she could. She also showed them how the computer worked and some of the features of the Internet.

"Also, you can use these for expenditures." She handed them each a thin plastic card. "These are credit vouchers that are provided to visiting members of the Imperial Alliance. As a member of the Alliance, each representative, up to a maximum of six at any given time per world, is given a credit for expenses while visiting Earth. That doesn't include this hotel room, or any meals in or outside the hotel. That is paid directly by the Imperial Alliance."

"So what do we use the cards for?" Irene frowned as she stared at the card.

"Shopping for one. Hiring legal council, except that is so far being care of by the NightHawk. The credit vouchers are normally used for entertainment due to the hardship of being far away from home. In reality, it is an open bribe to vote for Earth's proposals in the House of Representatives."

"How much money are we talking about here?" Aaron turned his card around, watching the hologram of the Alliance member stars.

"Lots. You don't know our credit system here, but I'll give you an example. For two hundred new Europe dollars, you could buy one or two shirts, or a pair of shoes. In your account, each of you has five thousand credits. And each day one thousand credits will be added, until you leave Earth. The remaining balance goes back to Earth's Visiting Diplomat Department, so you might as well use it up."

"Glora, can you show me where to shop?" Irene put her shoes on.

* * * *

"Shannon Crouts returning your call, Premier Duggan." The smiling woman gave him a moment to acknowledge her and then the screen went blank. A moment later, a short, heavyset man with a grim face appeared beside Shannon Crouts.

"Premier Duggan, Shannon Crouts. Do you prefer Premier Duggan, or Mr. Duggan?"

"Let's make this less formal. Call me Aaron, Shannon."

He looked surprised for a moment and then caught himself. But his grim face turned into a friendly one. White teeth broke through in contrast to his dark skin. "That sounds great. Look Aaron, this Charter thing is something not to be taken lightly. I will personally be dealing with you but I want you to know I have several other lawyers working with me. So don't think that we are going to be out gunned by the prosecution."

"I'm not familiar with the legal system here. What is going to happen?"

"The first time we go in court is for about half an hour where they'll read the charges to us. At that time we will plead not guilty and probably ask for a judge and jury."

"Why a jury?"

"Slows down the whole trial process for one and therefore gives us more opportunity to work on their facts. For another, the jury doesn't always understand the exact wording of the Charter, a judge would. And if the jury is a bit confused, they will not convict."

"A jury is more favourable for the defendant?"

"Absolutely. Since even before the Wave if the defendant could afford a long trial a jury was usually chosen. They have a harder time understanding the finer technical points of a case and as I mentioned they will not convict if they aren't sure."

"Better for the rich, it would seem."

"True, but the justice system allows us to use the jury and we will take advantage of any opportunity. The downside of the jury is that they are also affected by public opinion. They aren't suppose to look at the news media reports during the trial but it is a given that they do. The court ruled long ago it was wrong to withhold people the right to use computers or tablets, and therefore the Internet, over the extended time to be on a jury. So for now the battle is to turn around the negative reports about Haven. Right now the articles are mostly negative, portraying your world as backward and barbaric. We have to work on changing that image."

"How is that going to be done? How bad are those reports?"

"I'll send you a copy of some of the reports. As far as changing their outlook, leave that to me for time being. But this is where half the case will be won."

* * * *

Aaron relaxed in the overstuffed chair and turned on a viewscreen. He flipped through the channels looking at the different programs. The viewscreen gave an illusion of being three-dimensional and he tried shifting from side to side to study the effects. Aaron had seen the similar shows on the Galileo and still hadn't gotten over the novelty of a flat screen that gave a three dimensional picture. The programs themselves were also interesting but he was caught off guard as to their content. It appeared censorship was not given much consideration on Earth. He checked his watch. The ladies were gone almost two hours.

He was a bit shocked by the fashions on the Galileo and had expressed that to Glora earlier. He felt that such exposure of the female body could cause problems. Glora looked amused at his concern; something an old woman would have said might have been on her mind. Instead she told him about the security cameras that were everywhere and people felt safe with the large number of public and private police.

"No matter where you go there are security cameras. They're located in all public places and are monitored by both computers and security guards."

"The cameras are monitored by computers?"

"Yeah, they're programmed to pick out suspicious activities. They're actually better at it than people in some instances. They can also monitor multiple conversations and will flag the security if they hear suspicious conversations and will sound an alarm if it detects cries for help."

"Good Lord. That sounds as if people are being replaced by machines."

She had laughed. "Don't be silly. Who do think monitors the computers?"

"Good point. But you said both private and public police?"

"Right. To the general population they're the same. Each building will have its own security and will hire a security firm to handle it. The security police have the same powers of arrest as the public police forces and enforce the laws the same way. For example they will give you a summons or fine for littering or placing a recyclable item in the trash."

"The public courts accept privately given tickets?"

"Uh, actually some of the courts are private as well and that includes private detention centers. If a person is convicted by the private court system they can always appeal to the public system, but that costs money and the detention centers are usually in poorer condition than the private ones."

"How odd to have a system like that. It sounds bad if you're a criminal. Not much escape from the cameras or police."

"Well, that's another thing. If someone, let's say, shoplifts a shirt and is caught on a security camera they may get away with it anyway. The shopkeeper will have to make a complaint to the security firm and they will decide if it's worthwhile to find this guy and prosecute. Cost factor and all that stuff. The shopkeeper is often given an option to either drop the incident or to pay for the cost to apprehend the individual."

"If they can catch him as well would be a factor I would imagine."

"Well with face recognition cameras technology they would find him if he ever left his apartment."

"Interesting justice system. Money rules everything."

* * * *

Aaron sighed. They might not be back for hours he thought with a shake of his head. The TV couldn't hold his attention for long, his nervousness on being on Earth, the upcoming trial and the strangeness of the hotel room caused him to pace. He decided to read the news media articles Crouts sent him.

They were interesting, at least on how Earth viewed his home world. Also there were some reports from his trip from Haven to Earth. Apparently, there were reporters everywhere. He wondered if Irene would be amused by what was said about her, "the long legged Amazon from Haven."

* * * *

Glora led Irene slowly among the shops. She noticed that she was staring wide eyed at everything, looking up at the high ceilings and then turning around to watch the hundreds of people as they moved past.

"This is unbelievable! Are all places on Earth like this?"

"More or less. What would you like to do? Do you still want to buy some clothes?"

"You bet. I have to be careful what I wear on Haven, mostly business suits. But on Earth, I think I should be able to wear what women wear here without causing a problem. The fun stuff."

Glora took her into a few stores, describing some of the fashions, past and present.

"I got a pair of these pants a couple of months ago. They feel great, really comfortable."

"Those are pants? They're not just leggings or stockings?"

"Pants. Hey, how about these? These ride low on the hips." She held another pair of pants.

"Good grief. Those are so low they didn't even put a zipper in them. Hey, what are those? Electric dresses?" She pointed to another rack.

"Electronic pattern dresses. There is a power source built in them. It can cause the dress to change color, or become transparent in a preset pattern. Usually the pattern is small squares or circles. But they can be quite elaborate. This one changes from blue to green to transparency on a black pattern in star pattern. These dresses are usually worn only as eveningwear on special occasions. You know, glamour wear."

"You have shown me a fair bit. A lot of these clothes are semi transparent, tight fitting, or rather revealing. Nothing that could be worn on Haven."

"A lot of women alter their bodies, especially as they get older by going to those body shops, like that one you saw earlier. For a few dollars and some pills, you can have pretty much the body you want. And if they have the body, they want to show it off. Of course, this shopping district is more for the well to do. In other shopping strips you are just as likely to see people wearing more casual clothes, jeans and stuff like that."

"What do they wear under these clothes?" Irene held up a dress that wouldn't hide much of whoever wore it. "Seems to me the underwear they sell on Haven would look silly under these fashions."

"Sometimes nothing. Body suits are popular. The underwear is usually worn to be complimentary to the clothes, same color or style."

"Well, it looks like I can't buy just a couple of outfits like I thought. There is so much to choose from and then I would also have to buy shoes and underwear as well."

"So, you're going to hold off for the time being?"

"You've got to be kidding. Let's start spending!"

They went from one shop to another, Irene picking up outfits and then sending them up to her hotel suite.

Glora was watching Irene model a dress when she heard her mobile. She flipped it on and saw the face of a security guard.

Irene looked at Glora's face change expression as she listened to the call.

Chapter Four
Amsterdam, Earth

Robert sat in the hotel lobby. So much for the surprise visit he thought. First, it took forever to get through the airport and then the transport to the Alliance Court Buildings. He hadn't realized that there was a security clearance requirement to enter Alliance Courts; while it was located on Dutch territory apparently it was considered a separate state by itself. To get in he had to produce proper identification and have someone of the proper security clearance vouch for him. That someone was Glora. So the surprise was gone and, to top it off, she was tied up in a meeting or something and couldn't meet him right away. He spent another two hours traveling to her hotel where she wouldn't be back for three more hours. The lounge was boring and expensive so he waited in the lobby, getting a suspicious look from the hotel security.

* * * *

Shannon Crouts took a quick glance around Aaron's hotel room before speaking. The room was one of the more expensive ones in the Regis Hotel. Someone was pulling strings for this leader of Haven. "I don't normally do personal visits but I have some concerns about security in this case. The news media are getting desperate for more news and they can be quite effective in picking up supposedly secure signals. In addition to our case there have been several business proposals directed to Haven through my office."

"What type of business proposals?" Aaron asked as he gestured for Shannon to sit down in the living room.

Crouts went on to explain that several organizations were interested in setting up trade and services with Haven. Wood products were apparently a hot item and many companies wanted a piece of that. There was also interest in the trade of various textiles and hardware items. Leather coats, shoes and garments had many inquires but this was usually followed by a note of concern about the legality of selling animal skins. Two large corporations wanted to have the rights to set a spaceport, as well as the repair facilities for spaceships at Haven. This would mean sending trained personnel to Haven as the planet did not have anyone who understood higher dimensional field generation.

"So what do I do with these?"

"Oh, nothing much for now. I will, if you agree, request that they send us a sizable deposit with their business proposal. The deposit would be refunded if the business venture were turned down. This will help our case indirectly if there is a financial incentive to support us from the business world. The spaceport and repair facilities are going to be needed regardless so take a look at their offers. General Energies is the bigger of the two and can do the job easily. But their revenue is higher than most planets and they would dominate Haven economically, perhaps too much. Underworld Power is a much smaller concern and may be a better fit. Both companies will eventually have spaceports but only one will be Haven's government designated facility. As you have some free time I suggest you may want to meet with their representatives."

"Okay. Set up an appointment for me. I might as well be doing something."

"Excellent. Now, another matter is requests for interviews and information about Haven. I think it would be best if we allowed some interviews; it may help turn the tide of the initial negative reports. And that reminds me, Scott Pearson and his sidekick, Cindy Lorncorft, wanted me to say hello. They also said for you to give them a call sometime. I'll give you Scott's number."

Shannon continued to pass on information, giving a little detail on how the case was going. Aaron was glad for the update, but as soon as he left he called the number Shannon had given him.

He was mildly surprised when Cindy answered instead but recovered to invite them to visit Irene and him at the hotel. Aaron relaxed in the living room when the door chime rang out. He crossed to the living room, opened the door, and stared with his mouth open.

* * * *

Robert shifted position on the chair. Doubt was increasing as he waited. *What was I thinking coming here without warning? Glora could well have another boyfriend, could have put me in the category of former boyfriends and now just a friend. Damn! This could be awkward for both of us. She would try to be polite and try to let him down gently. This was going to be rather embarrassing.* Then he saw her enter the lobby, looking more beautiful than ever. He stood up and gave a hesitant wave.

She looked at him, frozen for a moment. Then dropped her shopping bag she was carrying and ran to him.

"Robby D! God I missed you!" She slammed into him, hugging and kissing him. "I am so glad to see you! Sorry for making you wait."

They babbled on how things were going. She held tight on to his arm as they headed to the elevators.

"Oh, we have an appointment to meet the Premier of Haven for dinner."

"What? I didn't bring any good clothes."

"That's okay. We're just having dinner in his hotel room. Probably pizza."

* * * *

Aaron's hotel suite

"Hi Aaron. Aren't you going to invite me in?"

Aaron stared at Irene. She was, as far as he was concerned, more than half naked. A skirt that was too short and didn't even come close to her navel at the waistband, and a short, semi-transparent blouse was the last thing he expected to see her wear. He gulped. What if someone was to see her? If she were to wear this on Haven, she would be thrown out of church. He would have to make sure she changed before anyone saw her. A few minutes later the door chime sounded again, and Aaron opened the door to Glora and Robert.

The two couples sat in the living room making small talk. Glora kept trying to bring Robert into the conversation but he still appeared to be too nervous with Aaron and Irene. Glora felt he would start relaxing in due time so in the meantime she chatted with them. She noticed Aaron was not quite himself; normally he gave the person talking his full attention but he now seemed to be distracted, especially towards Irene. It wasn't too hard to determine why.

She was wearing a skirt that had an uneven hemline that went from mid-thigh and then higher. Her short blouse, coupled with the skirt's low waist, meant a lot of midriff showed. It was normal informal wear on Earth but obviously, Aaron was not use to such sights. She wondered what he thought of her own ultra low rise pants with a top that had a rather open weave.

Eventually Aaron seemed to relax about the women's dress and Robert began to join in the conversation. It turned out that Aaron and Robert had a common subject; Underworld Power wanted to be Haven's choice to develop spaceports and spaceship repair facilities, and it was one of a dozen companies that had made an offer of employment to Robert.

Robert was considering their proposal, a standard training period on board spaceships, and then a progression on various space stations and repair facilities. It meant he would be in the more remote areas of human space for several years.

Aaron listened carefully to what Robert thought of them and of several other companies that wanted to do business with Haven.

The evening went better after dinner, and the four talked about the differences on Earth compared to Haven. Aaron was dismayed on what was allowed on Earth as far as fashion was concerned. Robert couldn't believe that civilians on Haven were allowed guns and did they really eat meat?

After Glora and Robert left, Aaron renewed his questions on Irene's wardrobe. But she refused to tell him what else she had bought and told him he would have to wait and see. She gave him a kiss goodnight and disappeared to her own room, leaving Aaron a little put out.

The next day things got busier for him; there were several appointments to discuss business and then a couple of calls from Shannon on legal matters. Irene went shopping in the morning but joined him in the afternoon to help in the interviews. She wore clothes more suitable to Haven than Earth. Aaron was relieved in her change of attire but she acted a little cool towards him.

After an early supper they relaxed when the hotel desk informed them they had visitors.

Ten minutes later the doorbell chimed and when he opened the door, Cindy waltzed into the room with a huge smile, giving Aaron and Irene a hug and kiss each. Scotty was behind her, extending a handshake to Aaron and a kiss to Irene.

"Guess what?" Cindy held up her hand, sporting a diamond ring. "We're engaged!"

Congratulations were extended, followed by drinks.

"So now what are you two going to do? I hear that you are making enough money to retire."

"Well, the money is certainly there. But I think we're too young to retire. Let's just say we're going on an extended holiday for the time being."

"Scotty was talking about us going on assignments for some of the more respectable magazines and papers. That would help keep us busy enough, but not too busy. Either that or start up our own paper if we can find some other financial backers."

"It sounds like you two are tired of the more sensational media."

"Yeah, kind of eats away at a person." Scotty's voice sounded resentful and he took a long drink.

The topic changed and then before long the four of them were talking about life on Haven like old friends. If Irene and Aaron had any resentment about being deceived by Scotty and Cindy's cover story back then, they didn't show it. Midnight came before their visitors left and Aaron and Irene encouraged them to keep in touch, telling them that Haven was always ready to have them again.

The following morning Aaron was up early and started to prepare for his interviews with some of the corporations that wanted to do business in Haven. This was put away before lunch, which he and Irene agreed would be taken together in one of the restaurants.

At just after noon Aaron knocked on her door. Irene still maintained it wasn't time for them to be spending the whole night together despite his efforts and she answered wearing a very short tartan skirt with semitransparent blouse. The bra was quite visible and matched her skirt.

"Is that appropriate dress for where we are going?"

"Of course. But you know you could use some new clothes. Those look stuffy."

"Well, I haven't been out much."

"No kidding. I don't think you have left the hotel room since we arrived. Do you like what I'm wearing?"

"It's very nice. Your blouse is a bit see-through though."

"It's supposed to be, silly. That's why the bra matches the skirt. The panties match as well, though they don't cover much." She walked towards the elevator, glancing back to see if he was watching her.

He was, of course. He noticed her walk had a bit more of a sway than usual and coupled with her telling him about her panties led him to suspect she was trying to tease him, or was trying to get him to think about her more. He wondered why for a moment, and then dropped it. Eventually he would figure out what to do about it. He did know that now that Cindy and Scotty were engaged, her mind had to be moving towards marriage as well. He thought she might be the right one for him. Just not right now as there were other priorities.

The elevator opened up on the plaza, a mixture of shops and restaurants. They walked hand in hand through the crowd, looking around as they moved. Aaron noticed most of the women dressed in rather revealing outfits. They looked relaxed as they walked, obviously not feeling conspicuous. Men wore casual clothes as well, open shirts were occasionally seen but full shirts with padded shoulders were more common.

He didn't notice anything unusual at first, just the odd person staring back at him. He thought that might be normal as perhaps he was looking around a bit too much, yet an anxious feeling came over him. Soon there was a throng of people around them, mostly women, trying to speak to him or simply to touch him. He looked at Irene and saw the same nervous look on her face. Voices grew louder and someone called out his name. A momentary squeal and shriek came forth from the encircling crowd.

"Aaron, we better get out of here. This is getting out of hand," Irene shouted even though she was standing next to him.

"Right, let's find someplace to go that's safe." He looked around. "There, Gary's Grill. Let's make our way over there." He felt her grab his arm and he pushed through the gathering crowd. Fortunately he was bigger and stronger than anyone around him and was able to push his way towards the restaurant, muttering, "Excuse me please, pardon me," as he went.

They reached Gary's Grill where a hostess wearing a poncho greeted them.

"Wow. That's quite a fan club you have Mr. Duggan." She held her hands out at the door to stop anyone else from coming in and then latched the door.

"Thank you. Could we wait here for a while until the crowd dissipates?"

"Sure. I'll get you a table. But they won't be leaving by themselves any time soon."

She led him to a table, away from the windows.

"Look, I don't mind keeping them out, but this might upset the boss a bit; loss of business and all that. So I may have to let some people in but I'll make sure they won't bother you two." She walked away, revealing lots of bare skin along the sides of the poncho.

"I can't believe that just happened. All those people around us."

"Around us? Aaron, all those people were young women and girls that were chanting out your name. They were all lusting for you."

"What?"

"Don't be so damn naïve. You are considered a sex object on Earth. A big, handsome male from a primitive world who, according to the tabloids hunts his own food and keeps a harem of women for his beck and call. Those females are going gaga over you."

"You're kidding."

"Do I look like I'm kidding?" She sounded annoyed. "You have another explanation for this?"

"Not yet. Let's eat. I'm hungry."

"Me too." Her voice softened. "Did you see what the hostess was wearing? She had absolutely nothing underneath that poncho."

"No, I didn't," he lied.

"I think I'm going to buy one of those." She watched his eyes, knowing he was lying.

After lunch, a security team from the shopping complex escorted them back to the elevators where they exited and returned to the hotel. The crowd followed them as they made their way back, but didn't present too much trouble. The security guard told them they were lucky they were in a protective area of Holland. The people here were not nearly as unruly as elsewhere. "Next time inform the police or a security firm if you want to go shopping in the common areas, sir. It's just not safe for famous people to wander about through crowds."

"Well, I guess that's the end of our shopping trips." Aaron didn't look too displeased by the turn of events at the mall.

"No. Just for you. I didn't notice any young ladies shouting out my name." She sounded annoyed as she said it but seemed to change her mind about the situation a moment later. "That's good because I enjoy shopping and you don't. We just better keep you away from all those wild women of Earth."

Aaron felt a moment of pleasure. It sounded as if she was actually jealous.

The following days were spent talking to various company representatives; some of the interviews were very promising while others showed the organization was only after money. Irene sat in on a few of them and gave her input. Aaron also managed to convince Shannon to join them in discussions with some of the larger concerns. Aaron was glad to have his expertise on the power companies; he needed advice. Technically, he would need the support of his councillors on his choice but he had no doubt they would follow his lead in the matter.

The date for the court arrived after another week of spending time in the hotel room. He was escorted by the hard nosed Imperial Guard, though Aaron wasn't sure if it was for his protection or to make sure he wasn't going to escape, or more likely just for show.

Shannon met them inside the high ceilinged room where after some delay a black robed judge appeared behind the court's bench. The whole process took only a few minutes where Aaron, on behalf of Haven, pleaded not guilty and elected a trial by jury. Then the Imperial Guard led the way back to the hotel.

The next two days he spent looking at the various proposed contracts. He decided that about a third were worthwhile for Haven to seriously look at. One thing he was pleased with was his ability to adapt to using the computer instead of paper. He would have liked to have paper to scribble on but had found that a writing tablet could serve the same purpose, using a pointer to write on a white surface that left a ghost image behind before vanishing. Meanwhile printed words copied what he wrote on the larger screen.

One of his first interviews with the media on Earth took place on 'Margette's Now Show'. The live interview took place in front of a noisy and full audience. Margette was known for her controversial interviews with equally controversial guests. Shannon was worried about possible negative reaction to the interview but agreed with Aaron it was also a good opportunity to also gain exposure as a positive popular figure, if he handled the questions right. She wasn't likely to try to ask too many questions in the area of politics as she wanted to keep the show light and appeal to as a broad an audience as possible.

After Aaron took a seat as the show's hostess welcomed him.

"Good evening Premier, and welcome to Margette's Now Show. Come on, people; let's give him a big Now Show hello!"

The crowd reacted predictably with applause, shouts and whistles.

Margette, a woman with flaming red hair, stood up and gave Aaron a hug and kiss. She sat opposite him in one of two over cushioned chairs, crossing her legs to give a bit of modesty to a tight, fake leather dress that slid high up her legs.

Aaron wondered at the intensity of her hug and tried to keep his eyes fixed above her shoulders. He couldn't guess her age, thinking she looked like she was in her early twenties but her voice sounded much older.

Margette gushed praise on him, asking him soft questions and tried to make him feel at home. Before long, they were on a first name basis. Aaron wasn't fooled by her friendliness; this type of behaviour wasn't how she made a living. He waited for her to strike, but was still a bit taken aback on her first topic.

"Aaron, you're so big and strong. Isn't he people?" They reacted with applause with a few shouts. "Say, Aaron, why don't you take off your shirt? Show our audience what a man from Haven looks like!" She laughed as the crowd went wild, chanting 'Shirt! Shirt!' "How about it, Aaron? Don't you want to make your fans happy?"

"I would, but this really is your show." He gestured towards her, keeping a smile from forming on his lips. "Say, why don't you lead the way by taking off your dress?" The chant from the audience was mixed between 'Shirt! Shirt! Dress! Dress!'

"Oh Aaron, you are so funny." Margette gave her best shy look as she giggled, quickly checking her notes for her next topic. "Aaron, you're much taller and bigger than the average size for men on Earth. Why is that? Does eating the flesh of animals promote more growth?"

He appeared to consider the question carefully and clasped his hands together giving an impression of forming a thoughtful response. This also slowed her down from her usual rapid-fire questions designed to put the guest off balance. "Well, a better question would be what caused the average size on Earth to drop. At one time, only a few hundred years ago, the average height of men on Earth was the same as on Haven. What do you think happened, Margette? Do you think it might have been the water?"

"Ha ha! Very good Aaron. You can shoot some fair questions yourself. Speaking of shooting, I heard you still use guns on Haven. How does it feel to go hunting?"

"You're right that guns are still in use on Haven. I, myself, however, am not a hunter. I don't use any guns, so I can't really tell you what it is like to go hunting."

Margette looked flustered. Someone had given her the wrong information about him. She crossed her legs the other way and put down her notepad. "So, how did rumours start about people from Haven being meat eaters?" She said meat eaters with a bit of disdain.

"Probably because we do eat meat as part of our diet."

"Why do people on Haven eat meat? Isn't that a little uncivilized? Even barbaric?" She leaned towards him, looking happy that she had him in a tough situation.

"I don't agree with that suggestion. But if you like, I'll inform you why we do eat meat." She remained silent, so he continued. "Meat provides certain nutrition that's difficult to obtain from other foods; on Earth that's easily done by manufactured food, such as enriched soybean. But on Haven we don't have the equipment to make these enriched foods; the Wave ruined our food manufacturing capability. We don't have the technology to make such equipment, so we turned to natural sources. It was to either eat meat or die."

"That helps people, but what about the cows, pigs, horses and chickens? They might not like being killed for food."

"Good point. Horses are not used for food. Chickens, I'm not sure they're smart enough to realize the difference." The crowd reacted with a bit of laughter. "Pigs are smart and could survive quite nicely by themselves. Cattle, however, do need human intervention. They have been domesticated for so long that they're dependent on people for survival. Incidentally, speaking of survival, did you know that Haven has more cattle and pigs than Earth? The cattle that do live on Earth, because they're not used for food, can only be found on protected game farms. And not very many at that. So as far as survival is concerned, these animals would probably prefer Haven over Earth."

Margette was getting tired of this direction of the interview. She decided he was just too good a politician to trap him in these open type of questions and she was aware how he didn't really answer her concern about how the animals felt about being used for food. She had underestimated him and now it was time to change the direction of the show.

"Aaron, could you share with us whether you are single or married? I know all these women here are dying to know." This was greeted by screams from the audience. Chants of 'Shirt! Shirt! Shirt!' could be heard again. "How about it Aaron, are you available for one or more of these ladies?"

He smiled shyly. "I'm not married …" The crowd reacted with more screams and a few calls of 'Marry me. Pick me. I'm free tonight!' "But I'm dating a lady right now."

"So does that make you unavailable to the rest of us? If so she must be very special to you."

"That she is." Aaron, for the first time during the show, looked a bit uncomfortable.

That made Margette feel a bit better although she knew he had won the interview battle tonight. "Dating? Does that mean you don't share an apartment together?" She smiled sweetly at him as she received the signal from the producer.

"No, we don't, we each have our own home in Oasis City."

"Aaron, thank you very much for being on the 'Now Show'." The applause started up again as Margette chatted with Aaron with the microphones turned off. "Good job, Aaron. I tried to corner you but you'd done your homework. You seemed to know what I was going to ask and were prepared."

"I'd watched some of your shows and made some deductions on what might be asked."

"Interesting. Were you aware that on the Now Show two years ago I had taken off my top to pay off a bet to another star?"

"No, I hadn't."

"So, I was considering taking off my dress to get you to take off your shirt. I am wearing a body suit underneath so I would've taken off my dress to get you to take off that shirt."

"I'm glad you didn't."

"Yes, well, I was concerned that the women may have rushed the stage. That would have been dangerous."

Aaron breathed a sigh of relief. What would have Irene said if he had taken off his shirt in public?

* * * *

The reaction to the interview was widespread, and generally very favourable to Aaron in the various media. Irene checked the stories as they came and seemed pleased as she read them out loud.

"Nice job, Aaron. The reports are favourable."

"Thanks." He looked at her lounging on the loveseat. She was wearing shorts that were high cut at the legs and a blue blouse. She didn't seem at all self-conscious unlike the last time she wore a revealing outfit.

"So how come you didn't take off your shirt? Modesty?"

"Well, it would have been inappropriate for a head of state. Plus I wasn't sure what your reaction might have been."

"Well, you're right that it would be unwise for a head of state to do so but I wouldn't have minded at all. As a matter of fact I wish you'd wear some more up to date fashions, especially those that show off your strengths a bit more." She watched him look at her as she stretched her arms above her head. "What's on your mind? It looks like you want to say something."

"I think we need to talk about something." He stepped towards her. "Do you feel about me as I do about you?" He started ask another question, and then stopped. She waited for him to finish the question. "Irene, I don't know how this trial is going to turn out. But if things turn out okay, would you marry me?"

She didn't say anything to him but got up and kissed him hard as a reply.

* * * *

The next interview he did was with 'New Reaches'. The news program interviewed people that related to business themes. The host Robert G. Richardson was a tall, thin man with oversized ears and a piercing gaze. After a quick introduction, Richardson quickly moved to questions that might be of interest to those in business and financial affairs.

"I understand the economy of Haven is based largely on agriculture and timber harvest."

"I suppose you can say that but our economy is a closed one," Aaron replied. "Currently we are not trading with any other planet and our resources are used primarily to sustain life on Haven."

"Fair enough. But according to the information I have the inhabitants of Haven have a good standard of living and some citizens seem to be quite wealthy. How is your tax system set up? Is it income based? What social benefits are provided?"

"The history of Haven was one of early struggles to survive. A large part of those early years was a barter-based economy; therefore, a normal type of tax wouldn't have worked. Today, because of those initial conditions we have a unique tax system. Haven basically taxes each person on the property value they own. The value of the property is negotiated between the owner and the government and a percentage is given as taxes."

"What if they don't agree on the value?"

"Oh, if a person undervalues their property for the sake of paying fewer taxes, the government can purchase that property for that price. I will point out churches and certain charities are tax exempt."

"Interesting. Your social programs?"

"Basic food, such as fruits and vegetables, is subsidized. Shelter is available to anyone who is in need in what you may call communal apartments. We also provide free medical, dental and education. Our churches provide strong support to those in need as well. To tell you the truth, very few people are in a difficult financial situation."

"Sounds like a healthy economy."

"We get by, though we don't really have a yardstick upon which to compare ourselves."

Richardson asked a few more questions but Aaron didn't say anything that could be called negative when he spoke about Haven.

* * * *

Irene discovered that there was a section of the hotel that was devoted to their special guests. These were normally for heads of states though popular entertainment stars were known to use the facilities as well. Five stories of exclusive shops, restaurants, entertainment venues and parks were available only to those with the correct credentials. Aaron acknowledged that he needed new clothes, especially suits for his court appearance. Glora and Robert were also interested in seeing the screened area as guests of Aaron and Irene.

The shopping and coffee shops were largely located on the top three floors and the foursome spent hours going in and out of the various stores. Most of the retail outlets didn't display the prices of the goods they sold, believing that a lot of the guests weren't concerned about such matters. Aaron was surprised that when he did buy some shirts, the clerk didn't ask him for ID, but merely informed him his purchase would be directed to his hotel suite.

"How do they know it was me? Am I that well known?"

Glora laughed. "Yes and no. He probably recognized you from the news sources but most of these stores use a video camera that scans faces. The information is sent to a computer that compares your features to a scan that was done when you entered the shopping complex, where the security station is. Your name comes from the computer that ran a recognition program and it relayed your name and hotel suite number to the store."

"That is both clever and a bit worrisome."

"Worrisome? How so?"

"Big brother; too much information about individuals."

Glora thought about what he said. It did have some merit she supposed. "But you have nothing to worry about unless you do something wrong."

"True. Unless the government changes the definition of what is unlawful."

The group passed by several stores and then went down, by escalator, to the second level. This level was more open, composed of coffee shops, souvenir stores and open tables where refreshments were served among trees and plants. They choose a table and a waiter presently appeared to take their order.

"Is it common to have these potted trees and plants around tables?" Aaron was eyeing the trees with interest.

"Depends on the area but usually there are trees or plants around food courts. Besides aesthetic reasons, there are also practical reasons for them. Each building is required to have so many trees and plants, depending on the size of the building itself and the number of people it serves, a green ratio of sorts. There are minor incentives for people to have plants in their apartments of a certain size and you may have noticed the potted trees in the hotel lobby."

"Yeah, and there's also a couple of small trees in my hotel suite." He suddenly looked surprised. "There're birds in these trees."

She turned to where he was looking. "There are usually a few types of birds around. A new type of ecology has formed around food courts that the Building Management Council is reluctant to interfere with, due in part to consumer relations and a possible reprimand from the Environment Safeguard Board. Several species of birds have developed that live among the area around food courts, along with a few insects and, well, I hope I don't scare you, a type of mouse."

Irene looked around on the floor. "Mice? They don't want to get rid of the mice?"

"Well these mice are small, about an inch plus a short tail. They avoid people completely and come out only at night, looking for food crumbs. It would be hard to get rid of them without affecting the birds and also there is the risk of the E. S. B. coming down on them."

Irene watched a bird fly to an unoccupied table and look around. "I take it there is a relationship between the birds, insects and mice?"

Robert broke into the conversation. "Right. That bird is the top of the food chain. It will fight off other birds for first choice of leftovers. It also will eat mice and insects. The other birds will take whatever is left over, including eating the small berries the trees produce. The mice will eat more of what is left over but also the eggs of the birds if they get a chance. There are at least a dozen types of insects but almost all of them live in the trees and plants. These trees, insects and animals have evolved so much from their ancestors outside of the buildings that they're classified as a different species. Some could no longer survive outside buildings and the controlled environment. In some locations, a small kind of lizard also survives. Those are almost impossible to find or see. In fact no one can determine how they manage to migrate from one building to another."

"You said the buildings are required to have trees. Why would that be?"

"One is for ecology. Earth has a lot of regulations that ensure there will be natural environments whenever possible. The other is more practical. Each building has a complex system of air filtering and replenishment of oxygen. Most of the structures here are a closed system and people would use up breathable air unless means were taken to refresh it. So we have huge computer controlled air systems. The reason for the required trees is in case of an air circulation failure of some kind, maybe an event like the Wave again. So the theory is that these trees and plants will help keep the air purified and provide oxygen."

"Good theory. But there doesn't seem to be enough trees here to do the job."

"Oh, you haven't seen the park yet."

* * * *

The park could be entered on the main floor, and was located in one corner of the building. For Robert and Glora it wasn't much different from other building parks other than they were usually located in the center of the structure rather than the sides.

"Now this is impressive." Aaron looked up and around. The 'ceiling' to the park was five stories above and gave the impression of a blue sky on a sunny day. Addition artificial lights gave the feeling of a warm sun.

"Come on. There are paths we can follow." Glora led the way. They followed the stone paths that snaked along, passing rest stops, waterfalls and streams and a small pond.

"This is huge. This must be what, a couple of acres in size?" Aaron asked as he looked around.

Glora pursed her lips in thought and then replied "I'm not sure; some parks are larger, or smaller, depending on the building size. The parks are usually also visible from the other floors through glass walls; we didn't see the park earlier because the hotel placed their prime suites along the park so guests may look out from their rooms to the park."

"Obviously I didn't have enough pull." Aaron said.

"You have enough pull but the costs are quite high. I had a budget to cover only so much for your stay here. But if you want I can make an application to cover the additional costs."

"Oh no. What we have is fine." Aaron stopped to look at a stream that slowly fed a pond. "Tell me, what types of animals live here? The same as in the food court?"

"No, there's a lot more variety. Again a different ecology has developed. There're – help me Robert – over a dozen types of birds?"

"Subspecies. There are about four true species but they seem to have varied a little bit from location to location. There's a type of small hawk that has adapted here but it's not the main predator normally. I don't know what is in this park, specifically, but some of the larger parks include birds, insects, small rodents, lizards, snakes and the largest have even had wild cats and dogs. The cats and dogs may have been someone's pets at one time that were let loose. All of the animals are smaller than those in the wild and have adapted quite well to the park. None of the animals bother the people, though if you break the rules and bring food into the park some of the birds, cats and dogs will approach cautiously. Oh, there's fish in the ponds as well."

"Do these parks require maintenance of some sort?"

"No, they're pretty well self sustaining. Sometimes one animal will take over completely. One park had too many rabbits so they were fed a chemical that reduced their ability to produce young. Some parks have lost a species entirely. Dogs, which usually are only slightly bigger than the cats, didn't seem to be able to adapt to some of the parks as well as it was hoped."

"Strange how life keeps adapting though to new challenges. Given enough time these parks could be sprouting off a whole new world of creatures."

"True. Scientists underestimated the time it took to change the plants and animals to the environment. They thought it would take a few thousand years but only a few generations caused a noticeable change in the species."

"Do you suppose that might be true of people as well?"

Robert looked up at Aaron and then over at Irene. "I guess the answer to that is self evident."

Chapter Five

The trial dragged on for several weeks. The prosecution started out strong, rattling off offence after offence. The defence didn't object much to some of the claims made by the Imperial legal team but merely made some minor corrections to their facts. Crouts explained to Aaron that while some of these facts were negative to them he didn't want the jury to dwell long on them by dragging out prosecution's strengths. Then the defence launched a strong counter attack, accusing the prosecution of ignoring the Charter of Conduct, specifically that all people have the right to choose their own government, unless forfeited by criminal acts. The people of Haven, they claimed, had not done any criminal acts because the Imperial Alliance had not properly informed them of those regulations prior to asking them to sign the document.

A second point was made that the Charter did not specifically disallow any activity that was required to ensure the survival of the people on Haven. The prosecution was upset about such a statement; it challenged the defence contention that hunting and the raising of animals were necessary for food. The defence insisted the people of Haven faced certain death if they did not eat meat, therefore, it was not illegal to do so.

This, of course, led to much objection by the prosecution about implied and written regulations. Both the judge and the jury were getting impatient with the various legal arguments on small and large points. The trial bogged down on whether the Charter provided for survival of people in special circumstances. The defence pressed on that it was wrong and therefore illegal to ask Haven to sign the Charter before they had a chance to study the document and get legal advice on its implications from attorneys within the Alliance. The prosecution found that most of the court time was spent on the Charter's right to dictate conditions on Haven, so soon after the planet was invited to join the Alliance. The defence asked why Haven was asked to join if it didn't already meet most of the Charter requirements.

* * * *

Aaron had sat in the courtroom but had not yet made it to the witness stand. This was just as well as far as he was concerned. Now he was trying to relax in his hotel suite, unsuccessfully. He gave up and started to read the business contracts and literature from the various companies that wanted to do business with Haven.

Crouts had been pressuring him to decide on two or three ventures. One, because some deals are better when the fire is still hot and for another it may have a bearing on the trial if there is a Earth based business involved.

His on again and off again reading was broken by the door chime and he opened the door to Irene, Glora and Robert.

"Hi," Irene said. "Glora and I were having a drink downstairs when Robert called her so we decided to save you from your paperwork. You do want to be saved, don't you?"

"I suppose so. What did you have in mind?"

Irene gave him a quick kiss before replying. "We found a place where we aren't likely to be disturbed. It's located in the secured area for special guests. It's kind of boring socializing only here because we have to protect you from those wild females."

Glora stood on her toes and pulled down on his neck to give him a kiss as well. "I guess congratulations are in order. Do I get an invitation to the big wedding?"

"I'm not sure just when and where and how big this wedding will be. But you will be invited."

Robert pushed through an opening between the two women. "Yes, congratulations." He shook hands with Aaron. "You have now eliminated half of the reading material in those gossip magazines."

The group made their way down two sets of elevators and through a short walkway before exiting into a small lounge. The lounge was upscale in its decor and prices, but ensured reasonable privacy. A small three-piece band played soft music in a corner stage.

The waitresses wore white beaded dresses that apparently were transparent except for those beads. This caused Aaron to take a second look as the waitress took their order. He saw Irene smiling at him as she walked away.

"I thought after going to Tarzan's you would be used to the underdressed women here. But your eyes bugged out the same as before."

"Caught me off guard, that's all. Too long in the hotel room." He realized he should be use to it by now. All the people contact he had so far had shown that the women were more often undressed than dressed when it came to evening wear. The men had a different set of fashions, which he thought was also a bit odd, but usually had lots of coverage. He was becoming more accustomed to it though. Irene wore a dress that exposed her whole back right down to the top of her cheeks. Glora wore white, semi-transparent pants and skin-tight blue top that looked painted on her body. At least she wore panties under her pants, though they didn't hide much either. And those outfits hadn't caused him to think it was all that unusual. Still the waitress wearing only beads caused him to stare harder and longer.

Irene was right about the lounge; it was a pleasant change from the hotel suite. He found that he was talking a lot to Robert. The young man was intelligent and pleasant and was able to tell him a bit more about some of the Earth corporations wanting to do business with Haven. Being a power engineer, he was also excited about the Regal and her generators that were no longer functioning. This turned the conversation towards some of the options he had on where he was going to work.

He indicated that he was leaning towards hiring on with Underworld Power; they had modern equipment, had a good name for quality and in safety and good benefits. The drawback was that he would be transferred to who knows where to start his career. That normally would not be a concern but his relationship with Glora would likely be over, or at least changed drastically. "I wish things could be worked out but it's not fair to either one of us to give up our career for the other," he said.

Robert also had an opinion about why people on Earth were smaller than they use to be. He admitted the idea was not his originally but thought it offered an explanation. The population grew faster than the available food supply and that lead to a smaller growth of the children and thus smaller adults. But he also found that the government building codes were changed that allowed buildings to lower their ceiling heights by a few inches. The higher density population, coupled with less room to live, led to the devolution of the human species. They shrank slowly over the generations.

The rest of the evening went by quickly, a few more drinks, some dancing and more talk. Glora also tried to educate Aaron on why women dress on Earth the way they do.

"You see, Aaron, we don't always walk around with half our body showing. There are certain social and cultural conventions that are taught on what appropriate dress is and when to wear it. For example, during daytime business, wear is what we call conservative. The skirts may be worn a bit higher than on Oasis City but the style is similar. Casual wear is good for daytime or evening and you may notice short skirts or short tops but is not anything too outrageous. The evening or exotic wear is what is causing your eyes to bug out. Anything goes. But the racier stuff is meant only for nightclubs and special evenings. The thing is women are expected to cover themselves during the daytime but at night they are expected to go around half-naked. It also means buying lots of clothes for special occasions." She took a drink. "And besides clothes there are jewellery and shoes to consider. Also underwear. One has to have the right bra and panties 'cause half the time they are visible. Bras are expensive too and one has to buy a new one for a new outfit half the time."

"I thought most women went without a bra."

"No, there are sheer bras that are hard to see; it can be hard to tell. The waitress I'll bet is wearing a sheer body suit, to help keep herself from jiggling."

"You make the fashion scene sound complicated."

"It's tough to understand but it is fun buying the clothes."

* * * *

The trial was getting a lot of publicity. Unfortunately, for those trying to sell the coverage to readers, there was little to report. The testimony on the finer points of the Charter of Conduct was now taking the front stage. Experts were explaining both the exact wording and the spirit of the Charter. The jury was caught slouching in their chairs and yawning.

Crouts continued to send them articles from the news media, and now the tide seemed to have turned in favour of Haven. Photos of Aaron and Irene were in several articles. Aaron was considered a sex object for the women and photos of Irene showed her in her more revealing outfits. Crouts indicated that this was good publicity. He wondered if she would reconsider the offer she turned down for her to pose nude in one of the more sophisticated men's magazines.

Scott and Cindy dropped by to visit as well. They apparently were still in their leave of absence and enjoying life. They were pleased that Irene and Aaron were engaged and offered their congratulations. They regretted they had missed Irene, who was out shopping, but said they'd try to get a hold of her in a day or two.

* * * *

Glora received a call for from her superior, Dr. Margaret Rishew, to meet with her in Dallas. She said a quick good-bye to everyone, telling them she should be back in a few days. Robert elected to stay behind, exploring Amsterdam on his own.

He also gave Aaron a call to go for a beer and the two went to a lounge in the secure area. Robert was a bit nervous about going for a drink with the leader of a planet but Glora coaxed him into making the effort. The beer helped him relax a bit and soon they were talking about various subjects, including the taste of the beer compared to Haven's.

"I have a question about the elevators here. It seemed to me that the elevator car would stop at floors for a few seconds and move, not up or down, but sideways and backwards. What was going on?"

"The car was moving back. Let me explain, if I can. If a building is only a hundred or so stories high, they usually use different banks of elevators to transport people from the ground to top. A person may have to change elevators a couple times to go from the, let's say, the fourth floor to floor 155. But now we have buildings a lot taller, and the size in area has increased as well. So the problem of moving lots of people got complicated, especially if you didn't want a huge bank of elevators. What they developed was several cars using the same shaft. A car will back up to allow another car to go by, and on even more complicated systems, they can actually go sideways as well to change shafts. The cars are computer controlled and won't always stop to pick up passengers, depending on their own load, schedule stops and how soon another car may arrive."

"That is really something. I take it they don't use cables any more."

"No, these cars are self powered. They run off storage batteries that are recharged as they move up or down the shafts. They use rails on the shaft to guide them."

The beer continued to come and soon Aaron was explaining how they made their buildings out of wood, bricks and stone.

"Fortunately they seem to be earthquake proof to some degree, because we have a few minor tremors on Haven. Of course we don't stress the situation too much by limiting the height of our buildings."

"Hey, I wanted to ask you about something. I read somewhere that there are sea monsters in Haven. Is that true?"

Aaron laughed. "Well there are some creatures out there that are big and ugly but hardly what I would call a sea monster. You better be careful what you read."

* * * *

The trial continued its slow progress. The reporting on the trial increased when the first witness was called by the prosecution, a veterinarian who gave his opinion on the livestock on Haven.

Dr. James O'Donnell, a rather thin man who looked even smaller hunched over while he sat in the witness chair, squeezed his hands together. The suit looked too confining and the back of his jacket pulled at his shoulders. He tried to focus on the heavyset man approaching him; the silver hair was full but added a comical rather than a distinguished appearance.

"Tell us, Dr. O'Donnell, have you studied the videos of the cattle, hogs, poultry and other livestock on Haven?"

O'Donnell swallowed hard. "Yes … yes sir, I have."

"Good. Now could you give us your expert opinion on how those poor animals met their demise?"

One of the defence attorneys leaped to her feet. "Objection. 'those poor animals' is leading the witness and jury to form a sympathetic opinion …"

It was first of many objections by the defence, some of the objections were legitimate as the prosecution let his own personal feelings appear but other objections were just to break up the thought process and flow of the prosecutor.

"Okay, Dr. O'Donnell, could you give us your expert opinion on how the life of the farm animals were ended?"

"Well, the farm animals, that is the cattle and the pigs, were led onto transport trucks and then driven to these, these special buildings, and then …"

"Please, Dr. O'Donnell, could you please describe the state the animals were in before they reached the stockyards?"

"Un, yes, of course. They were in a state of agitation, very nervous … very frightened." He used a white cloth to wipe his forehead.

"Agitated, nervous and frightened. Hmm, now why would they be agitated, nervous and frightened Dr. O'Donnell?"

"Uh, because they were going to be killed? I mean, because they were about to be killed."

"And how was the cattle and pigs murdered, strike that, I mean killed?"

"They were given a shot to their head, and then, and then their throats were slit so that they would bleed to death. Horrible."

The prosecution then exhibited pictures of animals being butchered as evidence. The jury studied the photos in silence as they passed them along. Russ Joestone walked back to his bench, nodded to the defence, and then sat down.

Cheryl deGruy conferred just a moment longer with Crouts before advancing to the uptight witness.

"Dr. O'Donnell, you said the cattle and the pigs were upset when led to the transport trucks?"

"Yes."

"Because they were to be taken to their death?"

"Yes."

"How did they know they were to be taken to their death?"

"Un, I don't know."

"You don't know? The fact is they didn't know where they were going either. Isn't that right?"

"Yes."

"The cattle and the pigs and any other animal is always nervous when taken out of a comfortable environment, isn't that true?"

"Yes, I suppose so."

"Good, I'm glad that little mystery is explained. Those videos you saw of the farm animals. Did you have a close look at them?"

"Yes, I did."

"Were the animals well fed?"

"Yes."

"Healthy looking?"

"Yes, they were."

"So you are saying the animals on the farm were healthy and well fed?"

"Yes ... but ..."

"Now Dr. O'Donnell let us review when the animals were killed. In your opinion, did the blow to the head cause the animals any undue suffering beyond the moment of the blow?

"Well, no. Not actually. But prior to..."

"Thank you. Would you agree that the animals were well taken care of and did not unduly suffer during their lives?"

"Yes, but really the image..."

"And in your expert opinion did the animals live healthier and less stressful lives than if they lived in the wild without any human intervention?"

O'Donnell sat staring at the defence lawyer. His forehead glistened and his Adam's apple bobbed up and down.

"Well, which is it? Which is better, living in the wilderness or protected on the farm?"

"Well, the farm might be safer and healthier, but…"

"Thank you. That is all."

The prosecution looked annoyed. Not at the defence, they were just doing their job. And certainly not at themselves; after all they were the good guys and just trying to bring criminals to justice. No, the source of the annoyance was directed at Dr. James O'Donnell who somehow let them down with his weak answers. Joestone scowled at the retreating figure making his way back to the general courtroom sitting.

The prosecution requested a recess until after lunch and regrouped to launch their next attack.

* * * *

"So Professor Gelinas, would it be correct to say that you have made a study of the social habits of the people of Haven?" Joestone smiled at his witness. The older gentlemen sat upright in the chair, giving an impression of an intelligent, learned individual.

"Yes, that would be accurate. I have compared their social life to that of early man and to our present high ideal as outlined in the Charter."

"And your impressions of the people of Haven?"

"Well, to summarize, and please understand there is enough material here that it could be the subject of an interesting book, that these people are quite primitive in many respects. Their laws, customs and moral behaviour to their environment is so regressive that I would hesitate to place them much above eighteen century Earth. Unfortunately they also possessed knowledge of some high technology, which made their impact on the planet Haven much more severe."

The professor leaned back in the chair and crossed his arms. "I am not a proponent of the theory that the human race has taken an evolutionary step forward since the Wave; that the race is better and smarter because the weakest was eliminated during the hardships. However, I would like to point out the primary population of Haven consists of white Caucasians, who are physically the size of our early ancestors. I would suggest that it is quite probable that the natives of

Haven represent a regressive step in evolution, both in their physical appearance and their moral attitudes."

"Could you elaborate on their moral attitudes?"

Gilinas shook his head. "One hardly knows where to start." He sighed. "They are destroying their environment by cutting down trees to use as common building material. They don't try to rehabilitate their criminals, but put them into slave labour. The women are obligated to produce babies; some of the women have been pregnant up to ten times. I would like to point out most of the births used the outdated so called natural method. The poor women and babies had to suffer the trauma of live birth. The people also had an unnatural craving for meat. They would eat the flesh of animals … why they were practically cannibals."

"Cannibals?"

"Yes, exactly. The DNA of most mammals is quite close to that of humans, and for a small percentage of change, we could well be same as those animals. Therefore to eat the flesh of the higher mammals is akin to being a cannibal."

The defence was hesitant about cross-examination on another hostile witness but to leave the statements he made without challenge would be detrimental to their case to the jury. Cheryl deGruy slowly made her way to Gilinas on the witness stand.

"Professor Gilinas you stated the DNA of some mammals match closely to humans?"

"Yes, essentially."

"So according to your reasoning a tiger eating its prey is practicing cannibalism as well?"

"No, that is quite different."

"No professor, it is not. The people of Haven are not cannibals by any reasonable definition are they? Or are you willing to stake your reputation that they are?"

Gilinas perched higher in his chair. "I was merely making an observation about their possible lifestyle by offering an analogy."

"So they are not cannibals?"

"No, I suppose they are not."

"Would you say, in your enlightened opinion, churches represent good moral behaviour?"

"Yes, I suppose so, but that would depend on…"

"Well, Haven has the highest number of churches per capita than anywhere else in human space. That would seem to be a contradiction to your immoral behaviour charge. Yes or no."

"Yes, but ..."

"The people of Haven are white and bigger than most of us. Is that sufficient cause to call them primitive or imply a backward step in evolution?"

"No, of course not. I was..."

"That is all, professor. Oh, was your upcoming book meant to be fiction?"

The prosecution now tried to bring their case forward by calling in Diplomat Beaumont's secretary, Charles Ring. Unfortunately, while he was able to state he believed Haven knew about the conditions of the Charter he had to also admit some indiscretions by the visiting Alliance personnel.

"So, on one hand you condemn Haven for using wood products and with the other hand your very own people were stealing wood furniture from your gracious hosts?" Cheryl deGruy raised her voice slightly.

"Well, some of them may have gotten a little over anxious. But ..."

"And what was this about Alliance Armed Forces being captured by a lone farmer when they were on a spy mission on the planet?"

"Oh that can easily be explained. You see ..."

"It seems to me that the Alliance should be careful who they are calling having immoral behaviour." Cheryl deGruy crossed her arms and glared at Ring.

After Ring stepped down the prosecution announced they would not be calling up Corporal Radison for her version of what transpiring on Haven.

The trial ended for the day.

Chapter Six

"You and your team did an excellent job today in court." Aaron sat with Shannon Crouts in his hotel room drinking coffee.

"Thank you," Crouts said. "But we have a long ways to go still. It was easy to ridicule those witnesses; they were too set on their opinions to suspect there would be alternative viewpoints and it was child's play to ambush them with questions. Unfortunately, the trail will boil down to if you broke the laws of the Charter. No, let me rephrase that. The trail will hinge on whether the jurors believe you were justified in breaking the Charter laws."

"But surely you managed to sway the jurors to some degree; you must have weakened the prosecutor's case by your cross examination."

"True. But try to remember that while most people don't profess to be prejudiced, indeed there are laws and social pressure to prevent discrimination, there is a concealed aversion to accept those who are too different. The people of Haven are doing things they would never consider, they look different and they live different. Somehow, those differences hint that there may be something wrong with them. That's why we're far from winning this case. The law states you are innocent until proven guilty; unfortunately, we've the reality of the jurors who have already formed opinions according to their own experiences. We have to change those built in opinions of what is normal."

"So what do we do?"

"I think I can raise doubt with any other witnesses they draw on. But I believe putting you on the stand might be the best way to go. I have seen you on those talk shows and you handle yourself well under difficult questions. I feel that you can sway the jury to our position."

The next day Aaron took the stand. He strode up to the witness box, smiled, and went through the swearing in ceremony. Aaron was dressed in Earth style business clothes; Crouts had told him it would make it easier for the jury to identify with him.

The prosecutor walked slowly towards the front of the court as he tapped on his notepad with his finger. "Premier Duggan, is it correct that you signed the Alliance Charter of Conduct?"

"I signed a Charter of Conduct, that is true."

"Did you, or your staff, have time to examine the Charter of Conduct prior to signing the document."

"I don't understand. Do you mean to read the document or to fully understand it?"

"To read it."

"Well, yes, it put me to sleep a few times."

The judge used his gavel to silence the small burst of laughter in the courtroom.

"Did you understand the intent and philosophy of the Charter of Conduct?"

"No, not really. It was rather vague."

Joestone looked up in surprise. "You mean you signed a document of such importance without understanding it?"

"You may have misunderstood my answer. We read the document, and we did our best on Haven to understand the various rules, policies and regulations within it. But the intent and philosophy of the Charter is something quite different."

"Okay, given that you have read the rules and policies within, you still signed the document knowing that your world was openly flouting them?"

"We had to sign. The Alliance showed up with warships that were quite intimidating. If we didn't sign I'm sure General Burgess would have been quite happy to use force."

"That is mere speculation. The fact is you signed the Charter, and Haven is openly ignoring the laws within it. Is that not true?"

"We obey to a higher authority."

"A higher authority? We are talking about the Charter here."

Aaron took a breath and then spoke towards the courtroom rather than Joestone. "Is it wrong for a starving man to steal? Morally or legally? The founders of Haven would have starved to death if they did not eat meat and more important, would have allowed their children to die as well. To me, it would have been morally apprehensible to allow one's offspring to die by refusing to do what was necessary. On Haven, we do not put ourselves above the environment; we are part of it and accept our role as both provider and consumer of life there. You ask us to stop eating beef. What would you tell the ranchers with two hundred head of cattle to do with their livestock? This is our culture that came about through necessity we are talking about, not some irritant that can be removed by a change in our bylaws."

The prosecutor looked stunned for a moment. He hadn't expected the leader of Haven to sneak in a speech during questioning. "All the same, didn't Haven receive an offer from the Alliance to help move Haven towards obeying the various laws and policies of the Charter?"

"Yes."

"So Haven signed the Charter, knowing it disobeyed the laws within it and then refused help to make the corrections?

"Yes, that is correct."

"That is all." Joestone returned to his seat feeling a bit uneasy.

Cheryl deGruy waited a few moments before walking up to Aaron, who still looked calm and confident. "Premier Duggan, why did you sign the Charter?"

"Because if Haven didn't we would have been run over by the armaments of the Alliance Forces."

"Haven refused help from the Alliance to make corrections in the areas Haven was in disagreement with the Charter laws. Why was that?"

"Other than the communication network, the Alliance wanted payment for their help in Alliance dollars. At that time we didn't have any and it would be wrong to accept services we couldn't afford to pay."

"Are you saying Haven refuses to change at all then?"

"Oh no. Anytime there is a mix of cultures there's bound to be change. Haven will change, but it can't do it at the rate the Alliance wants it to. Haven is only doing things it needs to do to survive."

"You mentioned the philosophy of the Charter. Could you expand on that?"

"Yes, the Charter wants all the worlds to be like Earth in its customs. Not, as the Charter indicates like all the other worlds in the Alliance, but like Earth. This gives Earth enormous power over the other worlds. Aside from that the problem with that is that worlds should be encouraged to be different, we can be one people without being clones of one another."

"So you believe it is okay for worlds to be different from one another?"

"Absolutely. If all the worlds were the same, progress throughout the Alliance will be in the same direction. Allow the worlds to be different and who knows what will be discovered that would never have occurred otherwise?"

"I see. It has been alleged that Haven is immoral. What do you say about that?"

"That would depend on your point of view. Some people on Haven would say Earth is immoral; the women walk around half undressed, people don't go to church on a regular basis, some of the entertainment might be considered sinful. I could go on, but all it means is there is a difference in our worlds. I would suggest there doesn't have to be a wrong or a right way, after all people only do what they are brought up to do."

"There was an earlier allegation that Haven used its prisoners to do slave labour. Is this true?"

"No. People convicted of a crime are offered an option to reduce their sentence by doing work, such as helping farms during harvest. If they choose not to work, or work only part of the time, that is fine as well. The sentence is adjusted accordingly."

"You indicated earlier that you believe there is a higher authority than the Charter. Please explain."

"The Lord. He is the one who ultimately decides what is right and wrong. If there is a contradiction between the Charter and what God tells us I would think the Charter would have to give way."

The defence continued to ask Aaron about life on Haven; the hardships, the struggle for survival and the strong family and religious beliefs. As the media reported later, the charismatic leader easily swayed the jury to sympathize with Haven. The media also reported that sales in meat flavoured soy meal had gone up dramatically.

* * * *

Aaron continued with business presentations and made an offer to Underworld Power. He felt that it was the best corporation to set up spaceport for Haven and wanted to get the ball rolling. Crouts had indicated to him that it was essential that a spaceport be taken care of as soon as possible.

Aaron asked Irene what she was going to do when they moved back to Haven and couldn't wear those fashions she fell in love with on Earth. She replied that she was going to try to change fashion on Haven by importing some of the more conservative clothes from Earth. Besides, she could continue wearing the underwear from Earth. Aaron didn't mind her trying. He was happy she decided that since they were engaged she was willing to spend the occasional night with him.

Aaron was also considering his own attitudes about the Alliance. He was confident the people of Earth were now seeing Haven differently than when he first arrived; telling those who would listen that Earth was being close-minded about other cultures. But he also realized that was a two edged sword that opinion could cut both ways. As a result, he was trying hard not to see the people he met as having lower morals but just a different set of rules they worked under. Certainly, Glora, despite wearing rather revealing outfits was an upstanding person. Therefore, he reminded himself that different people were only that, different but not necessarily wrong.

* * * *

"I'm sorry that you had to travel all the way to Dallas to meet me Glora. But the situation is getting out of hand and we have to act quickly. According to our legal experts, the Haven's defence team has out manoeuvred the prosecution and there likely will be a full acquittal. Therefore, Haven will keep full planet status. After considering a number of possibilities, we decided that we need someone who is on positive terms with the administration on Haven. You fit the bill in that regard and in all other categories."

"I don't understand what you mean. Are you offering me a position on Haven?"

"Yes. I'm sorry. I should have been clearer. Haven is small, so we don't necessarily need someone with a lot of experience. This would normally be considered a first step into the diplomat ranks. However, it is considered by some a bit of a plum, a new planet and the special circumstances surrounding it having increased interest in it. What we do need is a resident diplomat to handle Earth affairs on Haven. And I wanted someone who could get along with the local government, in fact I insisted on it. Are you interested?"

Glora was speechless.

* * * *

Irene answered the door. Robert was there alone, looking both happy and nervous.

"Robert, what a pleasant surprise! Do come in."

"Thank you. Is Aaron in as well?"

"Yes he is. I'll get him. Please sit down."

A minute later Robert was telling them his good news. "… and they offered me the power generation installation job. Not only at a higher salary than that I expected but on Haven itself! That means Glora and I will continue to be together. But it seems to me that you must have a lot to do with their offer."

"Yes, well, I figured that if a company was going to build a spaceport on our planet I wanted at least one man working there I could trust."

"Aaron! You never said a word to me. How many other secrets are you holding out on me?" Irene stood with her hands on her hips in mock annoyance.

"None. No secrets. Well, hardly any. Robert, it will be good having you around on Haven. Maybe you can find a way to fire up the old Regal."

"Count on it."

Aaron relaxed back in the easy chair. Things were going along pretty good. Now if that trial would only work out as well as Crouts promised.

Chapter Seven

Boston Globe-Times
HAVEN NOT GUILTY

The celebrated trial of the new planet Haven came to a surprisingly quick end on Tuesday. The jury had deliberated less than an hour before returning a not guilty verdict. The prosecution looked on in stunned disbelief over the verdict. It appeared that Russ Joestone, who headed the prosecution, had all the cards in his favour at the beginning of the trial but continually gave up ground to the defence. Near the end of the trial the jury were shown pictures of animals being killed for food. The defence asked for a recess at that point and when the trial resumed put Aaron Duggan, the Premier of Haven, on the stand. Even during the prosecution's strong questioning, Duggan gave an impassionate defence of Haven. At the end of the questioning Joeston could be seen shaking his head as he returned to his bench. The not guilty verdict means there will be no reprisals against Haven, though there will be negotiations concerning some of the infractions alleged at Haven to bring it closer in line with the Charter of Conduct.

MidNight View-America's News Source
Haven Set Free By Jury

Aaron Duggan, the tall, handsome charismatic leader of Haven leaped in the air and hugged his defence team as the jury read out a not guilty verdict on all charges. MidNight View covered the trial and had reported how the prosecution was continually outwitted by the slick, high-powered defence. The verdict may mean Haven can continue its program of eating flesh of murdered animals. In addition, MidNight View has learned Duggan may also keep his harem of beautiful women. The jury did not rule on the validity of the reported sex orgies Haven is noted for.

Nighthawk News
Haven Celebrates Not Guilty

Haven and Premier Aaron Duggan were rewarded with a not guilty verdict from the jury. The jury considered the arguments for fifty minutes before returning to the courtroom. The speed of their decision seemed to catch even Judge Climonts off guard.

Duggan stated that after he finished a few business deals on Earth he would leave for Haven as soon as possible. The leader of the defence, Crouts, has agreed to give an exclusive interview with NightHawk. Please watch for details in the up coming editions.

NightHawk News
<u>Pearson, Lorncroft To Wed</u>

Scott Pearson and Cindy Lorncroft have announced their wedding plans in an exclusive interview with NightHawk News. The couple met on assignment on Haven and have not been apart since. Together they have been responsible for almost all information about Haven and have provided several exclusive pictures and interviews from Haven. A reliable source has indicated that the revenue from those reports has given them financial independence as well.

The exact date is being withheld until a church date can be confirmed, but in a surprise announcement, Cindy Lorncroft admitted the wedding was to take place in Oasis City on Haven. More details to follow in coming issues of NightHawk News.

Chapter Eight
Starship Galileo, travelling to Haven

The waitress smiled a tired smile. Table number 3B was having a good time. The three couples were drinking as if there was no tomorrow. Of course, they would find out that there were would be indeed a tomorrow, one that may well include a hangover.

"Jane, when is the next show? Are you going to be in it? And we need some more wine, please."

"Sure, the red?"

"Right, the red. Better make it two."

"The next show is on in about ten minutes. I'm in the show after that, about a poor girl who falls victim to some head hunters. I hope you'll stay to watch." The last comment was unnecessary; the group looked like they would be there until close.

"Aaron, that's the second time you have asked her when she would be on. You must really like her," Irene scolded.

"Naw. I just can't remember what she told me before."

"Right. Just that your eyes keep bugging out every time she wiggles past in that short little Jane costume."

He grinned a drunk's grin. "Maybe a little, Irene. But you are the love of my life."

"And it better stay that way." She leaned over to kiss him. "Though I'm sure her show will be a good one." She got up from the table and headed to the washroom, followed by the other women. Aaron watched Irene walk away. She sure had changed her walk since she had come to Earth. The sway of the hips was quite interesting, especially in that short, loose skirt she wore.

Robert and Glora ignored the interplay between Aaron and Irene and concentrated on themselves, grinning at each other and sipping their wine. They were enjoying each other's company as much as was possible. That was true of Scotty and Cindy as well, of course, though they both had been through relationships before and had not become fascinated with themselves to the point of not observing the rest of the universe.

The show started. The group was making much more noise than usual; the effect of the alcohol that had taken over their thinking. They yelled and clapped, though the performance wasn't special compared to the previous shows.

The three couples joined in the general applause, and continued with their drinks and munches. The next act was the same comedian who pretended to be an over aged Tarzan last time. This time he acted as a pompous great white hunter and told a funny story on how to hunt lions and elephants.

Their waitress was in the next show. She did the same show Glora, Irene, and Aaron had seen a few months ago but with some minor changes. She was captured by cannibals and then was also put in a giant pot. Aaron and Irene thought the new performance was better.

Another show featured a couple who refused to pay for their drinks. The tribal council heard their case and pronounced them guilty. This time the woman was carried off by a male gorilla and the man was ordered to serve every lady in the room a glass of wine.

"About time, right Irene and Glora?" Cindy nodded as she spoke.

"No kidding. You would think that he would be a bit embarrassed to walk around in his underwear."

"He looks like a Martian. They don't get embarrassed by anything."

Scotty raised his glass. "I propose another toast. May we remain friends long after we get married and never forget how to get drunk!"

The glasses were raised together and another bottle was ordered. The waitress was happy to oblige and thought that there was a good tip coming from the group. She flirted with the men as well as she could without offending the women. She leaned against one man and then reached across the table, causing the short dress to expose the bottom of her cheeks.

One woman, the waitress thought her name was Cindy, gently pushed her away from the guy she was leaning on.

The Jane shifted her position slightly and pulled down her dress. She turned and whispered to the woman who had pushed her. "Oops. Sorry honey. Just part of the show."

The men looked disappointed when she left.

Irene smiled at Cindy's protection of Scotty, but knew how she felt. Women were always flirting with Aaron and sometimes making rather indecent propositions. It was annoying but fortunately, Aaron seemed immune to their advances. She turned her attentions to Scotty.

"So, Scotty, are the rumours true about you setting up a business in Haven?"

He laughed. "Now where did you hear that one? I suppose there would be some merit in that. Though it may be Haven may not let us settle there."

"I think you have some pull there from the higher ups. What type of business were you thinking of?"

"Selling liquor. That way I'm always close to my vice."

Cindy punched him in the shoulder. "Be serious, Scotty."

"Okay, I'm going to start up a newsmagazine on Haven, on real paper. It should be great fun."

Tarzan's Jungle slowly emptied out and soon only a few customers were left. The staff didn't mind them staying. There was still lots of cleaning up to do before they got around to the tables. Still, the staff was referring to their table as the hangover special.

Chapter Nine
Oasis City, Haven, 2614, fifteen years later

President Duggan's intercom chimed and the female voice announced the arrival of the two o'clock appointment.

"Send him in, please," Irene said.

A moment later, the door open and Scotty entered, smiling away.

"Scotty, it's nice to see you again. How was your trip to the East Continent?"

"Excellent. I got back on Tuesday. Looks like the magazine is ready to roll out there."

"That's quite a publishing empire you have now. Four dailies, a weekly news report magazine, and now a second edition of this – what do you call it, entertainment for men?"

"Ah, well, gives me a chance to practice a more diverse side of my photographic talents."

"Undressed young women."

He laughed. "It sells the magazine. It seems to me that you would make a good feature in the magazine."

"Oh no. My mother would die of a heart attack. Well, maybe not her but my dad would. Besides, those girls you need are young and beautiful. But what brings you here? Business?"

"Business with pleasure when it's with you." He paused for a moment. "Rumour has it that you are about to call it quits as President. Any comments?"

Irene looked stunned, but just for a moment. She stood up from behind her desk, walked to the front of it and sat on the edge. She looked down at Scotty as he sat in the leather chair. "Tell me where you heard that and how." She looked friendly as ever but her voice carried some tension in it.

Scotty didn't hide the fact his eyes ran up her legs before looking up to her. "I didn't hear it. I deduced it. Is it true then?"

"Tell me more before I confirm or deny."

"My reporter's instincts tell me you have just confirmed it but I might be willing to tell you how."

She smiled. "Might be willing? What do I have to do to get that information from you?"

Scotty laughed. "I tell you what. I'll give you the how and you can decide yourself what it is worth. Perhaps you would like to buy dinner for Cindy and myself.

"Dinner? That's fair. I am looking forward to seeing Cindy and the kids as well."

"Actually the kids are up at the space station with Auntie Glora and Uncle Robert. Speaking of kids, how are Michael and Sandra doing? Still on Mars with Dad?"

"They are. I miss them and Aaron." She paused a moment "Start talking about this rumour and how you came to this thing about my resigning."

"Aaron was both Premier and Haven's representative for several years in the beginning. I remember how taxing it was for him to be able to handle both duties. So after a few years he decided to resign from the Premier's office and concentrate on the position of representative. He had done a marvellous job for Haven and when he left the economy was booming."

"That I already knew." She smiled.

"When he stepped down, there was a political vacuum for the leadership. You split between the two opposing agendas and promised to carry on as Aaron did, which you did do. The economy continued to boom and suddenly Haven was being promoted as the wealthiest planet on a per person basis. So Aaron moved up to the Executive Council largely due the success of Haven's economy."

"Accurate history, Scotty, but nothing new."

"Right. But now he is in the inner circle of power. People across the galaxy love him. He's squeaky clean. He has not established enemies with other planets through biased trade practices. Never had a war of words, except with Tri Star Enterprise, and no one likes them anyway. Haven was one of the few to be able to thumb their noses at them. He is not necessarily anyone's first choice as president. But he is almost everyone's second consideration." He paused, looking at her reaction.

"Scotty, you are dragging this out, aren't you?"

"A little. President Tormachuk is about to resign. His health is not a secret to anyone. The new president is not going to come from Earth, despite their control of the House of Representatives. There would be far too much resentment from the rest of the planets. Ever since your husband steered through the amendments to the Charter of Conduct Earth has lost its big stick to enforce its way. So now a new

President is going to be elected and that will be done before the end of the semester." He took a breath and re-examined her legs.

"My sources on Earth and Mars tell me that your husband is a virtual shoe in for President. Some say the vote is only a formality. If he were President, it would not look proper for his spouse to be a leader of one of the worlds, favouritism and all that. Therefore you are about to resign."

"Very good, Scotty. You're right. I'm going to ask you not to print the story for a least a week. Please."

"All right. I can do that."

"And what would you like me to do make up for that?"

"Eighteen years ago was the first time I met you. The six of us have stayed good friends. We even share a wedding anniversary. Why don't you come over for dinner tonight and bring a bottle of wine. We can talk over old times together. Cindy hasn't seen you in a month. That will be good enough for me."

Chapter Ten
New Brazil Domecity, Mars, year 2615

Robert G Richardson shook hands with the newly elected President of the Alliance government. "President Duggan." He grinned at the taller man. "Thank you so much for giving me the first interview of the new President."

Aaron smiled. "I remembered the first interview I had with you. You were fair and asked good questions. I had a good feeling about you then and since then. Therefore you were the choice for my first interview as President."

Richardson nodded. "Thank you, but it is an honour to be chosen for this. It will be the highlight of my career, the first interview of the President of the Alliance Worlds." He paused as a technician attached a wireless microphone to his suit jacket. "I admit I am nervous."

Aaron laughed. "Probably no more than I was with my first interview with you." He made his way to the two chairs and the desk where the cameras and lights were set up. "Let's try to be easy on each other here. I'm a bit anxious about my new position too."

They sat facing each other and then waited as a countdown was signalled to them. Robert fiddled with his collar and then suddenly Galaxy News was on air. Aaron looked on as Robert suddenly became calm and relaxed. He looked straight at the camera and in a smooth voice introduced the newly elected President of the Alliance Worlds. His first questions were friendly and he inquired on Aaron's rapid rise to being the powerful man in human space.

"I have been in the right place at the right time. The Alliance Worlds were looking for someone not living on the dominate worlds, namely Earth, Regis, Titan and New Costania."

"You left being the leader of Haven to stand for that world in the House of Representatives. That must have been a difficult decision to make, to leave a young family so that Haven could be effectively represented."

"It was a heavy price to pay to be away for long periods of time but I was worried at the time that Charter of Conduct Office was still looking for ways to take away Haven's independence. We had a lot of political enemies when we first joined the Alliance."

Robert eased back in his chair and smiled. "Those political enemies must be a little concerned right now."

Aaron chuckled. "I would imagine they would be, but I want to be clear on this. I will not be pursuing any retribution against those who have stood in Haven's way. The Lord has told us to turn the other cheek and that is the philosophy I will use."

"You have promised changes in your campaign. What will be your first initiatives?"

"The economy is always the first consideration for a new leader. I do believe for the most part taxation has been fair and used appropriately. However, I want to point out the government does not have any money. We use taxpayer's money to run programs and the government. We must be prudent on how we spend those monies."

"Are you planning changes to how taxation is done in any way?"

"There are actually two forms of taxation. People pay a tax to their government, but hidden inside that is the tax paid to Charter of Conduct Office. This is a tremendously powerful organization and I believe they work hard to promote unity in the Alliance Worlds. Unfortunately, they are not accountable to anyone but the President of the Alliance Worlds. They tax Alliance Worlds directly and, therefore, the taxpayer indirectly, but do not provide accounting of their expenditures. I plan to introduce a motion that will require the Charter of Conduct Office to submit a yearly report of their operation to the House of Representatives."

"I'd suspect it will cause a lot of concern in the Charter Offices."

Aaron chuckled. "Sometimes to make progress we have to make a few waves."

Robert paused before asking his next question. "You are taking over the presidency at turbulent times. Though some Alliance Worlds are prospering, some are having difficulties. That does create friction between the have and the have not worlds. There has been open criticism of the Charter of Conduct. Some suggesting the document and the Charter of Conduct Office is outdated and is more of hindrance than a help to galactic peace."

"The Charter of Conduct has been an effective document for over two hundred years. While there are challenges to some of the wording and their implementation, I believe we have to work with the Charter and not try to reinvent another method of uniting humanity."

"To change subjects a bit, Haven is one of the most prosperous worlds. Your wife, Irene Duggan, is the President of Haven. Is that going to cause a conflict of interest?"

"I don't believe so. Irene announced she is resigning as president. She's done a tremendous job leading Haven through these difficult times and deserves to be able to take a break from public life."

"Besides the economy, there is the sensitive issue of Praxton. This is a prosperous world and so far has refused all overtures to join the Alliance Worlds. Praxton is also known for having their women virtually as slaves to their male guardians. Some Alliance Worlds are demanding that this planet be taken over and free these women. Others are saying the women are not asking to be set free and the women on Praxton want the Alliance Worlds to leave them alone. What are your views?"

"I do have first hand experience on what it is like when your home world is told it must change to conform to the rest of humanity. In the case of Praxton, this world was colonized by humans as long as many of the Alliance Worlds. Many of these worlds trade with Praxton and it receives many Alliance visitors each year as tourists. In that regard we are giving partial approval to the Praxton lifestyle." Aaron paused and leaned forward. "I believe we have to careful when we say the women are slaves on Praxton. It sounds outrageous but in fact it is not an entirely true assessment of their culture. It would be prudent for us to first demonstrate that Praxton would reap benefits if they were to join the Alliance Worlds and accept the Charter of Conduct as a way live."

"Mr President, one last thing before we wrap up. The media has been touting you as the man who will lead the Alliance Worlds to greatness, that you have a vision for the future. Do find those sentiments too much weight on your shoulders?"

"No. I sought out this job and knew what it entailed. I will do my best and I trust that others in positions of power will do the same. As we learned on Haven, God wants us to succeed and all we need to do is to work hard and do what we believe is right."

Robert smiled. "Thank you for your time, President Duggan. It's always a pleasure talking to you." As he watched Aaron walk away he felt strange sense that this was indeed a man who was going to make a difference. He remembered reading about a prophesy on Haven that Aaron Duggan was to be the one to save humanity. 'I don't doubt he can do it.'

The End

www.ingramcontent.com/pod-product-compliance
Lightning Source LLC
Chambersburg PA
CBHW050042180626
46810CB00002B/855